SO-AJQ-422

A CHANCE ENCOUNTER

"Mrs. Hunt," he called. He dismounted and led his horse over to where hers stood. "I was hoping I might encounter you."

His voice was a caress and it was all Diana could do not to move to lean against him. "I needed some time to think," she stuttered as she turned to face him.

"Did you think at all of me?" he asked.

"Your lordship should not ask such a thing of a widow," she replied.

He tethered his horse then offered her his arm. "Would you care to walk?"

She took it and they strolled farther into the spinney where the light was sparse and the smell of moss and damp strong. At last, when they came to a secluded spot, he stopped and took off his coat and spread it on the ground for her. "Let's sit awhile," he said.

Diana sat, looking straight ahead, her heart beating wildly again.

Woodham seated himself next to her. "I've thought of nothing but you since the last time we met in these woods."

"Your lordship is too kind," said Diana.

"And you are too beautiful," he murmured. He brushed away a curl from her neck and replaced it with his lips, causing her skin to come alive at his touch . . .

ZEBRA'S REGENCY ROMANCES
DAZZLE AND DELIGHT

A BEGUILING INTRIGUE   (4441, $3.99)
by Olivia Sumner

Pretty as a picture Justine Riggs cared nothing for propriety. She dressed as a boy, sat on her horse like a jockey, and pondered the stars like a scientist. But when she tried to best the handsome Quenton Fletcher, Marquess of Devon, by proving that she was the better equestrian, he would try to prove Justine's antics were pure folly. The game he had in mind was seduction—never imagining that he might lose his heart in the process!

AN INCONVENIENT ENGAGEMENT   (4442, $3.99)
by Joy Reed

Rebecca Wentworth was furious when she saw her betrothed waltzing with another. So she decides to make him jealous by flirting with the handsomest man at the ball, John Collinwood, Earl of Stanford. The "wicked" nobleman knew exactly what the enticing miss was up to—and he was only too happy to play along. But as Rebecca gazed into his magnificent eyes, her errant fiancé was soon utterly forgotten!

SCANDAL'S LADY   (4472, $3.99)
by Mary Kingsley

Cassandra was shocked to learn that the new Earl of Lynton was her childhood friend, Nicholas St. John. After years at sea and mixed feelings Nicholas had come home to take the family title. And although Cassandra knew her place as a governess, she could not help the thrill that went through her each time he was near. Nicholas was pleased to find that his old friend Cassandra was his new next door neighbor, but after being near her, he wondered if mere friendship would be enough . . .

HIS LORDSHIP'S REWARD   (4473, $3.99)
by Carola Dunn

As the daughter of a seasoned soldier, Fanny Ingram was accustomed to the vagaries of military life and cared not a whit about matters of rank and social standing. So she certainly never foresaw her *tendre* for handsome Viscount Roworth of Kent with whom she was forced to share lodgings, while he carried out his clandestine activities on behalf of the British Army. And though good sense told Roworth to keep his distance, he couldn't stop from taking Fanny in his arms for a kiss that made all hearts equal!

Available wherever paperbacks are sold, or order direct from the Publisher. Send cover price plus 50¢ per copy for mailing and handling to Penguin USA, P.O. Box 999, c/o Dept. 17109, Bergenfield, NJ 07621. Residents of New York and Tennessee must include sales tax. DO NOT SEND CASH.

The Adventuress
Sheila Rabe

ZEBRA BOOKS
KENSINGTON PUBLISHING CORP.

ZEBRA BOOKS are published by

Kensington Publishing Corp.
850 Third Avenue
New York, NY 10022

Copyright © 1996 by Sheila Rabe

All rights reserved. No part of this book may be reproduced
in any form or by any means without the prior written consent
of the Publisher, excepting brief quotes used in reviews.

If you purchased this book without a cover you should be
aware that this book is stolen property. It was reported as "un-
sold and destroyed" to the Publisher and neither the Author
nor the Publisher has received any payment for this "stripped
book."

Zebra and the Z logo Reg. U.S. Pat. & TM Off.

First Printing: January, 1996

Printed in the United States of America

For Myrle, the world's best mother-in-law

For money has a power above the stars and fate, to manage love.

—Samuel Butler

One

The cry of "Help!" carried on the wind, faint as imagination. Julian Warrington Brentwood, fifth Earl of Woodham, pulled out his pistol and spurred his horse into a gallop. He came up the rise to see Woodham Heath stretched before him like a gigantic stage, sparsely decorated with heather.

Day perched on the edge of night, making the kind of gray light that spawned dreams, and what Julian saw was every traveller's nightmare—a carriage stood center stage, its coachman slumped on the box. A giant ruffian had heard Julian's approach and was mounting his bay and wheeling away from the carriage, leaving a small female huddled against it.

"Stop, thief!" cried Julian.

The man refused to oblige and the earl closed the distance between them, aimed and fired. The bay reared and the thug toppled from it and fell to the ground, a heap of broken flesh and filthy clothes.

Ignoring him, Julian rode to the coach and dismounted before the frightened lady.

She was young, surely no more than eighteen. Her bonnet covered curls the color of pirates' gold. Her face was a perfect oval with very blue eyes. Fear made them unnaturally wide, but no less beautiful. Her terrifying experience had sucked all color from her face, and it served to make her look as fragile and tempting to the hands as his mother's Dresden shepherdess had appeared when he was a boy. He saw her torn pelisse and felt a desire to grind his heel on the dead man's head.

"Are you all right?" he asked.

She looked to the dead highwayman. His coat was torn at the back seam. A spring of blood seeped through the tear, spreading out into a dark pool, and a crimson stream trickled away from him into the dust. "Is he dead?" She whispered it, as if fearful her attacker might hear and rise up after her.

"Yes," said Julian.

She began to crumple, like a marionette when the puppeteer lowers the strings. He caught her and she clutched his coat.

Fearing she might faint, he scooped an arm under her legs and picked her up. He entered the carriage and laid her on the seat. She looked at him, dazed.

"I must leave you for a moment," he said gently.

She took a death grip on his arms and begged, "No!"

"I must see to your coachman," he said. "I assure you, you are perfectly safe now."

She bit her lip and looked at him doubtfully.

"I will return as soon as I have bound his wound," promised Julian.

"Thank you," she said. Her voice was small and breathy, and he wondered if it held that same quality even when she wasn't frightened. Slowly, he pulled away, giving her a reassuring smile, and she let the fabric of his great coat slip through her fingers.

What, he wondered as he climbed onto the box, was such a glorious creature doing travelling about alone in old miser Hunt's carriage? Who was she? A distant relation, perhaps?

The coachman held his bleeding arm and smiled at Julian through gritted teeth.

"Had yourself a bit of adventure, I see," observed Julian as he removed his pearl stick pin and untied his cravat.

"Just a bit, sir." The man looked at Julian gratefully as he used his cravat to bind the wound.

"I should say you are lucky the brute did not put a ball through your heart," observed Julian as he worked. "Where were you bound?"

"Spinney Hall, between Otter and Great Spinney."

"Yes, I know it," said Julian. So, he had been right. "Your master is Hunt."

The man nodded.

"And who is the girl?"

"Miss Brown," said the coachman. "She's to marry the master."

Julian raised a surprised eyebrow. This young thing was going to marry that fat old pinch purse? What a waste of beauty. "I can see he values her highly," said Julian with a hint of sarcasm in his voice.

"The master is a tight one with his money," admitted the coachman. "I tried to tell him Woodham Heath ain't been safe these past few months."

"So I have heard," said Julian.

"Woodham should have done something about it long ago," muttered the coachman.

"He has now," said Julian.

The man looked at him and his eyes widened and a deep flush stained his face. "Begging your pardon, your lordship. I didn't recognize you."

"I've been in these parts little enough in the last few years."

"We heard you was fighting the Frogs."

"That I was, but I can see I should have sold out sooner and come home and battled the highwaymen." He looked to where the dead man lay. "This should discourage anyone else with similar inclinations."

"That it should," agreed the coachman. "And thankful I am you came along. How is Miss Brown?"

"A little shaken, but she's a game one. She'll be fine. And how about you? I'll wager that arm hurts like the devil."

"Not so much I cannot do my job," said the coachman.

"Do you think you can handle the reins as far as Ottershaw Park?"

The man nodded.

"Good," said Julian. "Take us that far, then I'll see you're fed and put to bed. I shall take Miss Brown the rest of the way myself."

"Yes, your lordship. And thank you."

"My pleasure," said Julian.

"Er, begging your lordship's pardon," added the coachman. Julian cocked an eyebrow.

"We was all sorry about the old earl's death."

Julian nodded curtly. No one was as sorry as he. He climbed down from the box, got his horse and tied the reins to the back of the carriage. Then he climbed inside.

The coach smelled musty, and Julian noticed its once luxurious red interior was faded to rust. The girl sat frowning, with her arms wrapped about her as if she were cold. He smiled reassuringly. "Your coachman will be fine."

"I am glad to hear it," she said. Her voice was stronger now, but still soft, like the gentle lapping of stream water. "Will you ride with me all the way to Spinney Hall?" she asked.

"Yes," said Julian. "We shall stop first at my home and put your coachman to bed. Then I'll drive you the rest of the way in my curricle. I shall have your carriage returned to you tomorrow."

"You sound as if you know where to send it," said the girl in surprise.

"I do," said Julian. "Your coachman is wounded, but he is not unconscious. I understand you are on your way to wed old Hunt," he continued casually. He noticed the girl lowered her gaze to her lap, as if embarrassed by the subject.

"Yes," she said in a low voice. "I'm afraid so."

"Afraid?"

Her cheeks turned pink but she recovered herself. "You must forgive me. I don't seem to know what I'm saying."

"After what you've been through that is not surprising," said Julian. "When do you become Mrs. Hunt?"

"This Saturday morning," she replied, and he noticed she

said it as if she were speaking of her execution and not her wedding day.

"Allow me to wish you happy," he said. "And allow me to introduce myself. I am Lord Woodhaven."

"Lord Woodhaven," she repeated, awed. She sighed. "I suppose you are married."

The corners of Julian's mouth twitched. "No. I'm not," he said.

"Such foul luck," the girl muttered, then blushed fiery red at his amused gaze. She bit her lip and looked at him wide-eyed, at a loss for words to cover such a gaffe.

Julian came to her aid. "I do not yet know your name," he prompted.

"I am Diana Brown."

"Diana," he repeated. She was well named. She looked like a goddess, with her creamy skin and delicate features and that fabulous golden hair. And it would appear she was named after the right one; Diana, goddess of the hunt. He could guess what this little goddess was after. He thought of what her married name would be and found it hard not to chuckle. Fate had a sense of humor. "Why are you marrying Hunt?" he asked, curious as to how she'd answer.

"Mr. Hunt was kind to me," she said.

"Surely a great many men have been kind to you," said Julian. "Why marry an old miser like Hunt?"

"We did not know he was a miser when he proposed," said Diana. This made Julian smile, and she looked at him in exasperation, as if it were his fault she'd betrayed herself. "My mother felt Mr. Hunt would make me a good husband," she ammended, and turned her face to look out the window.

He studied her averted face. It wasn't the first time a beautiful girl had been sold to an old man. What a farce of a wedding night she would have! She deserved better—a young man with a flat belly, and fire in his loins, one who could stir her to passion. *Someone like yourself?* came a mocking voice from the corner of his mind. "Surely you could have done better than Hunt," he observed.

Diana grimaced. "Not in Bath," she said. "It is all gouty old men."

Julian chuckled. The chit was refreshingly honest. And amusing. "You should have gone to London," he told her.

"We could not afford London," she replied. She closed her eyes and sighed. "Oh, but I should love to see it." She smiled at Julian. It was a child's smile. "Perhaps Mr. Hunt will take me there for a visit one day."

"Perhaps," agreed Julian, and added silently. *When he has forgotten the value of a pound.*

"I've never met an earl before," she volunteered. "I thought that to be an earl, one must be old."

Julian smiled and stretched out his legs at an angle. "I suppose a good many of them look like your groom," he agreed. Now, why had he said that? At the mention of Hunt, her face had fallen. "Forgive me," he said. "That was a thoughtless thing to say." Her lip was trembling. She tried to avert her face, but he saw a tear trickle down her cheek. Before he could think sensibly, he was next to her on the seat, taking her in his arms, and she was sobbing. "There now," he murmured. "Don't cry. I'm sure Hunt will make you a very good husband."

"No, he won't," sobbed Diana. "He is stingy. And fat. I've never been married before, and I'm afraid. I. . . ." She broke off and bit her lip. "Oh, dear," she said. "What must you think of me?"

"I think you are the most beautiful creature I've ever seen," said Julian honestly. His gaze fell from her eyes to those beautiful, soft looking lips. Hypnotized, he slowly lowered his head.

Diana's eyes closed and she moved her face closer to his. The scent of lavender teased his nose.

He moved to kiss her, but she came out of her trance and pulled away. Refusing to acknowledge the blush on her cheeks, she dropped the curtain of honey brown lashes over her eyes and said, "What brought you out on the road this time of day, your lordship?"

The earl smiled. A regular coquette, this one. He leaned back into the corner of the coach and said, "I was visiting friends, discussing the problem of the highwayman who has been plaguing these parts, in fact."

She bit her lip and turned to look out the window.

"I'm sorry," he said. "I didn't mean to upset you afresh."

She gave him a shy smile. "I am so glad you happened along," she said. "Do you ever go to Bath?" she asked suddenly.

The earl grinned. Did the lady wish to torture herself over the prize that escaped or reconfirm the wisdom of the choice she'd made? "I have not been to Bath in recent years," he said.

"So I would not have met you last summer," she sighed, then muttered, "Pooh."

This made Julian chuckle again.

She chided him with a haughty look.

He sobered himself and begged her pardon. "It is just that I have never felt quite so much like the fish that broke line and got away," he explained.

She opened her mouth to speak. Her brows knit and he could tell she was debating what words to let escape. None did and the pretty lips clamped closed.

Julian laughed. "I hope your husband appreciates his great good fortune," he said.

She raised her chin and gave him a saucy smile, a hint of what she must be like when not thinking of dangerous highwaymen or inappropriate future husbands. "So do I, your lordship," she said.

Julian had never been one to poach on another man's property, but here, he thought, was a lovely piece that begged to be an exception. Anyway, he didn't consider Hunt much of a man, and the poor care he'd taken in bringing home his bride showed his lack of concern for her.

The carriage slowed and turned onto a long, tree-lined drive, drawing the girl's attention out the window once more. "It would appear we have reached Ottershaw Park," said Julian.

"My," she breathed, watching spellbound out the window.

The carriage stopped. Julian stepped out, let down the steps, and held out his hand to her. "Come. I shall send someone to help your coachman, then we'll continue on to Spinney Hall. But first you must allow me to offer you some refreshment."

Diana found herself inside the biggest house she'd ever seen. Not a house, she decided—a palace. She was vaguely aware of her host giving instructions to the butler. Before her stretched a long hall. At one end, a great staircase ran down each wall from a landing above. She had a quick vision of herself coming down that staircase in a fine gown. If only she had met the earl in Bath instead of Mr. Hunt.

But the earl had told her that he hadn't been to Bath in some time. Fate had chosen for her, and only in coming to the groom it had chosen had she met the man of her dreams, someone young, handsome and wealthy. Fate deserved a hearty kick in the shin, she thought sourly.

"Her ladyship is in the drawing room," the butler was saying.

"Thank you, Hansen," said the earl. "You may bring sherry there for my guest."

The earl ushered Diana into a large sitting room. Heavy gold velvet drapes hung at the windows and the furniture was all gold brocade. Diana's eyes widened. Surely she'd strayed into one of the Prince Regent's palaces.

"Mother, I'd like you to meet Miss Brown," said the earl.

Diana turned her attention to the dark-haired woman sitting on the sofa. She looked to be near the age of Diana's mother, only this woman was much thinner. Her white complexion, combined with the cold expression on her delicately chiseled face made her look like a marble statue. She murmured a greeting, giving Diana no smile.

The earl motioned Diana to a chair and she perched on it nervously. The cushions felt stiff and unyielding beneath her.

"Miss Brown had the misfortune to be set upon by our local highwayman," said the earl.

"How horrible for you," said her ladyship mildly. She cocked an enquiring eyebrow at her son. "And did you rescue her, Julian?"

"Yes, fortunately."

"I hope you killed the creature in the process. I am quite tired of hearing complaints about him."

Julian nodded. "Yes. I fancy the neighborhood will return to normal now."

"I am glad to hear it," said her ladyship. She returned her attention to Diana. "Are you visiting someone in these parts, Miss Brown?"

This woman made Diana feel like she was again at Miss Spooner's School for Young Ladies, with Miss Spooner scrutinizing Diana over her spectacles. "Mr. Hunt," she managed. "I am visiting Mr. Hunt."

"Oh? He is a relative?"

"He's to be my husband," said Diana, feeling somehow ashamed as she said it.

"I see," said her ladyship slowly, and Diana shifted uncomfortably in her chair.

"How very fortunate for you that my step-son happened along when he did," continued Lady Woodham.

"Yes," agreed Diana, venturing a smile at the earl.

The butler appeared with a tray, bearing not only sherry, but a plate of small, iced cakes and sandwiches as well. The earl poured some sherry in a crystal goblet and handed it to Diana, saying, "This will help to calm your nerves."

Diana drank it gratefully, realizing that being in the presence of this daunting woman was nearly as terrifying as her encounter with the highwayman.

Lady Woodham said nothing more. She nibbled a cake and allowed Diana to eat in silence. When Diana had finished her sherry and eaten a sandwich, her ladyship observed that Miss Brown must be anxious to be on her way.

"Yes," agreed the earl. "Mr. Hunt must be getting worried by now." He pulled a cord and the butler appeared again. "I need my curricle," Woodham stated.

"Yes, your lordship," said the butler, and disappeared.

Diana spent another awkward ten minutes in the beautiful gold room before the butler returned to announce that his lordship's curricle was ready and waiting. She thanked her hostess for her hospitality and made good her escape.

It was only when she was outside the great house that she realized she still wore a ripped pelisse, a souvenier from her encounter with the highwayman. A fine way to go to her future husband, with torn clothing! Why hadn't the earl's mother offered her a chance to change?

Even as Diana posed the question she knew the answer. Lady Woodham had not wanted to have her in her house any longer than was absolutely necessary.

Diana reined her thoughts down a more pleasant avenue. Perhaps when Mr. Hunt saw her torn garment, he would offer to buy her a new pelisse. Small chance of that, she told herself, reality quickly dousing hope.

What a fine catch Mr. Hunt had seemed when they first met him, so finely dressed and well mannered. But once the betrothal was arranged, Diana and her mama had quickly learned that fine manners did not necessarily denote generosity. She remembered his words to her mama when Mrs. Brown had hinted he might like to buy his betrothed an engagement present, "Once we are married she will be housed and fed, all at my expense. That should be present enough."

The sight of Lord Woodham's curricle did not make Diana feel any happier about the husband she'd chosen. Here was a smart-looking equippage—bright yellow with shiny black upholstery. If the musty carriage Hunt had sent for her was any indication, there would be nothing so fine as this in his stables.

"You mustn't mind my step-mother," said the earl as he set his horses in motion. "She sees every woman as a fortune hunter, out to trap me into marriage. It doesn't matter if the girl is engaged or not."

Diana felt the blood rushing to her cheeks. Fortune hunter was exactly what she was, and they both knew it. She wasn't even a very good one, it would appear, for she'd only managed to secure a fat old man with no title. If only Mama had taken her to London to seek a husband. Perhaps she would have met a man like Lord Woodham.

And ladies like his step-mother, who looked down on her because she wasn't as highly born as they, because she was nothing but a cheap adventuress out to feather her nest?

She'd overheard those words about herself at a Bath assembly. The sting hadn't lessened with time, but she continued to use the same balm. *I won't feel badly,* she told herself. *Some people are born with plenty. Others must use their wits and find a way to survive. I am merely doing what I must. Let that stuffy old Lady Woodham think what she wishes. It is of no consequence to me.*

The old wound attended to, she turned her attention once more to Lord Woodham, bestowing on him her loveliest smile. "This is a fine carriage," she observed. "To sit so high up above the rest of the world is a pleasant sensation." *If only my friends in Tetbury could see me now.*

Her contentment lasted until Spinney Hall came into sight. What would have appeared a fine enough home only a few hours ago now seemed rather shabby. The Hall was only half as big as the earl of Woodham's home. It was red brick, trimmed with woodwork once painted white, now faded to a weathered gray—a poor relation to the grand house from which she had just come.

As the earl helped her down from the curricle, and set her

feet on the ground, she realized she had come to earth in quite another way.

Charles Hunt looked surprised to see his bride-to-be escorted into his presence by none other than the new earl of Woodham. "Young Lord Woodham, is it not?" he said. "I thought you still out of the country." Without waiting for a reply from the earl, Hunt turned to Diana. "My dear Diana. I am glad to see you safely arrived. I was becoming worried."

The earl inserted himself into the conversation before Diana could reply, "And so you should have. To bring your bride here with none but your coachman to guard her was risky."

Mr. Hunt's brows lowered. "How is it I find you with Miss Brown?" he asked. He seemed to take in Diana's ripped garment for the first time. "What has happened?"

"I was set upon by a highwayman," said Diana. "The earl saved me."

"Highwayman! My coach—is it damamged?" demanded Hunt sharply.

Julian was disgusted. "Your coach is undamaged. Would that I could say the same for your coachman."

"Is he dead?" asked Hunt.

Julian shook his head. "He took a ball in the arm. It has been dressed, and he is recovering at Ottershaw Park. I shall have your carriage delivered to you tomorrow, and your coachman as well."

"I am in your debt, your lordship," said Hunt with a bow. "And thank you for rescuing my bride for me." He patted Diana's shoulder. "We will have a nice meal and you will feel much better," he told her. Then he turned with a smile to Julian. "I am sure his lordship must be anxious to return to the comforts of his own hearth, so we won't keep him. My humble thanks," he added.

There was nothing for the earl to do but promise Diana he'd have her trunk delivered later and take his leave. "Good-bye,

Miss Brown," he said, and bowed over Diana's trembling hand.
He smiled encouragingly at her and she smiled back, but her
eyes seemed to plead with him not to leave her. As there was
nothing he could do, Woodham turned and strode quickly from
the Hall.

Diana watched him go. She said nothing, but she wanted to
cry out, "Don't leave me!" That is cowardly, she told herself.
She turned determinedly to her husband-to-be, a smile pinned
on her face.

He was frowning. "Just what tricks were you playing, young
lady?" he demanded.

Two

Her experience with Lord Woodham in the carriage immediately sprang to Diana's mind and a betraying guilty flush warmed her face. "What can you mean?" she stammered.

"I mean I sent my coachman to fetch you and you come to me instead with that young puppy in tow, him looking like a schoolboy with a bad case of calf love." He shook a finger in her face. "I'll not be cuckolded, young woman! I'm marrying you to provide me an heir!"

Diana was shocked, both by Hunt's language and his insinuations. "I am a woman of honor, sir," she said, her voice wobbling under the heavy weight of nervous exhaustion. "I told you I would marry you, and so I shall, and I'll be a good wife, too. My mother taught me well how to run a house."

Hunt softened. "Of course, of course. What a fool I am to scold you after the ordeal you've experienced!" He took her hand and patted it. "Now, you mustn't cry, my dear. I'm a jealous fellow, and I just don't like to have my beautiful bride arrive with some young jackanapes sniffing 'round her skirt."

"If the earl hadn't come along when he did . . ." Diana began. The thought of what would have happened was too horrible to put into words. That, combined with her future husband's scold, caused the threatened tears to finally spill.

"There, there. Never you mind, my dear," soothed Hunt. He put a pudgy paw on her shoulder and hugged her to his side. "You're safe at last." He fished out a handkerchief and handed it to her. "Now, come sit by the fire in the drawing room and warm yourself, then we'll have our dinner."

Diana drew back. "My pelisse."

"Nonsense. You look perfectly fine," said Hunt. "Williams!" he barked, and a red-haired girl in maid's uniform came bustling down the hallway to bob a nervous curtsey. "Take my bride's pelisse and see if you cannot mend it," he commanded, helping Diana out of the close-fitting coat.

The girl did as she was bid and Diana shivered in the cold hallway.

"You will be warm once you are in the drawing room," said Hunt, and led Diana off. "My sister, Mary Barnes, and her son are here," he continued. "The vultures. Came down to see me marry." He grinned and lowered his voice. "I invited them," he confided. "That smarmy little leech, David, always thought to step into my shoes and enjoy the fortune I spent my life building. But I served him a trick by bringing you here, my dear. The money I have made I made with my own hands, and I'll have an heir for it from my own seed, not some greedy spawn of my sister's and that wastrel she married. Now they can watch me wed and think about the fortune slipping through their hands." Hunt chuckled.

Diana felt she should say something to this outrageous speech. Her husband-to-be was obviously proud of himself and expected her to be, also. "That was very clever of you," she managed.

He smiled approvingly. "I am a clever man," he informed her, and led her into the drawing room.

The room was supplied with fine, old furniture, and a blazing fire kept at bay the chill of a September evening.

A plump, middle-aged woman and a man who looked to be in his early thirties sat on the sofa. At the sight of Diana, the man rose and came to bow over her hand.

"This is my sister, Mary, and my nephew, David Barnes," said Hunt. "Come to see his old uncle set sail on the pleasant sea of matrimony."

David Barnes was tall and lean, with a handsome, fair face, and hair cut to fall dramatically over his brow. He smiled appreciatively at Diana. "I'm delighted to meet my new aunt," he said in a soft voice. "I see you are every bit as beautiful as my uncle told us."

"Thank you," she murmured.

The woman held out a plump hand to her. "I don't know why Charles didn't take a bride years ago." She shook her head. "Of course, now that he is old, he must make a cake of himself over a pretty young woman."

Diana didn't know what to say to this. Fortunately, she was spared, for her future husband answered. "A man must do things in a certain order, Mary. First he makes his fortune, then he can find a lovely young bride and enjoy himself the rest of his life. Those who squander their money indulging themselves when they're young have nothing in their old age but regrets. You can't expect some rich uncle to die and leave you his money, for that rich uncle may just marry and have sons of his own." Hunt bestowed a gloating smile on David, who merely smiled politely back and nodded.

"My, but I'm hungry!" exclaimed Mary. "I do intend to do justice to that rack of lamb you promised me, Charles."

Her brother pronounced himself equally ready to eat. He rubbed his hands together in anticipation. "Not only a fine rack of lamb, but turtle soup, a nice turbot, and Rhenish cream for dessert."

Ten minutes later, Diana found herself seated at a large dining table, without having been given so much as a chance to freshen up or see her room. It was obvious to her whose comforts were the most important in this household.

Dinner was an exercise in gluttony like none she'd ever seen. Both brother and sister did ample justice to every course set before them, and there were seven.

After dinner she was obliged to make up a fourth for whist. When Diana confessed she didn't know how to play the game,

Hunt looked vexed and said he supposed they'd have to teach her.

It had been too long a day and too much had happened. She found herself unable to concentrate and the remonstrances from her future husband every time she misplayed a card made her nervous and even more prone to error. At last he gave up. "I wonder if we shall ever make a card player out of you," he said, sighing like a man who had been sorely tried.

"I am sorry," said Diana. "I'm afraid I am simply too tired to concentrate."

"Poor thing," said her new sister-in-law. "It was a long, exhausting trip for you. We should have allowed you to find your bed long ago."

Diana turned to Hunt. "I should very much like to retire," she said.

"Of course. I'll conduct you to your room myself."

Diana had enjoyed quite enough of Mr. Hunt's company for one evening, but could think of no polite way to discourage him from going with her to her room. She said goodnight to the others and preceded him out of the drawing room.

"I have instructed Williams, my housemaid, to help you with your hair and gowns," said Hunt as they made their way up to Diana's bedroom. "I felt there was no sense in going to the expense of hiring a lady's maid when Williams is already here."

"Of course," murmured Diana, hiding fresh disappointment. Not even a maid of her own. How little this man valued her!

Hunt stopped and threw open a door. Diana walked inside. It was a small room, sparsely furnished but clean. Someone had thought to put flowers on the bedside table. "It's lovely," she said.

"After we're wed you will, of course, have the room that adjoins mine," said Hunt, strolling into the room after her.

Diana suddenly felt very nervous. "Well, goodnight," she said.

Hunt didn't leave. Instead, he rocked back on his heels,

studying her as if she were a painting. At last he nodded. "You will do very well," he said. "I chose wisely. It stirs me just to look at you."

Diana felt a blush staining her cheeks. She lowered her eyes to the thick carpet.

Hunt strode over to her. "Yes," he continued, "I think I should like a kiss goodnight from my bride-to-be."

The thought of kissing this fat old man on the mouth made Diana's heart give a sick flop. *He's to be your husband,* she told herself. *He certainly has the right to ask for a kiss.* "Of course, if you wish it," she said. She dutifully closed her eyes and pursed her lips.

With a chuckle, Hunt folded his beefy arms around her. She was aware of his paunch protruding against her. His breath smelled like wine, his body of sweat. He gave her a great, smacking wet kiss. "Such a sweet little thing," he said. "I must have one more."

Not until I absolutely must, thought Diana. Before he could touch his lips to hers again she launched herself into a violent sneeze. "Oh, my!" she exclaimed. "I do hope I'm not coming down with something.

Hunt's face registered disgust as she sniffed and looked around as if searching for a handkerchief. He pulled out his and handed it to her and she trumpeted into it.

"I should hate to be too ill to enjoy my wedding," she said. A violent cold, a putrid sore throat. . . .

"I am sure after a good night's sleep you will feel right as rain," said Hunt in a voice that strongly encouraged her not to disappoint him.

Diana held up her hand to be kissed. "Goodnight, dear sir," she said sweetly.

The endearment seemed to put him in a better humor. "Goodnight, my dear," he said, and the wet lips landed on her hand, making her shiver in distaste.

Misinterpreting her reaction, Hunt grinned at her lecherously. "Ah, we shall have a wonderful wedding night, shan't we, my little dove?"

Distaste must have shown on her face, for Hunt frowned. "I expect you to be a proper bride," he informed her. "We'll have no female hysterics or other such silliness. I am a man of the world and I certainly know how to treat a woman."

Diana couldn't help comparing what she'd experienced with Lord Woodham to Mr. Hunt's sloppy excuse for a kiss. It was with great difficulty that she smiled and said, "I am sure we will."

He seemed satisfied with this. "Well then, my dear, you have but to ring and Williams will come help you get ready for bed." He gave her another pat on the shoulder and went to the door. "I have business to attend to tomorrow, but you may go for a walk if you like. And, of course, Mary and David will be on hand to entertain you. Goodnight."

"Goodnight," said Diana weakly, and watched the door close. The moment it shut she collapsed, weak-kneed, onto the bed. What a day this had been, like some horrible jumbled dream!

Unbidden, the memory of the highwayman's manhandling came to her. She could almost feel his great paw tearing away her pelisse, hear again his wicked chuckle and his threat to fish whatever jewels she was hiding out of the bodice of her gown.

"I have no jewels!" she'd protested. "Not even paste. I'm not a rich woman. I haven't even a lady's maid travelling with me."

"What kind of looby do yer take me for?" he'd growled. "This is a swell's carriage. I'll have yer jewels or I'll cut out yer heart."

Only the threat of approaching hoofbeats and her cry for help had saved her. Would the man have really killed her?

Diana felt herself beginning to shake and grabbed the bed pillow, hugging it to herself. It had all been so terrible. And

Mr. Hunt hadn't even offered to replace her damaged pelisse—as if it could be mended and ever look the same again!

This last thought brought her back full circle to her impending nuptials and pushed tears from her eyes. This was a mistake, a terrible mistake. She knew that now. She should have cried off! The very thought of Mr. Hunt touching her again made her flesh quiver. What to do? What to do?

She got up and began to pace. She could go home. But how would she get there? She had no money to buy a seat on the mail coach. Of course, a gentleman would allow a woman the use of his carriage to get home if she changed her mind. But Diana suspected Mr. Hunt was a gentleman only as long as it cost him nothing. She could almost hear him now. "You certainly won't return home at my expense, young woman!" No. Mr. Hunt wouldn't send her home if she told him she'd changed her mind.

And what would Mama do if she returned unmarried? What would become of poor, simple Mathilde? Diana could hardly find a husband for her sister if she were unmarried herself.

Oh, but surely it wouldn't be such a terrible thing if she cried off. It had been easy to snare Mr. Hunt. She was young and beautiful. She could find another rich husband, someone more generous and in a better position to help care for Mathilde.

Something heavy settled on her rising spirits, pushing them down. The kind of suitor she wished to find was in London, and Mama couldn't afford another summer in Bath, let alone a season in London. There was no hope. She was trapped. She fell on her bed, buried her face in her pillow and sobbed herself into a sleep world, where the landscape was wavey and soft, like a lady's watercolor painting.

It was a soothing dream until the highwayman rode into it. He sat a blood-soaked horse, and at the sight of her kicked the animal into a gallop. There was no Earl of Woodham to rescue her, and she ran for miles through a dark forest, tripping over roots and scrambling back to her feet, sobbing as she heard the sound of the horse's hooves cantering behind her. At last her pursuer caught up with her in a clearing. She tried to run, but her legs were weighted and she was unable to move. The highwayman raised his pistol and fired.

Diana sat up in bed, panting, and looked wild-eyed around the room. At first she saw only darkness, which made her frantic heart pound harder. Then the darkness presented shapes. There was the chair by the fire. There was the wardrobe. She forced herself to breath slowly and lay back down in her bed. When was the last time she'd had a nightmare? She couldn't remember.

She lay still for some time, afraid to close her eyes. At last, her eyelids became too heavy to hold open and she had to let them fall, hoping as she did so that the horrible apparition she'd met earlier had ridden on. Exhaustion pressed her deep into sleep, wrapping her mind in blessed darkness.

She awoke the next morning with an aching head and depressed spirits that demanded gray, brooding skies, but the weather refused to oblige. The world outside her bedroom window was bathed in cheery sunlight. It had texture and substance. The highwayman was dead, the birds were singing. It was an ordinary day and no great harm awaited her.

Diana rang the bell for her new maid. After breakfast she'd take a walk. She'd be safe enough from her future husband's attentions outdoors, for Diana was sure he was not fond of any activity that did not involve his mouth and his stomach.

A scratching at her door signalled the maid's arrival and Diana called for her to enter.

The girl she had seen the night before entered the room and bobbed a curtsey. Diana saw the girl carried her pelisse over her arm. "I'm Williams, miss. The master said I was to be yer maid."

"Hello," said Diana.

The girl ventured over to her and timidly proferred the garment. "I found some buttons to match," she said timidly.

Diana took the pelisse. "I can hardly tell where it was ripped," she said, amazed.

A smile bloomed on the girl's round face. "I've never been a lady's maid before," she confessed nervously.

"I've never had my own lady's maid before," said Diana, "so we are starting out even."

Diana found herself grateful for the presence of the other girl. In making Williams feel at ease she was able to take her mind off her own problems.

The girl looked to where Diana's trunk sat. "I should have come and unpacked your trunk last night."

Diana heard the worried tone in her voice. "It makes no difference." She looked down at her crumpled gown. "I suppose I should have rung for you last night. Truth to tell, I was too exhausted." She shrugged and smiled. "Well, we are both starting out fresh this morning. Let's see if we cannot find some way to make me presentable."

"Oh, I'm sure that won't be hard," said the girl admiringly.

When Williams had finished with Diana's hair, she studied her reflection in the looking glass. With a little ribbon and a great many pins, her new abigail had achieved a fairly modish hairstyle. It was not as elegant as what Diana had seen on some of the fine ladies at Bath, but it would do nicely. She smiled and thanked the girl, then went downstairs in search of the breakfast parlor.

After peering into several rooms, she at last found it. Hunt's sister was there, sipping a cup of hot chocolate. At the sight of Diana, Mary Barnes set down her cup and called a cheery good-morning. "How nice to meet another early riser! My slugabed son is still sleeping, and Charles has already had his nose buried in his account books this past hour, so I have been quite alone. I must confess, I enjoy having someone to talk to at breakfast. I hear ladies of the nobility have their breakfast alone in bed. I think that a perfectly horrid habit, eating in bed. And all by yourself. Can you imagine?"

Diana thought it a wonderful idea, but she dutifully said

that she could not imagine such a thing and helped herself to eggs from one of the chafing dishes on the sideboard. She turned to find the other woman studying her.

Mary smiled. "Yes, I can see how Charles would want to marry you. You are amazingly lovely, you know."

"Thank you," said Diana, and took a seat.

"Of course, it is quite silly of him to wed at his age," continued Mary. "He does have heirs."

"I believe he wants children of his own," said Diana and quaked inwardly at the thought of what she'd have to endure to produce them for him.

Mary shook her head as if her brother's desire was incomprehensible. "The foolish man. Ah, but there was no talking him out of his decision." She studied Diana. "You appear to be a delicate thing," she observed. "I do hope you'll be strong enough to bear children."

This statement drained the color from Diana's face. She hadn't thought about the possibility of dying in childbirth.

"Oh, but I'm sure you are," continued Mary comfortingly. "You mustn't listen to me. I do ramble on sometimes. I'm afraid I do much of my thinking out loud." She went on with her breakfast, her placid manner unruffled.

Diana, however, found she had no appetite left. "You will excuse me?" she said. "I think, perhaps, I'll take a walk. I feel the need for some fresh air."

Diana made good her escape from the house without encountering anyone else. With a little effort it could be a lovely home, she thought, as she walked down the drive. There was a time when she'd thought all she needed to be happy was a fine house, and a rich man to care for her. What a fool she'd been!

As she wandered down a country lane, her mind wandered back to Lord Woodham. Mr. Hunt, who had not seemed so terribly unattractive when she'd accepted him, now looked like a fat old bullfrog when placed next to the earl in her mind's eye. Lord Woodham was slim and hard-bodied, with rich, chestnut hair, not fading into gray like Mr. Hunt's. Lord Woodham had large brown eyes, deepset, and a wide forehead, with not even a whisper of a wrinkle. Mr. Hunt's lips were thick and wet, and Lord Woodham's lips were . . .

Just remembering the nearness of those lips sent tingles rushing through her body in all directions. What madness had possessed her that she had almost let a stranger kiss her? She'd acted no better than a common tavern maid. What must he think of her? And all the stupid things she'd said. Well, it was a wonder she'd even known her own name after her harrowing adventure. Still, she must have appeared very common.

Oh, what did it matter what Lord Woodham thought of her, anyway, she concluded crossly. She was marrying Charles Hunt and that was that. She'd never see the earl again.

The sun climbed higher and the morning wore on as Diana continued her wanderings, reliving her dramatic rescue from the highwayman. Before she knew it she was in the spinney and lost. She sat down on a log and looked around in dismay.

The approaching sound of a horse made her start. She jumped up, ready to run from whatever ruffian approached.

Lord Woodham came into sight. "Good morning," he called, jumping from his horse and walking toward her.

Diana put a hand to her chest and let out her breath. "Oh, thank God," she sighed.

He shook his head at her. "Again, I find you alone and unprotected, Miss Brown. Does that groom of yours value you so lightly?"

Diana shook her head. "Of course, not," she said. "He was busy working this morning, so I went for a walk. I must have gone farther than I realized. I'm afraid I am a bit turned around! It would appear you've come to the rescue again," she said lightly.

"I am an earl, but I have the heart of a knight," he said.

"It is fortunate for me that you do," replied Diana. "Perhaps your lordship would be good enough to point the way back to Spinney Hall."

"I shall be happy to see you safely there. Would you care to rest for awhile first?" He indicated the log where she had just been sitting.

Diana felt her heart skipping excitedly. She shouldn't be alone with this man. It wasn't proper. But it might be the last chance she'd ever have to see him before she married Mr. Hunt. She sat down.

The earl sat next to her. "I've sent the carriage back to Spinney Hall," he said.

"How is the coachman?"

"Well enough," said Woodham. "He is returned, also."

"I don't know what would have become of us if you hadn't happened along," said Diana. "I am so grateful. I wish . . ." She broke off. It was hardly proper to say she wished they'd met under different circumstances.

Suddenly, he was leaning close to her, smiling wickedly, and she could feel her heart thumping wildly. "What do you wish, Miss Brown?" he asked softly.

"Nothing," she said, looking away in consternation.

"Please tell me what you were about to say," he begged.

"No," she said. "I think not."

He moved closer to her. She felt his thigh touch hers, and the contact produced a tingle which tempted her not to move her leg. She yielded.

"Tell me, Miss Brown," he murmured, "Do you find me attractive?"

His warm breath teased her cheek like a summer breeze, reminding her how close his lips were. Diana swallowed. "I am sure most ladies do," she replied.

"What do I care for most ladies?" he retorted. "I only wish to know how this lady feels." He caught her hand and brought it to his lips. They brushed the skin softly, teasingly.

"This lady feels that you are in the habit of behaving most improperly," Diana said primly, but she let her hand remain. His mouth slid caressingly up to her wrist and pressed another kiss there. He stole a glance to see what effect this action had on her.

It seemed to leave her with no life, no capability of moving her hand out of his grasp. Diana bit her lip. She must stop him. She would stop him. In just a moment.

He smiled and slid an arm around her shoulders and drew her slowly to him. "My dear Miss Brown," he murmured, and pressed his lips to hers. He continued the kiss until, no longer able to hold their prim stiffness, her lips softened and molded to his. Sensations seemed to rise from the depths of her soul like ghosts from a graveyard and she felt her body going limp, her mouth relaxed. As if the strength which had left her had gone into the earl's body, he tightened his embrace and his tongue invaded her mouth, tickling and exploring.

At last he ended the kiss. "You are well named," he whispered, caressing her cheek with his mouth. "You are truly a goddess."

Diana finally managed to break the enchantment. She pulled away and rose before she could yield to the temptation to kiss him again. Turning her back to him, she feigned great interest in adjusting her bonnet. "I must go."

He came and stood behind her. "Don't go yet."

Diana shook her head. "If I stay I will only say or do something I shouldn't."

"Then, by all means, stay," he teased.

Diana was not amused. "I am not some tavern wench," she informed him.

"No tavern wench could be as lovely as you," he agreed.

"You think I am a woman of loose morals," she accused.

"I think you are incomparably beautiful."

"Beautiful, but loose," she persisted. "You think I have no character, that I am merely a fortune hunter."

Woodham chuckled. "And a poor one, at that," he added.

Diana raised her chin to a haughty angle. "Your lordship is quick to judge."

Woodham caught her hand and kissed it. "Please forgive

me." The twinkle in his eye made a mockery of his humble words.

"I wish to go home now," Diana said grandly.

"As you wish," returned the earl, the dimple at his cheek betraying his amusement.

He fetched his horse and lifted her onto it. Then he surprised her by climbing up behind her. "I apologize that I have no side saddle for you to ride," he said, "but I promise to do my best to keep you from falling off." He slipped an arm around her middle and pulled her against him, making her heart thump wildly once again.

She tried, but found it impossible to ignore the sensation of his hard midriff against her back, of his arm intimately circling her. "Perhaps you should walk," she suggested as he urged the horse into motion.

"Ah," he said. "You had thought I would lead the horse while you sat on it like a great lady."

"I thought nothing of the sort!" declared Diana. "I simply thought it would be more proper."

She heard him chuckle and, earl or no, her palm itched to slap his face. "Is it not a little late to be concerned with propriety?" he asked.

Diana decided not to dignify this remark with an answer. "It is a lovely day," she observed, and he burst into laughter.

"You truly are wasted on Hunt," he said.

His words brought back the black cloud of her future and made her want to weep afresh.

"How do you like your new home?" he asked, his tone of voice mockingly conversational.

Diana wanted to cry out that she hated it. Instead, she said, "It will do well enough." That sounded calculating! She tried again. "It is a nice house. I am sure I will be happy there."

"We'll be neighbors," said the earl.

"Will I see you?" she asked, and instantly regretted the eagerness in her voice.

"Would you like to?" he countered.

It would be torture. "No," she said.

"No?" he echoed, amazement plain in his voice.

Diana shook her head. "I would rather not."

"You can kiss me as you did just now in the wood and yet say you don't wish to see me?"

"That is why I don't wish to see you," said Diana simply.

"I see," said the earl, and she wondered if he did.

They came to the edge of Hunt's property and Diana, recognizing it, said, "Please, let me down here. I shall walk up the drive alone."

"I don't mind escorting you all the way home," he said.

She shook her head. "Mr. Hunt might think I arranged to meet you. I shall go on alone."

The earl got off the horse and lifted her down. He should have let her go the moment her feet touched the ground, but he stood with his hands still on her waist.

She looked up at his face. He was smiling at her, and it looked to be a mocking smile. She took a step back, forcing him to drop his hands. "I thank you for bringing me safely back," she said. The earl seemed to be studying her. She waited to see what he would say next.

"I'll wager your groom plans no wedding trip for you," he predicted. "If life becomes tedious, you can always walk in the woods. I should be happy to meet you and bear you company." He caught her hand to his lips and as he kissed it, watched her for an answer.

The pleasant vision of walking through the spinney with the Earl of Woodham begged her to throw caution to the wind, but she dared not make such a promise while she was still unwed. *You dare not make such a promise at all!* she scolded herself. She said primly, "That would hardly be proper."

"That is my hope," he said and grinned.

She snatched her hand away. "I am not a loose woman," she reminded him.

"You are not a woman at all," he replied, "but a goddess. And a goddess may do as she wishes."

"Then I wish to return to the house," said Diana, the picture of moral rectitude.

"Your wish is my command," said the earl. "But first . . ." He pulled her to him, looking down at her with laughing eyes. ". . . I shall give you a wedding present."

For a moment, she forgot where she was, leaning willingly toward him, allowing him to press his lips to hers and produce that delicious surge of excitement in her chest. Only when he broke the kiss did she remember to be outraged. "Your lordship is a rake!" she accused.

He chuckled, taking her accusation as if it were a compliment. "Goodbye, fair huntress," he said. "I wish you good fortune."

Mocking her! He was mocking her! Earl or no, she would slap his insulting face.

But before she could do so, he stepped back and mounted his horse. He swept off his hat and bowed to her with a flourish, then trotted off, leaving Diana struggling for an epithet to hurl after him. With the memory of his kiss so fresh on her lips, she found it hard to think of anything. Too late. He was already almost out of sight. Diana sighed and turned to walk slowly back up the drive.

She didn't see the man leaning against a poplar tree until he spoke. "Hello, dear Aunt," said the soft voice of David Barnes. He sauntered over to her. "Was that the same noble gentleman who rescued you from the highwayman? My uncle told us all about it after you went to bed last night. Quite an exciting tale it made."

Diana's heart stopped. David had seen the earl kiss her. At a loss for what to say, she quickened her pace.

He matched his steps to hers. "Why the hurry?" he asked, smiling cynically at her. "Don't you wish to talk more about your new friend? It would appear he admires you greatly."

Diana made an exasperated noise. "What you saw was not what it appeared. The earl was merely bringing me back. I was lost in the spinney and he found me."

"How very convenient," said David. "And how very grateful you appeared just now. I wonder how much you showed your gratitude out there in the woods." He cocked an eyebrow at her.

She felt the blood rise from her neck to the roots of her hair, turning her face a guilty red. "You are rude, sir," she said.

He bowed. "I do beg your pardon. Of course, you must admit, it looks a little odd, your chancing upon the same man who rescued you and brought you home yesterday. I wonder what my uncle would think."

"You wouldn't tell him!" cried Diana.

"He would beat you if he learned you let another man kiss you," said David casually.

The same blood that had so recently flushed Diana's face fled, leaving it death white. She swallowed. "I am afraid you misunderstand the relationship between Lord Woodham and myself," she said weakly.

David nodded. "Of course," he murmured. "As would my uncle." He smiled down at Diana. "I would hate to see such lovely skin marked in any way. Perhaps we should let this be our secret."

"Thank you," she said stiffly.

"I'm happy to oblige." David took her hand and kissed it, looking slyly at her. "It's nice to see my new aunt is such a warm-hearted creature. I'm sure we'll all be one happy family."

"We had best return to the house," said Diana.

He nodded. "An excellent idea. Uncle was worried about you. He sent me to look for you."

"Oh, dear," fretted Diana. "I didn't mean to be gone so long."

"I believe he feared you had come in harm's way. Won't it be nice that we can tell him you did not?"

The look David gave her made Diana very uncomfortable. She began to suspect that he felt they had come to some sort of illicit agreement. What price did he expect to exact from her for her silence? And when?

Later that night she discovered he expected her to pay him for his silence as soon as possible. She heard a gentle tapping at her door not long after the household had settled for the night. Thinking it to be her new maid, she opened the door only to find David standing there in his dressing gown.

Before she could protest, he slipped into her room, shutting the door after him. "I'm glad to see you weren't asleep," he said, and added sarcastically, "dear Aunt." His eyes swept over her, and she saw in them the same greedy desire she'd seen in the highwayman's. "And how lovely you look." He reached out to flick the ribbon at her neck, and she took a step back. "Although we must see about getting you something a little more flattering," he continued. "Such high necklines and thick material are not at all the thing for a fashionable lady to wear at night, especially when she's expecting a visitor."

Diana moved away. "I was expecting no visitor, I assure you."

David cocked a disbelieving eyebrow. "Come now, there's no need to play coy with me. Did we or did we not come to an agreement this afternoon?"

"We did not!" Diana ran around the bed, putting it between them. "And if you come near me I shall scream."

David frowned. "What kind of game is this you're playing?" Sudden understanding showed in his face. "I see," he said slowly. "You play for higher stakes. Why have me when you can have a titled gentleman for a lover, eh? Well, I wonder what my uncle will think about your little game."

He turned to leave, and Diana ran around the bed and grabbed him by the arm. "Don't you dare tell your uncle such a thing!"

He smiled down at her and put his arms around her. "That's better," he said.

"Take your hands off me," she commanded.

He was shocked into obeying.

"Don't think you can force me to bed with you," she snapped. "And if you try to tell Mr. Hunt anything about Lord Woodham and myself I shall tell him about tonight. How do you think he would feel if he were to discover his nephew trying to bed his wife? He already dislikes you. He would never let you come here if he were to learn of this. And he wouldn't leave you so much as a farthing in his will."

David's eyes narrowed. "You little tart," he spat. Then he turned and stalked from the room, leaving Diana limp and shaking.

She sank onto her bed, wrapped her arms around her middle and rocked herself, letting the tears fall. She had never felt so alone and unprotected in her life. How she longed for her mama's comforting presence. What would happen to her in this house? If only Lord Woodham would come and take her away. . . .

No, she told herself firmly. To spin such fairy tales was silly. Men like Lord Woodham had pretty women throwing themselves at them all the time. Kisses obviously did not mean marriage to fine, titled gentlemen. At least, not kisses from little nobodies like Diana Brown. It was one thing to save her from a highwayman, quite another to save her from a miserable marriage. She was merely someone with whom to dally in the woods.

Diana got under the covers and wrapped them tightly around her. She would marry Mr. Hunt and be grateful for the security he offered her. And she would count herself well rid of Lord Woodham, who offered her only kisses, caresses and ruin.

Three

The next morning Hunt offered to show Diana some of the surrounding countryside. Anything was better than hanging about the house in the company of his odious nephew, so she agreed. Besides, she had a hankering to see how far her future husband's lands extended.

"Change into your riding clothes, then," said Hunt. "I have an old mare who should do admirably for you."

To call it old was a kindness, thought Diana, when she saw the decrepit animal. She felt guilty putting even her small weight on its swayback. The nag should have been turned out to pasture long ago. Not even a decent horse to ride—this was what her life as the rich Mrs. Hunt would be like. The thought made her fall into a dismal silence.

As they rode along, Hunt commended her on what a quiet, biddable woman she was and again congratulated himself on his wise choice of a bride. Diana swallowed the sick feeling that rose in her throat.

Two more days, she thought, and I'll be wed to this man—a prisoner of circumstance, with no hope for escape.

Her husband's estate, she realized, was not large.

As if reading her thoughts, he said, "It is not a huge estate, but have no desire to be a farmer. I am a man of business, and my fortune comes from my wit and wise investments. I'm not dependent on the whims of nature for my living." He smiled on her. "We shall live comfortably without having to bother about the spring planting or whether or not there will be rain."

Diana suspected that if she wanted to live as comfortably as her future husband predicted, she'd have to exert as much cleverness on her own behalf as he did in his mysterious business ventures.

She didn't see David until nuncheon. He greeted her with a smile on his face and scorn in his eyes, and she knew she had made an enemy. Well, soon he and his mother would be gone. He wasn't worth wasting thought over.

"We had a delightful drive this morning, didn't we, my dear?" demanded Hunt as he cut into a thick slice of beef.

"It was a beautiful morning for a ride," said Diana.

"Did you ride by the spinney?" asked David with a mock innocence.

Diana felt the blood drain from her face. Would he really tell Hunt about Lord Woodham, or was he toying with her? She'd confess the truth before he could spin out a lie and cause trouble. "Yes, we did," she said. She turned to Hunt. "It was my second time in that wood, sir. I'm afraid I walked farther than I realized yesterday and found myself lost there."

Hunt laid down his fork and looked at her in amazement. "My dear child, to walk such a distance! You are stronger than you look."

"I was foolish to go so far," said Diana. "I was very frightened when I discovered I was lost. And I wished I had taken you with me," she added. That was a lie, but it would appease her future husband.

"But you found your way back all safe and sound," said Hunt with satisfaction.

"Only because Lord Woodham happened on me in the woods. I'm afraid we are in his debt again, dear sir."

Hunt's brows narrowed and his face took on the reddish tinge of anger. "That young jackanapes again! Because he is nobility he thinks he may dally with every pretty woman around. Well, he won't be dallying with my wife."

"But he wasn't dallying with me," protested Diana. Even as she protested, she hoped the flush on her face would be interpreted as merely strong emotion and not guilt, for dallying was exactly what Lord Woodham had been doing. And she had allowed him to! She rushed on, fearful of what David might have to say on that subject. "I don't know how long I would have wandered in that wood if the earl hadn't happened along."

Her husband shook his head at her. "You are such an innocent," he said. "The man most likely rode out in the hopes of encountering you. He wishes to seduce you. His kind do it all the time. They spy some pretty girl, take her and use her, then leave her to deal with the consequences alone." Hunt shook his head. "The nobility in this country are a disgrace. But what can you expect from men who are handed everything and not expected to do an honest day's work?" He turned his attention again to Diana. "From now on you will not leave these grounds unless I accompany you."

"As you wish," said Diana. Across the table from her, she saw David wearing a smirk and wished she could throw her plate at him.

The rest of the meal was consumed in near silence. Both Hunt and his sister preferred to concentrate on the pleasures of the plate rather than the company with whom they ate.

This was fine with Diana. Hunt had given her enough food for thought with which to occupy herself. Of course, what he had said about the nobility was true. The earl was living proof. He was no better than the man she was marrying. In fact the earl was *worse*. At least Hunt was prepared to pay, and pay respectably for her. The earl was nothing more than a selfish poacher, intent on possessing as much of her as he could with as little cost to himself as possible.

She'd thought him so noble at first, simply because he'd happened to come along in time to save her from a highwayman. But he'd turned that to his own selfish purposes soon enough. Besides, he'd most likely have saved anyone caught in such circumstances simply for the adventure of it.

The only difference between Mr. Hunt and Lord Woodham, she concluded, was looks and circumstance. The earl happened to have the good fortune of being able to hide his selfishness behind a handsome face and a title.

The sound of a loud belch brought Diana's attention back to the table in time to hear Hunt pronounce himself satisfied. "I've neglected my work too long today." He wagged a finger at Diana as if it were her fault and said, "A man does not hang onto his fortune by spending his days in idle pleasure."

"It was kind of you to take valuable time to make me feel welcome in my new home," she said meekly.

"It was," agreed Hunt. "But now I'm afraid you must entertain yourself. Get my worthless nephew to show you the garden. There are some things still in bloom out there, I believe."

The mother of the worthless nephew looked highly insulted by this unflattering reference, but David smiled, unruffled. "I should be happy to show my aunt about the grounds."

"That is very kind," said Diana, "but I think, perhaps I shall take a rest."

David nodded. "Perhaps after you have rested," he suggested.

"Perhaps," she said noncommitally, and resolved to stay hidden in her room for the rest of the day.

But she found it impossible to remain holed up all afternoon. After an hour she was bored and decided to venture out in search of the housekeeper. She should start becoming familiar with how the house ran, and it would feel good to be doing something useful.

David intercepted her on the stairs, and she wondered if he'd been waiting for her.

"Rested now?" he asked.

"Yes, thank you," she said stiffly. "And now I am going to go speak with the housekeeper."

"Not even a bride yet and already taking over as mistress of the house," observed David.

"Once I am a bride I shall be expected to run this house," said Diana. "I wish to do a good job of it."

"I'm sure you will," said David, "But there is plenty of time to meet with the housekeeper, and plenty of work ahead in the future. Believe me, my uncle will get his pound's worth out of you soon enough. Best enjoy your freedom while you may," he concluded. He took her hand and threaded it through his arm and began to lead her down the stairs. "I think you'll enjoy the garden."

"I don't wish to see the garden," said Diana firmly, trying to stop.

But David drew her on. "Oh, I'm sure you do," he said pleasantly. "Not with me, perhaps, but one must take what company one can find. Wouldn't you agree?"

"No, I would not," snapped Diana, and tried to yank her hand free.

David merely smiled. "Come now," he said in a lowered voice. "I can hardly ravish you in plain view of anyone who wishes to look out the drawing room window. You'll be safe enough."

Diana clamped her lips shut and went with him. It was foolish to make a scene on the stairs, but when she had this man outside they would settle things once and for all. He opened the French doors for her and she proceeded him out onto the terrace. Refusing his arm, she preceded him down the steps to the lawn, then turned and said, "I hope I won't be forced to repeat what I told you last night."

"I think this sort of intimate conversation deserves a more private spot, don't you?" suggested David.

Diana pressed her lips into an angry line and marched ahead of him into the garden. He smiled and strolled after her.

"Would you care to sit?" he asked, indicating a small, stone bench.

"I don't intend to stay that long," she informed him.

He came behind her and put his hands on her shoulders and she squirmed away. "Dear Diana, why do you so dislike me?"

"Because you are unprincipled and sneaky," Diana informed him.

A smile spread broadly across his handsome face. "Why, my dear, you have just described yourself!"

Diana's eyes flashed with all the anger of one who suspected the accusation against her to be true. "I want nothing to do with you. Do you hear me? Nothing!"

She turned to leave and he caught her arm. "Don't put all your eggs in one basket, fair one. The nobility are an inbred and selfish lot. You cannot expect anything from that quarter. And you have only one ally in this family—myself."

"Don't be ridiculous," Diana said haughtily. "I have my husband. And your mother," she added. She looked David up and down as if she were a princess and he a commoner. "And I must say I vastly prefer her to you."

He burst into laughter at that. "Oh, yes. My dear, sweet mother who is so fond of you, she'd happily murder you before your wedding day if she could think of a way."

Diana was shocked into silence. She stared at David as if he were mad.

"My mother has no love for you," he continued casually. "Don't let her pleasant demeanor deceive you."

"What cause would your mother have to hate me so?" demanded Diana.

"Surely you cannot be so stupid. Should she like you because you are to marry her brother and give him an heir who will take away her only son's inheritance?" David shook his head. "No, don't count my mother your friend. And your husband-to-be has no real love for you. To him you are only a pretty breeding toy. He'll plough you, get you with child and then go back to pursuing his one true love. Money."

Diana's cheeks and neck pulsed with the hot throb of embarrassment. She turned her back to David and sank onto the bench. "What a horrid man you are to say such things to me."

He sat down next to her. "I speak to you bluntly, as a friend," he said.

"You are not my friend. You only wish to use me, just like Mr. Hunt, for a toy."

"I wish you for my mistress," he admitted. "My God, Diana, who would not? You are the most beautiful woman I've ever seen."

"And you are the most odious man I've ever met," she retorted. "You're not my friend. You are only a man who wants what is not his. Why don't you go earn some money of your own?" A red stain crept onto David's cheeks and Diana saw that her barb had hit a nerve. She rose and looked at him scornfully. "You sicken me," she said.

Slowly, he rose from the bench, an unpleasant smile on his face. "That was a foolish little speech you made. I shall try not to hold it against you when the time comes you need my help." Diana turned her back to him, but he continued, "And the time will come. Your fine earl will go off to London to enjoy the social season and find himself some little ballet dancer. Hunt will tire of you and leave you to molder in this place. When next we are alone, you'll be so starved for affection you will take any crumb I give you. Until then," he leaned over and planted a kiss on her shoulder, ". . . allow me to wish you happy." Diana made no reply and he left her. She heard the sound of his retreating feet crunching on the gravel path and shivered in the sunshine.

David didn't seek Diana out for any more intimate conversations before the wedding, and she found herself extremely thankful. She spent her mornings with the housekeeper and her afternoons walking the grounds. She was tempted to leave Spinney Hall—just to see more of the countryside, she told herself. But she dared not risk Hunt's displeasure, so she tried to be content with prowling the garden and walking to the edges of the vast lawns that surrounded the house.

In the evenings she played whist with her husband and his houseguests, and as she became more proficient at the game she found this was something that could give her pleasure.

Perhaps Mr. Hunt would play cards with her in the evenings. Life at Spinney Hall wouldn't be so miserable after all. The night before her wedding day she went to bed with a flicker of hope in her heart. She might be able to find a small portion of happiness with Mr. Hunt. And, perhaps, just perhaps, after she'd borne him an heir he would take her to London and allow her to introduce her sister to polite society.

Julian sat at the desk in his study, staring at nothing in particular and seeing Diana Brown. It was silly to be so pre-occupied with a woman, even such a stupefyingly beautiful one. Of course, if she'd been a young woman of means, he could have justified his preoccupation. But Miss Hunt was a nobody, a cheap adventuress. His stepmother had been quick to inform him of that obvious fact.

He sighed. A pity she was to be shut away at Spinney Hall. She would have made a delightful mistress. Life was unfair, indeed! That a fat old windbag like Hunt should find such a lovely creature. Bah! He'd ride her and be done in five minutes. Women, like expensive wine, should be savored, and that old glutton savored nothing.

Julian poured himself another glass of Madeira from a nearby decanter, now only half full. At this rate he'd be foxed in no time. He raised his glass to the future Mrs. Hunt and said, "To your success."

Half an hour later he sat in an intoxicated fog, his head buzzing lightly, and still the image of Diana Brown wouldn't leave his mind. He closed his eyes and she danced before him, wearing a thin muslin gown that showed her curves. The girl had had a lovely bosom; full, but not gross. And a slender waist. He'd nearly been able to circle it with his hands when he lifted her down from his curricle. He'd caught a glimpse of a nicely turned ankle as well, and longed for a look at the rest of her leg.

The vision he saw didn't show it to him. Instead, she looked at him with pleading eyes and cried, "Help me!"

Julian would no more let himself be taken in by a vision than he would a flesh and blood female. He shook his head and muttered, "I have already rescued you once. You have made your bed, now you will have to be bored in it."

As Williams lovingly laid out her wedding gown and veil, Diana stood by her bedroom window, reflecting on how little excitement she felt—so different from her feelings when she'd first received Mr. Hunt's marriage proposal. Of course, that was before she'd discovered him to be such a selfish man. That was before he'd kissed her with his great, wet lips. And that was before . . .

No. She would not think about the wicked Earl of Woodham and the way his kisses made her feel.

She turned from the window to find the maid waiting patiently for her. " 'Tis a lovely gown," ventured Williams. "All those little silver roses embroidered on the hem."

Diana moved to the bed and ran a finger over the white and silver gown. "Mama and I spent many hours sewing it," she said.

"It is as fine as anything I ever seen in a shop window," said Williams.

Diana smiled. "Mama is an excellent seamstress. She took in ladies' gowns to alter, even made a few." Diana sighed. "How Mama would have loved to have been here today."

Would offering a few days of hospitality have cost Mr. Hunt so very much? She should have insisted he allow her mother and sister to accompany her. It was her wedding day, after all.

And now, here she was to be married among strangers. Only
Mary Barnes and her son would be present at the church, to
act as groomsman and matron of honor. The guests coming to
share the wedding breakfast were few; Mary and David, the
squire and his wife, Mr. Bellows, the rector, who would marry
them, and his wife. All people she neither knew nor loved,
and who cared nothing for her.

She suddenly felt like crying and blinked hard to stop the
insistent tears from escaping her eyes. One managed to spill
free and danced down her cheek, and she tried surreptitiously
to wipe it away.

Williams gave her a sympathetic look and said, "I'm sure
your gown will look ever so nice."

Diana sighed. "Yes, you are right, Williams. I had best put
it on. There can be no postponing what will be. The only thing
that will save me now is death."

"Oh, miss, you mustn't say that," said Williams nervously.
" 'Tis bad luck, I'm sure."

"The only bad luck I see for myself today is in having to
go through with this marriage," said Diana miserably. "Well,
let us dress me and be done with it."

Williams fussed and fretted over her mistress, alternately
trying to encourage her and worrying aloud over her state of
mind. She played with Diana's curls and fussed with the long
gauze veil which fell down her back until Diana thought she
would scream. "Enough," she said at last. "I must go down."

She scolded herself as she made her way downstairs. It was
silly to act as if she were going to her execution. Her life
would not be so very bad with Mr. Hunt. She had to stop
behaving like such a baby.

Baby. Heirs. The consummation of her marriage. Once,
when cutting across a field in Tetbury, Diana had stumbled on
a half-dressed couple nestled in a hayloft. The thought of being
taken into Hunt's bedroom and being fondled in such a manner
by those fat hands brought the cold sweat of fear to her brow.

I cannot do this, she told herself, but her legs moved stoically onward.

Perhaps she could feign illness and, at least, postpone doing her wifely duty. She had easily been able to put him off with a sneeze. Of course, once they were married, something so small as a sneeze might not deter him. She could put her finger down her throat and retch after the ceremony. That, surely, would do it. She might not even need to use such measures, for just the thought of Mr. Hunt's hands on her body was making her stomach quesy.

She had reached the drawing room. "Ah, here is our bride," said Mary, coming to greet her. "And don't you look lovely?" The room had been filled with flowers in honor of the occasion. Their scent crept up Diana's nostrils like a spreading poison, making her feel increasingly unwell.

"David has already gone with your groom to the church," said Mary. "The stable lad has just returned for us. Are you ready?"

Never, thought Diana, but she nodded.

"Then let us be off," said Mary. "My brother won't like to be kept waiting."

Hunt stood at the door of the church, in dress attire. The silver buttons on his black coat were so severely strained they should have groaned, and his satin breeches looked as though they encased two gigantic sausages. His fat calves shone in clocked silk stockings, and his feet were stuffed into evening slippers. Diana had forgotten how ridiculous he looked in formal attire. He patted her hand and told her she looked lovely.

"She looks more than that," put in David. "She looks unforgettable."

This seemed very brazen, and Diana looked to her groom, sure he'd put his nephew in his place.

But Hunt smiled maliciously. "Yes, she does," he agreed. "And I'm sure you'll never forget her or this day. Will you, my boy?"

David smiled, but his eyes were ice. "I certainly won't," he said politely. This must be as hard for him as it is for me, thought Diana. All his hopes die once the vows are said. Remembering how hard her own family had struggled along on their limited funds she could almost pity David.

Hunt turned to the rector. "Well now, Mr. Bellows, let's begin the ceremony. We have a fine wedding breakfast awaiting us afterward, and I must confess all this excitement has made me hungry."

The ceremony was torture. Once during the vows, Diana felt faint, but Mary had her vinaigrette ready and was able to revive the bride to say, "I do." The rector pronounced the couple man and wife and instructed the groom to kiss his bride. Diana shut her eyes before turning her face to be kissed, preferring not to see the approach of the sickening, wet lips.

She felt them, though. They slid over her like some horrible forest snail and she shuddered.

Her groom misinterpreted it and patted her shoulder encouragingly. "We'll be alone soon enough, my little dove," he whispered, and she kept her eyes closed to shut out the sight of his face.

The ceremony at an end, the little group made their way back to Spinney Hall. Soon after, the rest of the guests arrived. Mary beamed and greeted one and all as if she were the mistress of the house. "Ah, Squire Irving. And your charming wife! Allow me to introduce you to the new Mrs. Hunt."

Diana let herself to be paraded around the room like a horse on show. The faces of the fat squire and his wife, and the rector and his boney matron were but blurs. Although the squire had a booming voice, she was only vaguely aware of him clapping Hunt on the back and congratulating him.

At last it was time to move into the dining room, where the best service was laid in honor of the special occasion. Crystal goblets waited to be filled with wine to toast the bride and groom, and napkins folded in the shape of mitres sat on the fine bone china plates.

It had been an overcast morning, but now the sun burned

its way through the clouds and sunlight invaded the room, making the silver shine and the crystal wink and sparkle. "Oh, the sun!" declared the rector's wife. She turned to Diana. "Happy the bride the sun shines on," she told her.

Breakfast was a glutton's delight. The sideboard was filled with tempting dishes from the kitchen; eggs, ham, sausage, kippers, devilled kidneys, stewed fruit, and naturally, a brides-cake.

Hunt employed neither butler nor footman, and Williams and another maid were attempting to serve. In her nervousness at having to serve such a grand meal, Williams managed to spill a bowl of stewed plums.

Mary clucked her tongue. "Clumsy girl," she scolded, and sent both maids off to the kitchen for towels.

The squire's wife commiserated with Diana on how difficult it was to find efficient servants. "A butler would be a wise investment," she told Hunt, "Now that you are a married man you'll want to entertain more, and one really cannot do without a butler."

"Paying a man simply to follow me around and open doors and tell me when my dinner is ready is a waste of money," said Hunt.

"Charles certainly needs no butler today when he has his sister and his new bride to serve him. Isn't that right, Diana?" Mary inquired.

"Of course," murmured Diana, taking the hint and rising from her seat.

"Perhaps you would like to take off your veil first," suggested Mary. "Mrs. Bellows," she said to the rector's wife, "would you be so good as to assist her?"

Mrs. Bellows was happy to oblige, and by the time Diana's veil was removed Mary had her brother's plate heaped high with food.

"Just the way he likes it," she informed Diana. "In fact," she added, handing Diana the plate, "I think you might add a few more kippers. Charles is so fond of them."

Diana obeyed, wishing she could slip something into the kippers to make her new husband lose interest in performing his nuptial duty.

A mortified Williams returned with towels, followed by the other girl bearing a pan of warm water. They quickly mopped up the spilled food, and within a matter of minutes order was restored, and all the guests served and happy.

But nothing looked good to Diana, and after forcing two bites of sausage down her throat she gave up.

Hunt looked at her untouched food. "You should eat something," he told her. "A bride must keep up her strength."

The squire smirked at this and his wife pretended not to notice her husband's crude behavior. Diana felt weak. She knew she wouldn't have the strength for what lay ahead no matter how much she ate.

"I'll admit the kippers are a little off," Hunt continued, "but this is fine ham."

"Where do you intend to take your new bride for your honeymoon?" asked the squire's wife. "Italy, Greece?"

Hunt looked surprised by her question. "Why, nowhere," he replied. "We shall be as happy as two peas in a pod here at Spinney Hall. Won't we, my dear?"

"Of course," murmured Diana. She felt David's mocking gaze on her and kept her eyes on her plate.

"Hunt's right," agreed the squire. "What sensible man would want go junketing about the world, when the loveliest corner of it is right here in Surrey."

"Always thought it was foolish of young Woodham to go haring off to the Peninsula," observed the squire. "Why the old earl allowed it I cannot imagine."

"I am sure the boy has regretted it many times since," said Mrs. Bellows. "Imagine how horrible he must have felt when he heard of his father's death. And, can you imagine, not to be able to get home until so long after the funeral? How his poor stepmama managed I cannot imagine."

"Of course, the news he'd been wounded was what probably

killed Woodham in the first place, mind you," the squire told her. He shook his head. "Bad business, that. Woodham should have put his foot down. After all, a young nobleman owes his first responsibility to his family."

"Hear, hear," said the rector.

"He has certainly made himself scarce enough in the two years since," continued the squire, his voice disapproving.

"Well, he is back now," said Mrs. Irving, "and I am sure he means to make up for his absence."

Seeing the wistful look that settled on Diana's face at mention of the new Earl of Woodham, the rector's wife misinterpreted it for homesickness and said to her, "It is lovely here in the spring. And there is always much to do. I think you will like it very much."

"Of course she will," said Hunt. "Being mistress of such a fine house, and with such kind women to befriend her, why shouldn't she be?"

Diana forced a smile.

No one seemed in a hurry to leave, and the meal stretched on. They had been at the table an hour already. Perhaps now would be a good time to beg her guests' indulgence and excuse herself. "Are you not feeling, well, dearest?" asked Mary.

Diana was about to reply that she was not when she realized her sister-in-law hadn't been talking to her. She followed Mary's gaze to Mr. Hunt. He had set down his fork and wore a pained expression on his face. He rubbed his stomach. "I must have eaten something that didn't agree with me," he said. "I feel rather billious."

There were many murmurs about the table at this news. How vexing! On his wedding day, of all days.

"Take a little wine," suggested the squire's wife. "That is the best thing for constitutional disorders."

Hunt gulped down the rest of his wine. He sat as if waiting for his stomach to feel instantly better, then shook his head. "That's not helping. I do believe it is getting worse," he added, and clutched at his stomach.

"Dear, dear," fretted Mrs. Bellows. She looked at her husband.

"Well, we had best be going," he announced. "Perhaps if we all leave, you will be able to rest."

"Excellent idea," agreed Squire Irving

Hunt rose from his chair to see his guests out and doubled over with pain, letting out a loud moan.

"Oh, dear!" cried Mary. "This is most unfortunate."

David rushed to his side. "Allow me to help you upstairs," he said.

Hunt's face was now screwed up in pain. He nodded and let David lead him from the room.

Mr. Bellows took Diana's hand. "What an unfortunate circumstance," he said sympathetically. "But I'm sure your husband will be feeling much better soon."

Diana was too overcome with joy to speak. It was nothing less than a miracle! She nodded and tried hard not to let her polite smile stretch too wide.

The guests left and Diana and Mary moved to the drawing room to await David's return. Fifteen minutes later he was with them, shaking his head. "Uncle was violently ill in his room just now, and I don't like his color at all. I think we had best send for the doctor."

"For a simple upset of the stomach? Don't be so silly," scoffed Mary. "May I remind you? This is not the first time this has happened. He has simply eaten something which disagreed with him."

"If that is the case it is a violent disagreement," observed David.

"David," said his mother firmly. "There is no need to be so dramatic. You will only frighten Diana." She patted Diana's hand. "It is a simple stomach upset," she said comfortingly. "I'm afraid Charles sometimes indulges a little too freely in rich food. It does not always agree with him."

"Perhaps we should send for the doctor," suggested Diana.

"If he isn't improved by morning," added David.

"Yes. That is a good idea," said Mary. "I'm sure by tomorrow he will be right as rain. But if not, we can fetch a doctor and perhaps get some powders for him." She gave Diana a kindly smile. "Such a disappointing wedding day for you, dear."

Diana tried to look regretful. "These things happen," she said stoically. She rose. "Perhaps I'll just go have a piece of cake. To keep up my strength," she added, and made good her escape to the dining room.

Once safely there Diana sighed in relief. No wedding night for her. She was saved. At least for this night. And who knew what tomorrow would bring? Maybe Mr. Hunt would still be ill. Williams and the other maid were there clearing the table. She shooed them off and took a plate from the table and cut herself a large piece of cake.

"Such a concerned wife."

Diana turned to see David, sauntering up to the table. She flushed guiltily. "He is not seriously ill, is he?"

"More so than my mother realizes."

Diana set aside her cake. "It was simply an upset stomach," she protested. "He must have eaten something that disagreed with him."

David looked at her in stoney contempt. "Yes. He must have."

She stared at him, wide eyed. Why was he looking at her like that? Was it her fault Mr. Hunt was ill?

"I shall leave you to finish your cake," he said coldly and turned to leave.

"You will tell me if he worsens?"

David's lip lifted in a cynical smile. "Oh, by all means, Miss Brown."

He was being deliberately rude to anger her. "It is not Miss Brown any more," she informed him. "I am Mrs. Hunt."

"Much good it will do you," said David, and left her.

She tossed her head, dismissed all thoughts of the horrid David Barnes from her mind, and took a large bite of cake.

* * *

Late that afternoon the two women sat with the tea tray between them when David entered the room and announced, "He is worse."

"One isn't always quickly well when the stomach is troubled," observed Mary.

"It is not just his stomach, Mother," said David. "It is his bowels. And he is complaining of dizziness. I tell you, he is a very ill man. We should send for a doctor."

"Really, dearest," said Mary, "I thought we agreed to wait until morning. I am sure it is nothing, and won't you feel silly when the doctor tells you the very same thing?"

David shook his head. "I don't like to alarm you, but I think it is more serious than we realize."

"Then we must send for the doctor," said Diana.

"Who can we send?" objected Mary. "We are dangerously low on servants."

"There must be someone," said Diana.

Mary shook her head. "We obviously cannot send Charles' man, for he is busy attending to Charles. The coachman is still lazing about, pretending his arm bothers him. . . ."

David looked put out. "Send the groom," he snapped. "He was able to manage the carriage this morning. He should certainly be able to fetch a doctor."

His mother made a face. "Very well," she said. "But I think you are making a great fuss for nothing."

"Nonetheless, I shall feel better after we've had the doctor here," said David and left them to go in search of the groom.

David had barely been gone when Hunt's white-faced valet came rushing into the drawing room.

"Good heavens, what has happened!" cried Diana, jumping up.

"He is dead!" cried the man.

"Nonsense! He cannot be," snapped Mary.

"I tell you, he is," insisted the servant.

Diana rushed from the room, Mary following her, calling, "Don't go up there, Diana. You won't want to see."

Diana rushed down the corridor to Hunt's bedroom and stopped in the doorway. He lay on his large, canopied bed, staring vacantly at its fabric ceiling. In spite of the open window, the room reeked of foul odors.

Diana felt the bile rising in her throat and put her hand to her mouth. She backed up and found herself backing into her sister-in-law. With a cry, she turned and pushed past Mary and ran to her room. She slammed the door after herself and leaned against it as if to keep death out, for surely it seemed to be pursuing her wherever she went.

How could this have happened? Mr. Hunt had seemed in perfect health that morning. Now he was dead.

And she was free. She began to laugh hysterically. The laughter turned to crying and she slid down the door and crumpled in a billow of silver and white.

Four

Diana remained holed up in her room long after the sound of voices and footsteps had ceased to whisper through her door. Long shadows crept across her bedroom floor and the room grew cold, but still she stayed, her body wrapped in a blanket, her mind wrapped in thought. How had this all happened so suddenly? Mr. Hunt had seemed perfectly fit. It was a miracle. It had to be. One moment she was married and dreading her husband's attentions, the next she was saved.

But she had never wished her husband to die. She'd wished illness on him, yes, but never death! She should never have thought such wicked thoughts. Was she, somehow, responsible for this?

The faint sound of the passing bell tolling from the parish church crept in under the bedroom window, reminding her once more of the immediate horror of death and its accompanying needs. Who would make the funeral arrangements?

Surely not her. It was all so grisly and horrible. The smell and sight of what lay in the room down the corridor made her shudder and swept her afresh with nausea.

When the shadows took full possession of the room she rang for Williams and requested a fire.

"And would you fancy a bit of tea, Miss, er . . . Missus," stumbled Williams, blushing fiercely.

Diana shook her head.

The maid looked earnestly at her, but said no more, and half an hour later Diana sat by a cozy fire, tallow candles scenting the room with the faint odor of sheep. She curled up in her chair by the hearth and slept.

That was when she saw Hunt, his head nothing but a skull. He came toward her, arms outstretched, bony, skeleton fingers reaching for her. "I was robbed of my life," he wailed, "robbed of my wedding night. I'll have it yet."

Diana screamed and woke up. Her heart was pounding as if she'd run for miles. She looked nervously about her and it seemed that while she'd slept the cozy little room had been stripped of its womb-like warmth and left with the miasma of the crypt. She threw off her blanket and hurried out, trying all the while to shake the feeling that some threatening spirit dogged her.

Once in the hallway she hesitated, uncertain what to do. She really had no desire to see David, but she needed someone to guide her, and she knew that he was the only one who could. Still, she lingered, chewing her lower lip. It would be unpleasant talking to David. He would, most likely, insinuate all manner of rude things. Well, there was no help for it. Best go downstairs now and be done with it.

She found him with Mary, seated before the drawing room fire. He turned at the sight of her and rose, saying nothing.

His mother had enough to say for both of them. "You poor child," she gushed. "Such a horrible nightmare experience! You should have let the doctor give you something to sleep."

"I have slept," said Diana, and the memory of what that slumber had produced made her shudder.

"You're cold," observed Mary. "Come, sit by the fire."

At these words, David moved his chair closer to the hearth and indicated she take it, then leaned against the fireplace mantle, regarding her.

"Thank you," she murmured, and sat down uneasily. "I don't know what needs to be done," she stammered. She looked to David. "Do you?"

"I have some idea," he said. "I have already notified the rector. Did you hear the passing bell?"

She nodded. "What else is to be done?"

"Mr. Bellows will come tomorrow morning and we will make all the arrangements for the funeral," said David.

"Must I be there?" asked Diana.

He shook his head. "As the bereaved widow, I am sure no one expects you to."

Diana caught the light seasoning of sarcasm in his voice and regarded her lap. At last she said, "I am truly sorry he died so horribly."

"Of course you are," said Mary. "It is a great shock to become a widow before you have even had time to be a bride."

Diana suddenly realized she didn't know what had caused her husband's death. She wasn't sure she wanted to, but she felt it was expected she ask. "Of what did he die?"

"Gastric fever," replied Mary. She shook her head. "My brother was very foolish in undertaking matrimony at his time in life, and with his weak constitution. The doctor should have cautioned him against such a rash step. If I'd known of his plans sooner I'd have had a plain talk with him myself. It's downright wicked to take a wife when one is in such delicate health."

Funny, thought Diana, the words "delicate health" seemed an inappropriate description of Mr. Hunt.

Mary continued, "It is a pity, though, that he could not have lived to enjoy a taste of married life." She dabbed at an eye with the corner of a lacy handkerchief. "He worked so hard all his life, poor man." Her son went to stand behind her and put a hand on her shoulder and she reached up to pat it. "Dear boy. Such a comfort to have my son with me at a time like this." She sighed. "There is so much to do." For the first time she seemed to notice that Diana still wore her wedding dress. She frowned. "We must see about getting you a proper widow's gown first thing tomorrow."

Diana nodded meekly, thankful the whole grisly tangle was being seen to by others. She leaned back in the chair and shut her eyes.

"This has all been too much for you," Mary cooed. "A good dinner is what we need."

Diana shook her head. "I couldn't eat."

"Well, you must eat something," insisted Mary. "We all must. David, do go and tell Williams to brew us a pot of tea. And tell her to bring some biscuits with it, and some bread and cheese. And some of those tarts I saw in the kitchen. That should tide us over. I vow, the first thing we must do when you are master of Spinney Hall is hire a butler. How on earth my brother managed without one is a mystery to me."

Diana remembered how, only that morning, Mary had observed her brother had no need of a butler. Her son, it would seem, was a different case altogether.

David left and Mary talked on, her voice becoming a background drone to Diana's thoughts. From wedding gown to widow's weeds all in one day. Only last summer she'd been so happy, so sure her life would be one of ease and laughter. At least, now that she was a wealthy widow there would be ease. But what of laughter? The next two years of mourning stretched before her like a prison sentence. And the funeral, what a torture that would be—people staring at her and whispering. Would she have to go through this funeral as she did her wedding, without any of her blood kin present, only strangers to bear her company? "I wish to send for my mother," she announced suddenly.

Mary, who had been interrupted in mid-sentence, looked surprised, then sympathetic. "Of course, you do," she said. "But we cannot wait on them for the funeral."

Panic seized Diana. "I cannot sit in that church pew alone," she said through gritted teeth.

"But, my dear, you shan't be alone. David and I will be with you."

Diana bit her lip and tried not to cry.

David had returned in time to hear his mother's words and put in, "Never fear, dear aunt. We'll help you through this ordeal." The smile he gave her was saturnine and she felt stung by his words.

"I want my mother here," she repeated, her voice threatening hysteria.

"Write her a letter in the morning and I shall include money for the coach fare and post it tomorrow," said David.

"By all means, send for her," agreed Mary. "She won't arrive in time for the funeral, but she will be a comfort to you when she does come."

"Thank you," said Diana stiffly. She rose. "I think I shall retire now."

"You should at least take a dish of tea," urged Mary. "And a biscuit, to keep up your strength."

How very like her brother Mary Barnes was, thought Diana. The solution to everyone's troubles lay in the larder.

"We cannot have you becoming ill," reasoned Mary. "Charles would certainly not want that, God rest his soul."

Diana sank back onto the chair, her nerves begging her to scream, while Mary alternately mourned the loss of her brother and catalogued the many fine possessions he'd left behind.

Mary's conversation seemed to make David as uncomfortable as Diana, for at last he said, "Mother, please. Let us talk no more of such things."

She sniffed. "Well, of course, if you don't wish to. I am sure I was only making conversation." Williams arrived, bearing a tea tray, and Mary greedily eyed the biscuits, the thick slices of cheese, and tarts. "Ah, now here's something to take our minds from our troubles. We shall all feel so much better after we've had a bite."

Diana drank her tea and ate her biscuit, and found she had appetite for another two as well.

"There now," said her sister-in-law. "I told you you were hungry."

"One can only mourn for so long," said David, causing Diana to set down her cup with an angry clink.

"David," snapped his mother. "You will show some respect to your uncle's widow."

David inclined his head politely. "Forgive me. It was a thoughtless remark."

Diana knew better than to believe his apology heartfelt. "I know why you talk so to me," she challenged. "It is because I have taken your inheritance away from you."

Mary gasped, and even David looked surprised. "My dear, you are tired," she said.

Diana sighed. She had been unacceptably rude. "I'm sorry," she said. "I think I had best go rest."

"We are all overwrought," said Mary.

Diana nodded and left. However half way up the stairs she realized the import of Mary's earlier comment about hiring a butler when her son was master of Spinney Hall. Did Mary think her marriage to Mr. Hunt not legal because she had been a bride for such a short time? Surely Mary couldn't be right.

Williams helped Diana into her nightgown and unpinned her hair. Neither of them said anything, and Diana wondered if Williams was remembering her comment that morning. Careless words about death, tossed out in desperation, that's all they'd been. Again, Diana had the uncomfortable feeling that she'd somehow brought her husband's sad fate on him.

She climbed into her bed, laid her head on the pillow and shut her eyes, determining to shut out her present circumstances. But they crept in behind her eyelids, bringing another bad dream.

This time she found herself on a London street, watching a hearse roll by pulled by four black horses. "Who has died?" she asked a passerby.

"Why, don't you know?" replied the woman. "It is your future that has died. Your greed killed it." With that the woman threw back her head and laughed, and Diana realized it was Mary Barnes.

She stopped her ears and ran into the street and turned just in time to see a curricle bearing down on her, pulled by wild-

eyed horses snorting fire. The driver stood and raised his whip
to urge the horses to a faster gallop and Diana saw the face
of Lord Woodham. She stood in the middle of the road, unable
to run, and screamed.

Her eyes popped open and she sat up, breathing hard. Nightmares. More senseless nightmares! Sleep was no friend to her
this night. She'd seek it no more.

Instead, she dragged the coverlet from the bed and went to
the chair by the hearth to sit staring at the dying embers and
think how like them her life was.

The next morning Diana appeared at the breakfast table
looking a proper widow in demeanor, if not in attire. The pur-
plish crescents under her eyes declared a sleepless night and
the listless toying with the food on her plate was all that
Charles Hunt could have wanted.

Mary encouraged her to eat, reminding her she must keep
up her strength. "David will be leaving soon to speak with
the rector. If you have the letter to your mother written you
may send it with him. Then he is going to Croyden to fetch
a seamstress for you. Williams told him of a girl who can be
got for a quite reasonable price."

It was good of Mary to see to these details for her, thought
Diana. David, too. His heart was obviously not completely
black. "Thank you for all you are doing," she said.

Mary smiled at her across the table. "I am only glad we
were here when it happened."

Mary and David took care of everything. Diana had only to
put on the hastily made black bombazine dress on the actual
day of the funeral and let herself be driven to the church, had
only to sit in the pew between David and Mary and allow
herself, the grieving widow, to be ogled by everyone for miles
around.

The Earl of Woodham graced the funeral, and by his presence gave Charles Hunt more distinction in death than he'd enjoyed in his lifetime. After the service, Lord Woodham bowed over Diana's hand and said all that was proper, which wasn't much at all. The look he gave her was kind but somber—very proper for a funeral, small comfort for a woman confused and frightened and feeling very much in need of a rescuer with broad shoulders and a large handkerchief.

Diana longed to tell him she had terrible nightmares, that she was afraid of the future. Instead, she let him offer his condolences and said, "Thank you," in a leaden voice, then allowed David to lead her off.

"Poor little thing," said Mary Barnes to the rector's wife.

"She is fortunate she has such a kind sister-in-law to look after her," said Mrs. Bellows.

Mary nodded. "We are certainly trying. Well," she added briskly. "We had best get her home. We still have to get through the reading of the will."

"Of course," murmured Mrs. Bellows. The show was over, the crowd was thinning. Mrs. Bellows found her husband and took his arm. "Such a saint, that Mrs. Barnes. How lucky the girl is to have her at a time like this."

Julian's stepbrother, Stephen, was lounging before the fire in the drawing room when Julian entered. The fire's glow cast an angelic light on his fine features and put a golden halo glow on his brown curls. "And how was the funeral?" he asked.

"Boring," said Julian.

"The duties of an earl are tedious," said Stephen with mock sympathy. His stepbrother ignored him. "And did you offer to call on the widow and lend her your support in her time of sorrow?"

"I said what was proper," replied Julian coldly.

"How very dull," yawned Stephen. "But cheer up, your lordship, you need only wait a year if you are discreet."

He was merely voicing the thought that had lingered in Julian's mind, but uttered in Stephen's voice it somehow sounded callous, slightly degenerate. Julian frowned.

"I hear she is lovely," said Stephen, studying his stepbrother.

"From whom?" asked Julian idly, pouring himself a drink.

"From my valet, of course, who heard it from the footman who heard it from the upstairs maid who heard it from. . . ."

"Spare me," said Julian, holding up a hand.

Stephen shrugged. "Of course, as Mother dislikes her that is probably reason enough for you to court her."

Julian sighed. "We need to find you an heiress and marry you off, brother dear. And when you go you may take Mother with you."

Stephen grinned and said, "You must not be so hard on her, your lordship. She can hardly help it if she thinks no woman good enough for you."

Julian knew perfectly well his stepmother's reason for discouraging him from marrying had nothing to do with his incomparable worth. So did his stepbrother. "Perhaps I should just give over the title to you," he suggested. "Then you would keep that adder's tongue still."

Stephen smiled at him angelically.

At Spinney Hall, the three mourners ate a late nuncheon, for Mary was sure she'd never have the strength to get through the reading of the will without something on her stomach. She remarked often throughout the meal how very much Charles would have approved the fare. "Poor Charles," she sighed. "He did so enjoy his food, even as a boy, but in the end his stomach was his undoing."

Diana pushed away her plate, what little appetite she had gone, as the image of her dead husband appeared before her mind's eye in all its putrid splendor.

An hour later the solicitor arrived and was shown into the library where the family joined him. As Mr. Hewitt pulled out a sheaf of papers, Diana twisted her handkerchief and wished yet again that her mother and sister were present to bear her company.

"Well, then," said the little man. "It would appear we are all here." He pushed his spectacles down his nose and regarded Diana over them. "It is most fortunate Mr. Hunt was such an efficient man, else we might have had a bit of a tangle, but he saw to it that his affairs were in order before his wedding, so I am sure everything will run as smooth as clockwork. Yes, as smooth as clockwork," he repeated.

David's sigh was not especially noisy, but in the quiet room it was easily heard.

The lawyer frowned, cleared his throat and began to read, "I, Charles Hunt, being of sound mind and body. . . ."

Poor man, thought Diana. He had seemed to be of sound mind and body when she first came to him.

"To my wife, Diana Hunt, I leave my establishment in Heptonstall, and a jointure of four hundred pounds per annum, to be paid out of the monies earned from my mill, located in said town and the rental of large looms in the surrounding areas."

Heptonstall? Where was Heptonstall? And what of this house?

"And to my male issue or closest blood male relative I bequeath. . . ."

Diana listened as the lawyer rattled off a list of investments and property, including Spinney Hall. "But Mr. Hunt had no male. . . . I mean. . . ." She stuttered to a stop.

The lawyer cleared his throat. "Yes, well, that is, indeed, most unfortunate. As Mr. Hunt left no children behind, his nephew, Mr. Barnes, being his closest blood male relative, will inherit."

David! Diana noted the closest blood male relative wore a vengeful smile. Poor Mr. Hunt had thought to teach his nephew a lesson. Now that nephew had the last laugh. It wasn't right.

"Mr. Hunt didn't want his nephew to inherit his house," she protested. "He told me."

"I am afraid, Mrs. Hunt, that you must have somehow misunderstood your husband, for his wishes are right here in his will, quite plain," said the lawyer. "It would be useless to try and contest it."

Diana blushed and settled back into silence. Well, what did she care, really? David could have this house. She had no desire to live in it. It was haunted with nightmares. And she did have four hundred pounds allowance and a house of her own. Along with Mama's jointure they could manage quite well. She would leave this place as soon as Mama and Mathilde arrived.

"To my female issue. . . ."

This bequest was much smaller than the first, Hunt obviously not being as concerned with the welfare of any daughters he may have had as he was with ensuring his dynasty be passed on to his son. Except for a paltry sum left to his cook, there were no other bequests.

Diana suddenly felt very sorry for Mr. Hunt. Nothing had turned out as he planned.

"Well," said Mr. Hewitt. "I should say that finishes it up." To Diana, he said, "I have the key and the directions to the house in Heptonstall, and when you are feeling able you may come to my office and collect them. The banker in Heptonstall holds your monies from the business there." Mr. Hewitt shook his head and tamped his papers on the library desk to even them up. "Sad thing, sad thing," he muttered.

Mary turned to Diana. "You look near dead yourself, dear. Perhaps you would like to lie down and rest a little."

Diana nodded and allowed Mary to shoo her out of the library. But once in her room she felt restless, and a short half hour later she was on her way back downstairs. There was no one in the drawing room and so she went to the library.

Just as she turned the knob she heard the crash of glass upon the hearth and David gasp, "Mother!"

Five

Diana nearly rushed into the room to see what horrible seizure had overtaken Mary Barnes. But Mary's voice came strong and clear and caused Diana to silently turn the knob back in place and let the door remain slightly ajar, taking up a position as eavesdropper.

"Well, what would you have had me do?" Mary was demanding. "Let him live to father an heir?"

Sudden terror grabbed Diana. She noted David's white face and the shattered glass and pool of wine on the hearth and wished she had something fortifying at hand to drink herself. Surely she must have misheard.

"You are telling me my uncle did not die of gastric fever?"

"My dear son, don't look so shocked. Haven't you been hoping these past ten years he would die?"

"I never intended you to assist him in it," protested David.

Mary went on calmly, "You know as well as I that your uncle was a stingy man. He never offered to help your father, never lifted a hand for us, even when we struggled so. . . ." Her voice drifted into silence.

"But to kill him."

"I did it for you!"

"But the doctor. . . ."

"Is a fool," said Mary. "Besides, you know your uncle had a history of stomach problems."

"Always when we came to visit." David's voice sounded low, thoughtful.

"Yes," said Mary with a complacency that turned Diana's stomach. "I suspected on my last two visits that he was planning something foolish. I thought it best to be prepared. I even made sure from that old gabblebox Hewitt of the wording of the will before I finally acted."

"And if the will had been worded so that I did not inherit?"

"I would have made it worth the man's while to change it."

"Oh, Mother," said David faintly.

"Stop!" snapped Mary. "You talk as if I am some monster. I did this for you."

David knelt before her. "But Mother, if someone were to suspect . . ."

"If someone were to suspect I can tell you who they would look to—it would be that little adventuress Charles married. Why, it was she who handed him the plate of food that killed him!"

Diana picked up her skirt and backed away from the door, the pulse of fear thrumming loudly in her ears. She ran up the stairs, feeling lightheaded, but afraid to indulge herself by stopping before she had reached the sanctuary of her room.

Once there, she rang for Williams, then collapsed in the chair in front of the hearth.

When Williams arrived, she found her mistress slumped in it, her head leaned into the cushions, her face pale. "Oh, Madam, you're not well."

"I shall be fine," Diana assured her. "But tonight I'll take my dinner in my room. And please make sure no one but you and Cook handles the food."

Williams looked perplexed, but said nothing and left to do her mistress's bidding. She returned a short while later with a tray, then stood hesitating, as if wishing to say something.

"What is it?" prompted Diana.

"Mrs. Barnes asked me why I was taking food to you in your room."

Diana broke off a bite of bread. "And what did you tell her?"

"I told her you wasn't feeling up to coming down to dinner." Williams flashed a look at her mistress.

"You did well," said Diana. "Thank you."

Williams flushed pink under her freckles and smiled, then lowered her gaze to inspect her apron. "Is there anything else you would like?"

Diana shook her head and Williams left her to herself, poor company indeed.

But her own company was infinitely preferable to that of her in-laws. Remembering afresh what she'd learned sent a flood of panic rising in Diana's veins, and she paced the room in an effort to stem it. How long before Mama and Mathilde would arrive and they could be on their way to Heptonstall? Surely no more than two weeks. Two weeks! She had no desire to spend another two hours with Mary Barnes, let alone two weeks. I must behave as if I know nothing, she told herself, else I will be the next one to die of gastric fever.

The next morning Diana forced herself to take breakfast with Mary. As she entered the breakfast room, fear tickled her skin and she shivered. She managed a half smile before turning to the sideboard.

"Are you feeling better this morning, dear?" Mary inquired. Diana nodded.

"Good. This sort of thing is always difficult, but somehow we manage to muddle through."

Which has been more difficult for you, wondered Diana in disgust, murdering your brother or pretending to be sorry he is dead? She caught herself frowning and schooled her face into pleasant lines before turning to join her sister-in-law at the table.

"The eggs are especially delicious this morning," offered Mary, and Diana determined to have only the muffin she had taken.

"If you continue to eat like such a little bird you will blow away."

"I am sure I will feel more like eating eventually," said Diana. "Where is David?"

"Off doing some sort of business or other," replied Mary, waving a dismissive hand. "When one comes into property there is always much to be done."

"Of course," murmured Diana. She turned her attention to her muffin, anxious to be finished eating and gone.

But where? Where would she go? How would she fill the long day? If only she had a black riding habit she would take a ride.

It was a few moments before she realized Mary was staring at her. "Have you been sleeping well?" asked Mary.

"As well as one could expect, I suppose," answered Diana.

Mary nodded. Slowly, she began to butter a piece of toasted bread. "I thought I heard you up walking last night. And the night before," she added. She was now smiling pleasantly at Diana, but her eyes were those of a cat, carefully watching a mouse.

A guilty flush warmed Diana's cheeks, warned her to think quickly of a reason to explain her sudden color, something to allay Mary's suspicions that Diana didn't trust her. None came to mind, and she stammered, "Truth to tell I was up last night. I'm sorry if I woke you."

"I know my brother's death was a shock to you," said Mary. She seemed to consider saying more on the subject, but let it drop, turning the conversation instead to the autumn weather and the turning of the leaves.

"It looks to be fairly nice out," ventured Diana. "Perhaps I shall take a walk."

"You could use the fresh air," advised Mary. "Spending all that time cooped up in your room is not good for you."

Spending all this time cooped up with my relatives is not good for me, Diana mentally amended. She excused herself and went to fetch her cloak.

Outside, the lawns of Spinney Hall were damp with cold dew. They stretched before her, uninspired, unwelcoming. The trees along the drive needed pruning, she noticed. She turned back to look at the house. It was grander than her little house in Tetbury, but its faded air reminded Diana of a child let to go about with dirty face and hands, tangled hair and unkempt clothes.

For this dirty child, Mary Barnes had killed.

Diana remembered the highwayman. He'd been willing enough to take her life in exchange for anything he could find on her.

She shuddered. This house. It brought out dark and gray thoughts such as she'd never had. She would ask David to fetch that seamstress up to the house and order herself a riding habit. Then she would take the dilapidated old pony Hunt had given her and ride, far out into the country where she could think of something other than Spinney Hall and murderers.

She found David that afternoon in the library which had served as her husband's study, sifting through a pile of papers. He looked up and smiled, his eyes assessing her as if she, too, were part and parcel of his inheritance. "I wish to have some more clothes made," she announced coldly.

He nodded. "An excellent idea. I must say, black becomes you, Diana."

She made no reply, but turned to leave.

"Stay a moment," said David. "I would have a word with you." She turned back. "Shut the door, please," he said.

Diana's eyebrows raised.

"I have no intention of ravishing you right here," he added. "Really, you have so little sense of what is proper."

Diana made no reply to this. Ignoring the chair that sat conveniently next to the desk, she took a seat across the room.

David smiled, shook his head, and crossed the room to sit opposite her. "I will be making Spinney Hall my new home," he announced.

"Really," said Diana, and the sarcasm in her voice made him frown.

But he refused to verbally acknowledge the barb, continuing,

"I must return to my old home to attend to several things. And, truth to tell, I have no desire to remain at Spinney Hall during the winter until I have some workmen in to fix the place. The fireplaces don't draw well and the roof leaks."

"I am sure none of this has anything to do with me," said Diana impatiently.

"But it has a great deal to do with you," said David. "I will wager the house in Heptonstall is in worse repair than this one, as my uncle rarely went there. I believe he has tenants living in it now, and rather than force them to vacate immediately I thought you might prefer to remain here through spring."

Spring! Stay in this grim house? Was he mad?

A sudden image of herself walking with the Earl of Woodham under trees frothy with pink and white blossoms sprang to mind. It was a tempting vision. She really had no desire to go haring off to yet another strange place.

Diana turned suddenly suspicious. "What strings do you attach to this present?"

"None," said David. "I imagine you have had enough upsets and changes to last you at least a good six months. This will give you a chance to find your feet."

Diana looked at him in surprise. "That is very kind of you, David."

"I am not a monster, Diana."

At that moment David's eyes held neither lust nor resentment, or any of the other ugly qualities she'd seen so much of in him, and Diana thought that, perhaps, he was, like her, merely a person who had been swept along by circumstances of other people's making.

He leaned back in his chair, smiling, sensing an unspoken truce. "I will caution you, however, to remember that you are in deep mourning."

Diana was ready to take up weapons again. "And what might you mean by that?" she demanded.

He shrugged. "Only that you might be severely tempted to

entertain . . . visitors. It would never do, you know. People would talk."

Diana felt herself blushing for the second time that day. "Gossip didn't bother you a few days ago," she pointed out.

David grinned. "Touché," he murmured.

"When will you leave?" she asked.

This made David's grin widen. "We'll remain until your mother arrives. I should hate to leave you alone in the house."

"Pray, don't remain on my account," said Diana. "I am sure you are anxious to be gone."

"On the contrary," he said in silken tones.

Diana decided it was time to end the interview.

She also decided that unless she wished to alert Mary to the fact that she knew her for a murderess, she had best quit avoiding both her and her son. So that night after dinner, instead of taking herself off, she forced herself to follow her sister-in-law into the drawing room.

"I see you are feeling better," observed Mary. "It is a hard thing to accept the loss of a husband. I know I had a most terrible time when my poor Harold died. Twenty-eight years we were together." She looked across the room, seeing the past. "Such a good man he was. Not clever like Charles, but he did try so very hard to make a success of himself. If he'd only had someone to help him along a little."

"How did he die?" asked Diana.

Mary returned to the present. "What? Oh. I'm afraid life simply became too much for him. He came home one day and dropped dead right in front of me."

Mary's eyes filled with tears and Diana wished she hadn't said anything. She bit her lip, feeling gauche and uncomfortable.

Mary blinked back the tears and said brightly, "But we mustn't be looking to the past. What's done is done, I always say, and one must live in the present." At that moment David joined them and she looked up to him and smiled. "Well, now. What shall we do to amuse ourselves this evening?"

"I suppose we could play solo whist," suggested David. "For that we only need three."

"Excellent idea," agreed Mary.

Diana sighed inwardly. The mention of cards reminded her of her arrival at the Hall, and that first horrible card game. But she forced her lips to smile and her head to nod. The best way to make Mary think she'd overheard no conversations of murder was to pretend to feel perfectly at home in the woman's presence. So, play cards she would.

And as the evening wore on, Diana became engrossed with the game enough to almost forget she played with a blackmailer and a murderess.

The day Diana received her mother's letter was a particularly drizzly one. The leaden sky had oozed rain all morning and dampened her spirit. But reading her mother's sloppy scrawl drove out the damp and made her dance.

"My, my. What good news is this?" asked Mary, coming into the drawing room and catching Diana in mid twirl.

"My mother and sister are on their way to me," crowed Diana, feeling new confidence now that she knew reinforcements would soon arrive.

"That is wonderful news," said Mary. "Then you may at last go to your new home in Heptonstall."

Diana looked at Mary, puzzled. "I don't plan to go to Heptonstall until spring," she said.

"Spring?" echoed Mary. "Why on earth do you wish to wait so long, child? I should think you would be dying to see your new house."

"Your son offered me the use of Spinney Hall for the winter."

Mary frowned. "He did?"

"He said he had no plans to stay here until he could get workmen in to make repairs," said Diana. "I assumed he made his offer with your consent."

"Why should he need my consent? This is, after all, his property. I'm sure he may do with it as he likes," said Mary peevishly.

"I am grateful for his generosity," said Diana politely.

The look Mary gave her was speculative, and Diana was sure Mary thought she and David had struck some sort of immoral bargain. But she said nothing more on the subject, instead asking when Diana's mother planned to arrive.

"Mama says they shall arrive in Croyden by the thirtieth. Oh, my! That is day after tomorrow."

"I shall tell David to have the carriage sent to meet them."

Day after tomorrow. Diana repeated it to herself like a liturgy. Soon Mama would be with her and all would be well.

And two days later when the carriage pulled up in front of Spinney Hall, Diana was waiting on the front steps, a curious David standing behind her. Mrs. Brown was barely down from the carriage when her daughter rushed into her ample arms. "My poor baby," she crooned, patting Diana's back. "Everything will be fine now. Mama's here." She let go of Diana and the young girl who had come down from the carriage behind her stepped forward. "And here is your Mathilde."

Mathilde was a shadow version of her sister. Her features weren't quite as regular, and while she had the same yellow hair and blue eyes, they lacked vibrancy, as if the lion's share of color had been spent on the first daughter, leaving less for the second.

Mathilde didn't seem to grudge her sister her beauty. She looked at Diana with loving eyes and said, "I missed you."

"Oh, darling. And I missed you, too!" Diana embraced Mathilde, then drew back and smiled at her.

Mathilde returned the smile. "I'm hungry," she announced.

Diana laughed and hugged her sister again. "Oh, goose. How good it is to have you safely back with me. Both of you." She hooked an arm through theirs and walked them back up the steps to the door. "First I will show you your rooms and then we shall find something for you to eat."

"But I want to eat now," protested Mathilde.

"You must take off your bonnet first," said her mother. "And we must make the acquaintance of this handsome man."

Her sister's simplemindedness had never bothered Diana in Tetbury, but in the presence of the cynical David she suddenly felt ill at ease. She stole a glance at him.

He was smiling tolerantly. Good. There would be no sarcastic remarks from David to spoil the moment.

Diana made introductions.

"I hope you will enjoy your stay at Spinney Hall," he said.

Mathilde cocked her head to the side, looking at him. "Mama is right. You are very handsome," she said at last.

Even this didn't shake David. He merely raised an amused eyebrow while Mrs. Brown fussed at her daughter for being so forward. "Come along now and let's get you upstairs before you say anything else to embarrass us," scolded Mrs. Brown.

"But Mama, you said he was handsome."

"I may say as I like. I am an old woman, after all." Mrs. Brown turned to David. "You must forgive my daughter. She is. . . ."

"Charming," said David and bowed.

Mrs. Brown smiled slowly. "You are a very well-mannered young man."

Again David bowed.

"Come, Mama," said Diana, tugging at her mother's arm. "Let's get you settled."

After her mother and sister had freshened up, Diana took them into the drawing room to meet Mary, who had been waiting there like a grand lady for them to attend her. Mary gave both mother and daughter an assessing look as Diana made the introductions, but her words were kind enough. "So at last we meet Diana's family. How very unfortunate it should be under such sad circumstances."

"It is most unfortunate," agreed Mrs. Brown, settling her plump form on the sofa. "We had no idea Mr. Hunt was in such poor health."

"I am afraid his constitution was always weak," said Mary. "If only I had known he intended to do something so foolish as marry I am sure I would have tried my best to talk him out of it. Now here is your poor daughter a widow before she even had time to be a bride." Mary shook her head. "Terribly sad."

Diana felt David's gaze on her and refused to look in his direction. "I will be fine now Mama and Mathilde are here to bear me company."

"We will be happy as peas in a pod," put in Mrs. Brown. She turned to Diana. "You gave me no direction for your house in Heptonstall, dearest, so I had to wait on sending our things."

"David—that is, Mr. Barnes—has offered us the use of Spinney Hall until spring," said Diana.

Mrs. Brown looked approvingly at David. "That is most generous."

"Not at all," said David. "I don't plan to move in until then. I'd as soon have the house occupied in my absence."

Mrs. Brown nodded. "It pays to have someone about to keep an eye on the servants."

Mary gave a contemptuous snort. "I'm afraid my brother had no notion of what constitutes proper staff for a gentleman's house. But when David is master of Spinney Hall he will change all that."

Diana watched her mama's thoughtful gaze rest on David and cringed. She knew that look. It was the same way her mother had looked at Mr. Hunt when they first met him. Well, she would soon disabuse her mother of any notions she had in regard to David Barnes. Diana had rather marry a thousand Mr. Hunts than one David. Mr. Hunt may have been a miser, but he at least had scruples.

Mrs. Brown managed a visit with her daughter in her bedroom before dinner. As soon as Williams had been dismissed, she brought up the subject uppermost in her mind. "Mr. Hunt's nephew is a handsome young man."

Diana picked up her hairbrush and fingered it. "I have no interest in David, Mama."

"Well, of course not," said Mrs. Brown. "After all, you are just widowed. It would hardly be proper to be casting out lures so soon."

"Even if I had been widowed ten years I would have no interest in him," Diana insisted.

"But dearest, he seems like a perfectly nice man."

"He is not a nice man, Mama."

"Diana! How can you say such a thing? He is allowing you to remain in his house these next six months."

"Mama, he . . ." Diana stopped, feeling suddenly embarrassed. She laid the hairbrush back on her dressing table and bit her lip. "He has no scruples."

Mrs. Brown's eyes narrowed. "Has he made advances to you?"

Diana nodded.

"Well, you must not allow him to do so. Make him wait. He will be all the more anxious to marry you if he knows he cannot have you under any other circumstances."

"I have no desire to have him under any circumstances!" declared Diana, rising.

"Of course, you needn't have him if you don't wish it," said her mother stiffly. "I was thinking only of you. And Mathilde, of course. I am sure, for myself I would be happy enough to get along on our jointures. It won't be much, and of course I cannot imagine anyone wishing to marry Mathilde when we will have so little money. And how we shall take care of her future without you being well connected I cannot begin to imagine."

"Mama, please!"

Mrs. Brown looked at her daughter as if Diana had just stabbed her.

Diana rubbed her forehead. "Forgive me. I'm afraid I am not myself these days. So much has happened."

"Of course," said Mrs. Brown soothingly. "There is plenty of time to worry about the future. And there is little enough we can do for the next two years at any rate."

"There is much I need to tell you of this family," said Diana. A knock at the door prevented her.

It was Mathilde, in a pale blue gown, a matching ribbon threaded through her faded golden curls.

"You look lovely, dearest," said Diana.

"Mama helped me with my gown and another lady put this ribbon in my hair."

"Williams," explained Mrs. Brown. "That girl truly is a treasure."

Diana nodded. "Yes, she is." She sighed inwardly. Well, there would be no telling her mother about the Barnes's terrible secret now. Not in front of Mathilde, who would be certain to repeat it in the middle of dinner. "Let's go down, shall we?" she suggested.

"Of course," said Mrs. Brown, and preceded her daughters out of the room.

They had barely gained the drawing room when the same girl who had been hired to serve the wedding breakfast slinked into the room to whisper that dinner was ready.

"Is the butler ill?" Mrs. Brown asked her daughter.

"There is no butler, Mama," said Diana.

"No butler? A fine gentleman like Mister Hunt living with no butler? I can hardly credit it," said Mrs. Brown.

David gave her his arm. "Truly amazing, is it not?" he agreed. "But let mè assure you, Mrs. Brown, I am taking steps to rectify that situation. I shan't leave you and your lovely daughters marrooned here at Spinney Hall without any servants. I intend to hire a butler and a maid, and a full time gardener as well."

"What a thoughtful young man," murmured Mrs. Brown.

Mary Barnes frowned. "Really, David," she said, as they took their seats around the table, "there is no need to be so extravagant. I am sure Mrs. Brown and her daughters don't wish you to go to any unnecessary expense on their behalf."

"It is hardly any great expense, dearest," said David. "We both know the grounds have needed a gardener these past six years." He smiled at Mrs. Brown. "And my aunt and her mama can break in the butler for me."

"Oh, we shall see to that," Mrs. Brown assured him cheerily.

"And as for a maid," he continued. "Why, it hardly seems fair to expect poor Williams to keep up the house, serve the meals and be ladies maid to three women."

"Well, I am sure Williams never expected to be caring for three women," said Mary.

"Is that the lady who put the ribbon in my hair?" asked Mathilde.

"Yes, dear," said her mama. "And a very sweet thing she is."

Diana sat through each of the six courses on the edge of her seat while the two mothers sparred verbally over everything from the merits of Spinney Hall's cook to whether it would prove to be a mild winter.

When she finally led the way back to the drawing room to wait while David enjoyed his port in solitary splendor, she went with gritted teeth, expecting more of the same. The women didn't disappoint her.

"You really shouldn't let David talk you into postponing your move to Heptonstall," said Mary in a mild voice. "I am sure if I were you I would be anxious to start settling into my new home."

"My poor child has had enough change to last her a good long while, I should venture," said Mrs. Brown. "No, I think we shall be most comfortable here at Spinney Hall, in spite of the fact that it has been let fall into a sad state of disrepair."

"My brother was not well these past few years," said Mary.

Mrs. Brown shook her head. "The poor man seemed in such fine health when we met him last summer."

"Well, you cannot always tell by his appearance what a person's constitution is really like," said Mary, and changed the subject.

David joined them soon, and the rest of the evening limped along, broken by a very short concert forced from Diana by her mother. Diana ended the evening before the supper tray ever arrived, convincing her mother that she was tired from her long journey and ready for bed. She noticed that neither David nor Mary begged them to remain.

Six

The following day a tall skeleton of a man with thin lips and a receding hairline of gray wisps arrived at Spinney Hall and Williams showed him into the library. After twenty minutes, David sent Williams to fetch Diana.

"This is Addison, Diana," he said, as she settled herself on a chair. "I have just hired him to be my butler. Addison, this is my aunt, Mrs. Hunt. She will remain at Spinney Hall until spring as your mistress."

"It will be my pleasure to serve you, Mrs. Hunt," said Addison.

Diana inclined her head in imitation of a great lady.

"Well then, Addison," said David heartily, "go fetch your things, and you can begin tonight."

"Very good, sir," he said, and left.

As soon as the door was shut, David turned to Diana. "What do you think of my new butler?"

"I should hate to meet him in a dark corridor," Diana replied.

David frowned. "He comes with impeccable references."

"From an undertaker?" guessed Diana.

"I should think, Mrs. Hunt, you would have a little more appreciation of people's efforts on your behalf," David snapped.

"This was done for me? Are you sure it was not to increase your own consequence that you hired the man?"

"I could have waited and hired someone in the spring," said David stiffly. "I thought to make your life easier."

"Then please forgive me for thinking ill of you," replied Diana, equally stiff.

David inclined his head. "Tomorrow I'll be interviewing for a gardener and a maid. After they have been installed here, Mother and I shall leave." He fingered the quill on his desk. "I hope that, once I am gone, you will realize my company was not, after all, so unpleasant. Perhaps, you will even miss me just the smallest bit."

"Perhaps," agreed Diana in tones which showed how very mistaken he was. "If you will excuse me, now I must return to sorting the linens."

David nodded and she left, relief bubbling in her that before the week was out, he and his horrible mother would be gone.

At the end of the week Diana stood on the front step and watched David and Mary climb into their carriage. Looking the picture of familial loyalty, she waved as their conveyance turned in the drive and Mary fluttered her handkerchief out the window. And she remained watching them all the way down the drive. When there was nothing left of them but a cloud of dust she turned and danced back into the house.

Just then Addison came into sight, and she felt fire rush up her neck and inflame her cheeks. "Addison." she stammered.

He held up a small basket. "I am sorry, madam. Mrs. Barnes left behind the tartlets and fruit Cook made up for her."

"Oh, dear," muttered Diana. "Then they will be back."

Addison cleared his throat and Diana looked up to see he was biting back a smile. "Perhaps madam is in need of a rest. I should be happy to convey all that is proper to Mrs. Barnes when she returns."

The crunching of wheels on gravel punctuated his sentence. Servant and mistress exchanged conspiritorial looks and Diana ran up the stairs to leave Addison to deal with her in-laws. She smiled to herself as she ducked into her room. *Well, David,* she thought, *for the first time I am truly grateful to you.*

On Sunday the three women went to church. Diana donned the solemn expression expected of a widow, and when Lord Woodham and his mother and stepbrother walked past her to take their seat in the family pew, she forced her eyes to remain looking straight ahead.

After the service, Mrs. Bellows was quick to find her. "Well, my dear, I see you are bearing up well," she approved. "And this, I would venture to guess, is your mama?"

Diana made the introductions and half listened to the conversation while watching Woodham out of the corner of her eye. He had just spoken to the rector and now he was leading his stepmother down the church steps, followed by a younger man with a slim body and an angelic face. One more moment and they would walk right past her.

"Ah, Lord Woodham," cried Mrs. Bellows, "And Lady Woodham. How kind of you to come this morning." She dropped into a curtsey.

Lady Woodham stopped. "Good morning, Mrs. Bellows," she said in a voice of frozen politeness. "I have just now complimented your husband on an excellent sermon. If there is one thing of which we need more, it is humility." She raised an eyebrow in Diana's direction. "Society is crowded these days with people who don't know the meaning of the word."

"You are so right, your ladyship," gushed Mrs. Bellows. "And I must tell you, my husband values your approbation highly."

These last words went unheard, for Lady Woodham was already gently tugging on her stepson's arm, murmuring, "Come, Julian."

"You go on. I shall be with you in a moment," said Woodham.

Her ladyship looked none too pleased with this, but she took her other son's arm and departed.

Woodham seemed oblivious to her departure. He smiled at Diana. "Is there anything you need, Mrs. Hunt?"

She shook her head. "My nephew, Mr. Barnes, left us well provided for before he returned home."

"So you remain at Spinney Hall?"

"Until spring. Then I shall remove to the house my husband left me in Heptonstall."

"Heptonstall?" he repeated, apparently puzzled.

"My nephew, Mr. Barnes, has inherited Spinney Hall," said Diana.

A corner of the earl's mouth twitched, and Diana knew instantly what he was thinking—her search for a fortune had failed miserably. "I am sure if you can somehow get through this trying time that the future will be brighter," he said. "Meanwhile, if you should find yourself in need of any assistance, I hope you won't hesitate to send word to us."

"How very kind," put in Mrs. Brown, who had been listening to the conversation avidly.

Her words seemed to recall the earl to his surroundings. He bowed and hurried after his mother.

"That is the new Earl of Woodham," said Mrs. Bellows unnecessarily. "He has only been among us a short while. I am sure he will be off for London soon."

She chattered on, but Diana heard none of it. London? Why should Lord Woodham wish to go to London? The Little Season, of course—that time before the Christmas holiday that she'd heard so much about, when the nobility went to stay in their fine town houses and dance in beautiful clothes and attend the opera and the theatre. She sighed inwardly. The only thing she and Mama and Mathilde would attend these next few months was church. And judging from Reverend Bellows' sermon this morning there would be little pleasure in that.

* * *

Julian set his jaw, determined not to quarrel with his stepmother, although her words begged him to.

"Really, Julian. Lending countenance to that cheap little adventuress—I am sure your poor father is turning in his grave."

"Well, you can hardly blame him," put in Stephen. "She's a lovely little piece." Her ladyship gave him a quelling look and he grinned mischievously and added, "If you don't want her, brother dear, I shall be happy to do what I can to keep the lady from grieving."

"Stephen!" snapped his mother.

But it wasn't Lady Woodham's sharp words that silenced him. It was his stepbrother's stony look. Stephen smiled and shrugged and said no more.

Lady Woodham sweetened her voice. "Surely you can see how very beneath you socially the girl is. I am sure you will find ladies of good breeding in London to flirt with who are just as lovely."

His stepmother was right, of course. London was a veritable sweet shop of pretty and willing young matrons who, having done their duty and produced their husbands an heir were now free to pursue amorous adventure. Julian supposed he did not need to entangle himself with this particular female. But it was rather like being told he could have only beef when he was hungering for fish or salt when his mouth watered for sugar. And what did position have to do with anything? After all, when it came to dalliance it mattered not whether the skirt a man lifted belonged to a dancer or a duchess.

On Monday Diana decided she needed fresh air. She came downstairs in her new black riding habit and encountered Mathilde idling in the hallway, eating a biscuit.

"Where are you going?" asked Mathilde.

"I am going for a ride."

Mathilde's eyes lit up. "May I go with you?"

Diana hoped for company in the spinney, but not her sister's. "No, dearest, not today.

Mathilde's face fell. "But I want to come, too."

"Next time," Diana promised, and slipped out the door before Mathilde could say more.

As she trotted her horse down the drive, Diana wondered if she was being foolish. What made her think Lord Woodham would come riding through the woods by chance? Still, she rode on, hoping against hope that she'd encounter him. She remembered how, before Mr. Hunt's death, the earl had hinted at meeting her in the woods. Would he remember that conversation?

She found the spot where she'd last met him, led her horse to a stump and dismounted. After tethering the animal, she went to sit on the same fallen log where Lord Woodham had kissed her. She sat and closed her eyes, letting the sunshine fall through the leaves and gently dapple her face with warmth while memory warmed her body with the recounting of Lord Woodham's embrace.

Half an hour passed and the spinney remained a solitary place. Diana sighed and rose. It had been a foolish thought. She was untying her horse's reins when she caught a faint sound of hooves. Or was it her imagination? She remained still, reins in hand. Another moment and the sound became more pronounced. Her heart picked up speed. It had to be Lord Woodham. A few more moments and he rode into sight. Her heart was thudding so that she felt weak and her mind scrabbled about frantically for some plausible excuse she could give for being out here. There was none. She turned her back to him.

"Mrs. Hunt," he called. He dismounted and led his horse over to where hers stood. "I was hoping I might encounter you."

His voice was a caress and it was all Diana could do not to move to lean against him. "I needed some time to think," she stuttered as she turned to face him.

"Did you think at all of me?" he asked.

"Your lordship should not ask such a thing of a widow," she replied.

He tethered his horse then offered her his arm. "Would you care to walk?"

She took it and they strolled farther into the spinney where the light was sparse and the smell of moss and damp strong. At last, when they came to a secluded spot he stopped and took off his coat, and spread it on the ground for her. "Let's sit awhile," he said.

Diana sat, looking straight ahead, her heart beating wildly again.

Woodham seated himself next to her. "I've thought of nothing but you since the last time we met in these woods."

"Your lordship is too kind," said Diana.

"And you are too beautiful," he murmured. He brushed away a curl from her neck and replaced it with his lips causing her skin to come alive at his touch.

Diana swallowed and turned her face to his. "Your lordship," she began, unsure what she was going to say next.

"Diana." He made her name sound like a prayer. His hand came to her shoulder and he gently guided her back until she lay on his coat and his face hovered over hers. She saw love in his eyes, she was sure. "I shall go mad from wanting you," he whispered and kissed her ear. He nestled his face into her neck and kissed it.

Diana bit her lip, trying to resist the sensation the earl's hand was causing as it slid down her shoulder. The desire in her blood was a disease. She mustn't give in to it. She remembered her mother's advice—*Make him wait. He will be all the more anxious to marry you if he knows he cannot have you under any other circumstances.* "Lord Woodhaven," she managed. "I am afraid I am too soon widowed to be entering into courtship."

The earl's hand froze. "Courtship?" he repeated.

Diana sat up and looked down at him. "Why yes," she said slowly.

"My dear Mrs. Hunt," he said, sitting up beside her. "It will be a long time before you are able to wed. And really, after your painful experience, I'm sure you are not anxious to consider matrimony again."

Diana looked at him, uncomprehending. "I am afraid I don't understand."

He inched closer to her and slid a hand around her middle. "Why, only that marriage isn't something we really need to worry about, is it? After all, your main concern is to be assured of a comfortable living. I can provide for you in ways your husband never could."

"But not," said Diana slowly, "as a husband."

He shrugged. "You already had a husband. Where was the benefit?"

Suddenly the only desire Diana felt was to slap this man's face. She did, and felt much better for it when she saw his shocked expression. "The benefit, my lord, would be in knowing that I am a woman of principle, wed to a man of principle, which I now see that you are not!" She gathered her skirt and scrambled to her feet. "Good day, your lordship," she spat, and marched off.

She hoped he would follow her, but the only footsteps she heard snapping the twigs and bracken were her own.

The autumn leaves flamed and fell and a chill crept into the air to whisper of winter. Diana saw Lord Woodham twice more at church, but he only gave her polite greetings as bare of words as the trees were of leaves. In November she looked for him in vain and learned from Mrs. Bellows after the service that he had gone to London for the Little Season.

"I suppose it is a wonder he remained with us as long as he did," said Mrs. Bellows. "But when a man moves in such exalted circles one can hardly expect him to be forever contented with a bucolic life. I imagine now that he has set things to rights here he intends to enjoy the London high life."

The London high life. As the carriage bumped back down the road toward Spinney Hall, David's words came back to haunt Diana: "Your fine earl will go off to London to enjoy the social season and find himself a little ballet dancer." She pressed her lips together in an effort not to cry.

"Isn't it a pity you did not meet someone young and wealthy like the Earl of Woodham before you met Mr. Hunt?" observed Mrs. Brown.

Diana didn't trust herself to speak and so said nothing.

This created no problem for her mother. She continued to soliloquize. "Of course, the earl is far above our touch. But if you gave Mr. Barnes half a chance . . ."

"He would never do," said Diana firmly.

"I certainly don't see why you must take that poor man into such stubborn dislike."

"There is something I must tell you of Mr. Barnes," began Diana.

"Lord Woodham is very handsome," said Mathilde. "I should like to marry him."

Mrs. Brown patted her daughter's hand. "Yes, I am sure you would, dear. But we shall find you someone else instead. You must be patient." She returned her attention to Diana. "Tell me one thing that is wrong with Mr. Barnes. He is well mannered and fine looking."

"You said after Diana was married you would find me a husband," continued Mathilde.

Mrs. Brown gave Diana a look which promised they would talk later, then turned her attention to Mathilde. "And so we shall, my child. We must all mourn the loss of Diana's husband before we can do anything."

Diana turned her gaze out the window and saw her period of mourning stretched ahead of her like an endless road.

* * *

"Why can we have no Christmas party?" complained Mathilde. "And no kissing bough? It is so quiet here. I want to have a party. And a new dress."

"We cannot have a party because I am in mourning," said Diana, stabbing at her needlepoint. "You know that, Mathilde. We have told you over and over again."

Mathilde hung her head and Diana immediately regretted her harsh words. "Now, dearest. We will still have our own little celebration on Christmas day. I already have a present for you."

Mathilde brightened. "You do? What is it?"

"You will have to wait and see," said Diana. "If I tell you it won't be a surprise."

Mathilde sighed and went to the window. "The snow is pretty," she said. "Will anyone come carol to us?"

"I don't know, dearest," said Diana.

"I wish you hadn't married Mr. Hunt," said Mathilde.

Mathilde spoke the same thought which had just come into Diana's mind, and hearing it aloud stirred the simmering discontent deep inside her.

"If you had not married Mr. Hunt we could have had a Christmas party," Mathilde continued. "That is what Mama said. I still don't see why we cannot have a small one."

"That is enough!" snapped Diana. "Really, you will drive me to distraction teasing me about this."

Mathilde turned and stared wide-eyed at her sister.

"And do stop looking at me like that!"

"Diana!"

Diana saw her mother standing in the drawing room doorway, displeasure written in every line of her face. "What can you be thinking of to talk to your sister in that way?"

"Mama, I vow she is driving me to distraction!"

"She is your sister."

"She is a trial and a burden!"

Mrs. Brown's displeasure turned to shock and Mathilde burst into tears.

"Now see what you have done," scolded Mrs. Brown.

"I am sorry, Mama," said Diana stiffly. She went to Mathilde and put a hand on her shoulder. "There now, dearest, don't cry. I didn't mean it."

"You did. Else you would never have said it," sobbed Mathilde.

"No, dear. People often say things they don't mean." Diana fished a handkerchief from the pocket of her gown. "Here now. Blow your nose and dry your eyes. There is no need to cry."

Mathilde took the handkerchief and smiled at Diana. "You're not angry with me any more?"

Diana shook her head. "No," she said wearily. "I'm not." And without another word, she turned and left the room.

Biting back tears of frustration, she hurried to her bedroom and rang for Williams to help her into her riding habit. As soon as Mama was done consoling Mathilde, she would be up to lecture, and Diana had no desire to face her mother's wrath until she had gained better control of herself.

Of course, it had been cruel and foolish to snap at Mathilde. Mathilde was hardly to blame for Diana's unpleasant circumstances. And poor Mama. How could she have known Mr. Hunt would die as soon as he married?

Diana sighed. It was to her discredit that the loved ones she'd longed for most when she married now irked her so greatly as a widow. What she needed was some time alone to think, to plan for the future. She would ride in the spinney until she forgot the burdens she carried, until the swirling cauldron of emotion inside her had cooled.

Once outside, she walked her nag slowly down the road, feeling chilled in spite of the wool cloak she'd put over her worn, black riding habit. The sky was an oppressive gray and the air was pregnant with the promise of more snow. Winter was a nasty time of year. Except for those who could afford to go to London for the Little Season and make merry in candlelit ballrooms.

The jingle of sleigh bells danced on the air long before Diana saw the sleigh. And even before it pulled into sight she knew who it was. She stopped her horse and braced herself.

It came over the rise, a picture of Christmas cheer with its bright red body and gold trim. The horses were decked out with wreaths, their manes braided with red ribbon, and greenery trimmed the harness. The four people seated inside were covered in rugs and laughing. As it swooshed by, Diana saw the dark haired woman in a fur trimmed bonnet and cloak seated next to Lord Woodham and Woodham, himself, smiling in recognition and tipping his hat. Then they were gone in a cloud of snow mist.

The Earl of Woodham had moved on to greener pastures. She'd had her chance to hold him, if even for a little while, and she'd thrown it away. Now she was alone, and her youth was buried with her husband. It wasn't right. What was she going to do about it?

By the time the first snowflakes fell from the heavy gray clouds, Diana had returned, her epiphany complete. She left her horse with the groom and hurried back to the house and ran up the stairs, lifting her skirt high and taking them two at a time. Inside her room, she rang for Williams, then went straight to the wardrobe.

Williams entered the room, looked at the pile of black cloth on the bed and gasped. "Mrs. Hunt. Begging your pardon, but what are you doing?"

"I am getting rid of these," said Diana, scooping the bundle into her arms. She walked to Williams and shoved them at her. "Take them away. You may have them yourself or give them away. I don't care. Just don't let me see them in my wardrobe again."

"But your mourning . . ." began Williams.

"I am going to half mourning," Diana informed her. "Take

away those things and then come help me into my gray afternoon gown."

"Oh, my," said Williams weakly.

"Oh, and Williams."

"Yes, Mrs. Hunt?"

"Have the gardener cut me off a sprig of holly from the tree at the corner of the house. I wish to wear some in my hair. And make sure it has plenty of berries!"

Williams bobbed a curtsey and hurried off to do her mistress' bidding.

Diana went to the window and looked out at the flurrying snow and smiled. Somehow, the gray skies didn't seem half so dreary any more.

An hour later she entered the drawing room wearing her gray gown, the holly secured over her right ear.

Her mother looked up from her sewing and gasped. "What is this?"

"I am tired of wearing black bombazine," replied Diana.

"Are you mad, child?"

"It is madness to continue to wear black for a man I barely knew."

"He was your husband."

"For only a few hours, Mama. Must I trade two years of my life for those few hours?"

"Yes," said Mrs. Brown sternly. "You must. It's not right . . ."

"It's not right to pretend any longer and keep this place like a mausoleum. It's not right that Mathilde should have no carollers and that we should not rejoice in Christmas all because I was married to a stingy man for a few hours!"

Mrs. Brown looked at her daughter as if she were a stranger. "You simply cannot do this, Diana. What will people say? And what will Mr. Barnes and his mama think?"

"I certainly don't care a fig for what they may think," said Diana.

"Well, you should. Mr. Barnes has been very good to us."

"And I know why."

"Well, of course. The young man has hopes. And you may come to see he is not nearly half so unsuitable as you think him now. If you will just be sensible and wear your black like a proper widow."

"I cannot marry David Barnes. His mother murdered my husband!"

Mrs. Brown sat very still. "Diana," she said softly. "What are you saying?"

Diana sat down next to her mother and took her hands. "It is true, Mama. I overheard them speaking of it in this very room. Mary Barnes poisoned her own brother so that her son could inherit this house."

"No. I cannot credit it."

"It is true. I swear it."

"My God," said Mrs. Brown. "Why did you not call the constable?"

"They were here in the house with me. How could I have?"

Mrs. Brown bit her lip. "It is not too late," she said at last. "We should have the body exhumed. You must tell some-one . . ."

"No! They will blame me."

"You?"

Diana nodded. "Mary made sure it was I who gave Mr. Hunt the food with the poison. That is what she told David. She must have slipped something in his kippers when no one was looking."

"There must be something we can do."

Diana shook her head. "No one would believe my story. And why should they? Mary Barnes was his sister. I was merely his wife, the adventuress who married Mr. Hunt for his money. Everyone would think I killed my husband."

Mrs. Brown sat staring across the room, and Diana knew it was her shattered plans for their future she saw.

"David Barnes is a man with no principles, Mama. I would

never have had him. I'd determined that even before I learned about his mother."

Mrs. Brown studied her daughter. "I hope you are not cherishing hopes in some other direction."

It was Diana's turn to look away. "I don't know what you mean."

"I suppose Lord Woodham will come back to his family home for Christmas," mused Mrs. Brown, still regarding her daughter, whose pinkening face was pretending nonchalance. "He is already here, isn't he?"

Diana pressed her lips together and nodded.

"I'll warrant he has houseguests."

Again, Diana nodded, unable to trust her voice.

Mrs. Brown sighed heavily. "My dear, simply because the man has spoken to you after church on occasion, you cannot delude yourself into thinking him interested. The earl moves in much higher circles." Diana's lips tightened, and her mother continued, "I've seen how you look at him, Diana. But you look too high. A squire's son you could get to offer matrimony, a knight or perhaps even a baronet, but not an earl."

"And why not an earl?" demanded Diana.

"Because you have neither position nor money."

"I am no shopkeeper's daughter. And I have some money."

"We both know there are women who spend more on gowns than your jointure will provide you in a year. And yes, you are gently born. But you have no title."

Mrs. Brown squeezed her daughter's hands. "Let us settle in Heptonstall come spring and be happy. We can travel to Bath after your mourning is over, or Brighton. You will meet some nice man. . . ." Diana was shaking her head furiously. "My child, don't try to catch at stars. The fall to earth can be mortal dangerous."

Diana remembered the dark haired lady in the sleigh and nodded. Her mother was right. There would be no more reaching for stars. Others were depending on her and she had to be sensible.

Mrs. Brown put a hand to her daughter's cheek. "And wear your black like a proper widow."

Diana sat stone still, a frown etched on her face.

"Diana." Mrs. Brown's voice was pleading now.

Diana shook her head. "I cannot continue like this any longer. Since I was never a proper wife, I see no reason to be a proper widow." She turned to her mother. "Allow me my gray dress and my sprig of holly, Mama. It's Christmas. No one should go about with a long face and wearing a shroud at Christmas. Why, it's practically an insult to God. And besides, no one need know. When we go to church I will still wear black. But here at the house, when it is just ourselves . . . what can it hurt?" The look on her mother's face told Diana she was wavering. "Let it be my Christmas present from you."

Her mother shook her head and smiled. "Diana, Diana. You know I never liked to see you unhappy."

"And I shan't be," said Diana. "We will all be happy yet. Wait and see."

"I don't know," said Mrs. Brown. "I hate to think what will come of this."

Diana didn't hear her. She was already making plans.

The following day, Diana sent for Addison. "Please tell the groom to go out in the woods and cut some greenery for the house."

The butler stared at her as if he hadn't heard correctly.

"You heard me," she said sternly, trying to put more authority in her voice. "My little sister needs something of Christmas around this house, and I intend to see she has it."

"As you wish, madam," he said. "Will there be anything else?"

"No," said Diana.

Addison made his stately exit, and Diana brushed all thought of his stiff disapproval from her mind with the reminder that she was the mistress and he was the servant.

Her next order of business was to write a note to the dressmaker and order three new gray gowns.

"Oh, dear," fretted Mrs. Brown after learning what her daughter had done. "I only hope Mrs. Bellows may not hear of this." Diana blanched and her mother looked at her severely. "I hope you do not live to regret your rash decision, Diana."

"What's done is done," said Diana stubbornly, trying to ignore the doubt nibbling at the back of her mind.

Christmas eve came, and with it the carollers.

"Carollers!" cried Mathilde, running from the drawing room as Addison opened the door.

The small group that sang "Good King Wenceslas" was a rag tag collection consisting of the groom, the gardener, Williams and the other maid, but it was enough to make Mathilde's eyes sparkle. And Diana had a punch bowl of wassail on the marble topped table in the entrance hall to wet dry throats after the singing was done, as well as small presents for each of the servants.

"That was wonderful," said Mathilde. "Now may we have our presents?"

"Yes, dearest," said Mrs. Brown, smiling approvingly at her eldest daughter. "Come back into the sitting room and we shall open them."

Diana turned to follow her mother and sister.

A throat cleared behind her, and the butler's voice said, "Mrs. Hunt?"

She turned, still smiling, a questioning look on her face.

Addison's somber visage bore the hint of a smile. "May I wish you a happy Christmas?"

"You may. And a happy Christmas to you, too, Addison." Diana started again for the drawing room.

"And Mrs. Brown."

She turned.

"May I make so bold as to say that . . ." He pursed his lips and stopped.

"Yes?"

"A sprig of holly here and there is not amiss."

Diana touched the sprig in her hair and smiled. "Thank you, Addison," she said.

He gave her a stately bow, and she went to her mother and sister, wrapped in warm feelings. Whatever the consequences, she would not regret having done all she could to make Mathilde's Christmas merry.

It was shortly after boxing day when Mrs. Bellows paid a call. Fortunately, Addison was able to forstall her while Diana pulled the blue ribbons from her hair and donned the one black gown she had kept for church.

"Mrs. Bellows, how very good to see you," said Diana, taking a seat next to her nervous mother.

"I shan't waste time beating about the bush," said Mrs. Bellows. "There has been talk, Mrs. Hunt."

"Talk?"

"It is rumored you have gone to half mourning."

"Who has said such a thing?"

Mrs. Bellows ignored this question. "You have ordered gray gowns from Annie Hubble."

"I have," admitted Diana. "I thought it would be nice to give her some extra business."

"Is that not a little premature?"

"Perhaps. But as you see, I am still in black."

Mrs. Bellows frowned. "Well, yes," she said. "And I assure you, Mrs. Hunt, I came here with no intention of creating trouble, but I felt it my duty to make sure all was well. After all, a widow owes a certain respect to her husband's memory. Wouldn't you agree?"

"Oh, yes," put in Mrs. Brown. "You are quite right."

"May I offer you tea?" asked Diana.

"No. I must not linger. I have much to do today."

Diana tried to look disappointed. "Of course, we mustn't press you to ignore your other duties."

As soon as their caller was gone, Mrs. Brown turned to her daughter. "Did I not tell you how it would be?"

"Another few months and we shall be living in Heptonstall where no one knows us and we shan't have to worry about what others think. Then I shall be able to wear my gray gowns in public."

"Oh, Lord. Where will it all end?" fretted Mrs. Brown.

In freedom, thought Diana. Sweet freedom.

Winter dragged on, and Diana only saw the Earl of Woodham occasionally. After church they would exchange polite greetings. Once she saw him in town. But he was with his stepmother, and the dowager pulled him ruthlessly away before they could come within speaking range of each other. It doesn't matter, Diana told herself firmly. The Earl of Woodham is no longer of any interest to me.

At the beginning of March Diana received a letter from David telling her he would be returning to Spinney Hall in April. Would she care to have him make arrangements for her move to Heptonstall or would she wish to remain longer at the Hall? Diana understood the message between the lines and immediately wrote Mr. Hewitt, the solicitor, of her intention to repair to the house in Heptonstall at the end of March. That, she thought, is that, and deposited the letter on the entryway table.

By the end of March the blustery winds finally lost strength and became mere breezes, still damp but free of the sting of winter. Diana took one final ride. She encountered Lord Woodham on the road approaching from the opposite direction.

He smiled at her and turned his horse to walk with hers. "How have you been, Mrs. Hunt?"

"Quite busy," replied Diana stiffly. "And I believe your lordship has been equally busy?"

The earl smiled at this. "Not so busy since the holidays ended."

"Ah, yes. You had houseguests, did you not?"

"We had a great many guests."

"I couldn't help admiring the lovely green bonnet one of your guests wore," continued Diana casually.

A corner of the earl's mouth twitched upwards. "Oh? I wonder which particular guest that was."

"The lady whom I saw in the sleigh with you," said Diana, her cheeks blooming pink.

"Ah, yes. Miss Sample. A very pretty young woman. An heiress, too. I fell ill during her stay. Fortunately for Miss Sample, however, another of my houseguests was in fine health. The two are now engaged."

"You were going to offer for her?" asked Diana sharply.

"That is what my stepmother asked me," replied the earl.

Diana busied herself with her reins. "And what did you answer her?"

"Why, I didn't," replied Woodham.

Diana frowned. "I am sure it is none of my concern whom you marry."

"That is exactly what I told my stepmother," said Woodham jauntily. His voice softened. "Would you hate to see me married to another, Mrs. Hunt?"

"I am sure I would wish your lordship to be happy," said Diana.

"Happiness and marriage have nothing to do with each other," said the earl. "As you, perhaps, have learned. Love, on the other hand, can give a man a happiness no legal joining of titles and lands ever could."

"Your lordship believes a man cannot find love and marry?"

"Whom one loves and whom one marries cannot always be one in the same," said the earl. "You have married without love, fair huntress. Tell me which you would rather have."

"I would have both," said Diana.

"If you could have but one?"

"I would have both or neither."

The earl drew his horse next to hers. He took her hand and raised it to his lips. "Half a dream is better than no dream, Diana. Remember that." He released her hand. "I will be leaving for London next week. Will you miss me?"

"I shan't be around to miss you," Diana informed him. "I am bound for Heptonstall."

"Heptonstall!"

"I believe I mentioned that my husband left me a house there."

"Oh yes. I had forgotten. So you will go there and wall yourself up like a proper widow and wither away."

"I shan't wither in two years," said Diana.

Woodham smiled. "No, I'll warrant you shan't. In fact, I am sure you will bloom even more lovely. Perhaps, after a year you will receive callers?"

"Perhaps," replied Diana, and added, "If they bring me sweets from London."

The earl laughed. "I shall remember."

Will you? wondered Diana. Well, no matter, she told herself firmy as she supervised Williams in the packing of her trunks. I shan't wear the willow for Lord Woodham any longer than I shall wear gray for Mr. Hunt.

Seven

It was the day before Diana and her family were due to leave when Addison came to the library, asking for a word with her. She set the letter she'd been writing David to one side and folded her hands on the desktop.

"I was wondering if, perhaps, madam might have need of my services in Heptonstall."

Diana blinked. "Williams will go with us. But beyond her. . . . You were hired to serve Mr. Barnes."

The butler nodded. "I would not wish to appear disloyal to my employer, but it seems to me that perhaps madam might have use of someone of experience in her new home."

"Are you saying I cannot manage on my own?"

The butler's thin face flushed an unflattering burgundy. "I am merely offering my services."

The sudden realization dawned on Diana that she would miss the old cadaver. And it would be good to have two loyal servants to help her in her new surroundings. She smiled. "We leave tomorrow."

A ghost of a smile haunted Addison's face. "I shall see that everything is ready."

"And Addison."

He turned. "Yes, madam?"

"Why did you leave your previous post?"

The long face seemed to lengthen before her very eyes, and the last of the burgundy stains disappeared, leaving his skin the color of dough. "There was a misunderstanding." He pressed his lips together.

Diana waited.

"Missing silver, madam."

"You did not take it?"

He shook his head, holding her look. "No, madam."

"And you never found who did."

Addison bit his lip. At last he said, "I did not."

"How long were you at your last post?"

"I was butler to the earl for seventeen years."

"You would do your reputation more good if you looked elsewhere for a position," said Diana.

"Meaning no disrespect, madam," replied the butler, "but I think, perhaps, we are well suited."

Diana nodded. "Very well. And Addison?"

"Yes, madam?"

"Thank you."

The next day they departed for Heptonstall, a new driver handling the carriage reins. On the desk in the library sat Diana's polite note thanking David for his kindness and informing him that, as he already had a carriage, she had relieved him of the bother of his uncle's old one. The postscript read, "I hope it may not inconvenience you, but I have hired away your butler."

It was the end of March, 1811, when Diana arrived at her new home. There had been much to see en route: villages built on high terraces overlooking the Calder Valley, scanty crops of oats and wheat on the edges of the moorland. Heptonstall, was small and picturesque, but the townspeople seemed to eye Diana's passing carriage with hard faces.

The house, itself, appeared nearly as unwelcoming as the faces of the people. A smaller, wood version of Spinney Hall, it sat apart from the rest of the village, an orphan with peeling gray paint and a garden overgrown with weeds. The rosebushes along the front walk were sadly in need of pruning. Inside, dirty windows cast a gloomy light, and furniture swathed in Holland covers lurked about the shadows like ghosts.

"Oh, my," said Diana faintly, surveying her twilight kingdom.

"It will look much better after we have the covers off the furniture and the windows cleaned and a fire in the sitting room hearth," predicted Mrs. Brown.

Mathilde wrinkled her nose. "I want to go home."

"This is our home now," said Diana. "And we will make it comfortable. You'll see."

Addison already had his coat off and was rolling up his sleeves. "Johnny Coachman and I will take the trunks upstairs, then I will see if I cannot find some rags to clean, madam."

Diana smiled and blessed the day Addison had walked into their lives. She removed her bonnet and tossed it onto a dusty table. "And Mama and Mathilde and I shall remove the Holland covers. Before the day is out we'll have this old tomb showing signs of life."

"I'm hungry," announced Mathilde.

Food. Here was something Diana had forgotten completely about.

"I saw a fine looking bakery when we drove through town," said Mrs. Brown. "Perhaps you had best send Williams for some buns before they close."

"I want to go," said Mathilde.

"Very well," said Diana. She fished in her reticule. "And get us some tea, also. Tomorrow we will make a proper shopping trip."

Williams took the money and left with Mathilde in tow while Diana and Mrs. Brown set to work in the house.

By the time the shoppers returned, the two women had uncovered a mishmash of faded furniture. A fire danced in the hearth, giving the room a homey glow. "It is hardly the first stare of elegance," said Diana, looking about, "but it will do for now."

Williams set off to brew tea and the three ladies settled in chairs in front of the fire. "Well, and here we are in our new home," said Mrs. Brown happily. "Granted, this is not quite what I envisioned for you, Diana, but a coat of paint and our own furniture will make a world of difference. And who knows what fine, upstanding man you may meet here."

Diana wasn't at all sure she wanted a fine, upstanding man. Marriage to one of those creatures was quite enough. But she held her tongue. Mama was right about one thing. This was a new start. Here in Heptonstall she would be able to put her disastrous marriage and previous misadventures behind her. She had a house, and it wasn't a bad house. She would turn it into something lovely. She, Mama and Mathilde would be happy here.

Williams returned with their tea. Diana noticed her plate was cracked.

"The buns are good," said Mathilde.

It was something.

The next morning, Diana and her mother and sister took the carriage into town. There wasn't much town to visit, concluded Diana, and found herself longing for a chance to live in London. What would it be like to reside someplace where fashionable modistes and miliners lived only a short carriage ride away, where one had easy access to linen drapers and furniture makers? "I suppose I shall have to make a trip to London to get the material for new window draperies," she observed.

"Once you are out of mourning we might consider it," replied her mother. "Here, let us stop at the apothecary. I should like to get some basillicum powder to have on hand, and I have a feeling we will need to purchase something for rats."

The young man who waited on them was all smiles and politeness, although Diana noticed his smile became tentative when her mother introduced themselves.

In the bakery, too, the baker's wife was friendly, but the young men lounging about the bakery door looked at Diana with hard eyes. And Mathilde they ogled rudely.

"I don't like it here," fretted Mathilde.

"Never you mind, dear," said her mama, patting her hand. "Those were just rude young men. We shall ignore them."

"They looked at me as if I were the devil himself," mused Diana.

"I am sure you are imagining things," said her mother.

Diana said nothing, but she knew she hadn't imagined those stoney gazes.

They arrived home to find they had a visitor. Mrs. Appleby, a graying, round woman, had a face shaped to complement her name. With her red, round cheeks she should have had merry eyes and a ready smile, but Mrs. Appleby's eyes were dull and her smile grudging. "I hear your husband is dead," she said without preamble. "My condolences. I suppose you've come to see that Hunt's mill keeps producing, keeping our men out of work."

Diana stared at the woman, at a loss for words.

Mrs. Appleby suffered no such loss. "You'll be needing a cook. My husband is one of those your husband's wide looms put out of work, so I figure that should even the score."

"Well, of all the nerve," huffed Mrs. Brown.

"Never mind, Mama," said Diana quickly. She turned to their visitor. "I know nothing of my husband's business. I have only just moved here."

"Your husband's business was to raise a pound and consider none but himself," said Mrs. Appleby. Here she gave Diana a thin smile. "But then, which of us can control what our husbands do?"

Now Diana smiled, sensing that this woman might not be as antagonistic as she appeared. "Can you cook?"

Mrs. Appleby patted her puffy girth. "What would you guess?"

Diana ignored her mother's wildly rolling eyes and said,

"You may have the position." She led the way from the sitting room. "I'll show you the kitchen. You may start immediately. Send Williams back to town for anything you might need."

"Whatever were you thinking of?" demanded her mother when she returned.

"My dinner," replied Diana.

"That woman is rude and insolent. Why on earth did you hire her?" persisted Mrs. Brown.

"She understands," said Diana.

For dinner, they had mulligatawny soup, followed by potatoes and a leg of lamb. Mrs. Appleby had also managed to make a blancmange for dessert.

"Please tell Mrs. Appleby that the dinner was wonderful," Diana said to Addison, when he had finished serving them.

"It could have been better," sniffed Mrs. Brown.

Diana remembered the two helpings of blancmange her mother had enjoyed and smiled.

The rest of the week passed quickly. There were financial affairs to attend to, and linens to order, a larder to stock, and help to be hired. Diana added a scullery maid and a gardener to her staff. The gardener was a young man named Charles Gint. He was not much older than herself, and had dimples and golden curls. He had a habit of whistling as he worked, and hearing him through the open window helped Diana ignore the fact that she was still in half mourning. She was already tired of gray. Come summer she would have a new dress made. Something in blue.

The following week the ladies had a caller. Mrs. Willoughby, the banker's wife, was a middle-aged stick of a woman with a thin, primly pursed mouth and thin curls. She had very little chin and her bonnet seemed to overwhelm her face. Diana didn't care. The woman was a caller, nonetheless.

"I felt someone should welcome you," Mrs. Willoughby said, after settling on the faded sofa. "It is such an uncomfortable thing to come to a new place as a widow. Naturally, people don't wish to intrude."

"It was very kind of you," said Mrs. Brown. "It has been terribly hard on my poor daughter to be widowed so young."

Mrs. Willoughby followed Mrs. Brown's gaze to Diana and shook her head. "Such a trial. And I am sure there are those who will do their best to make you feel unwelcome. But you mustn't pay any mind to them. Common people simply don't understand progress."

"Progress?" repeated Diana.

Mrs. Willoughby turned to her mother. "You know how it is. Lazy people will look for any excuse to be lazy. These men lounge about and drink spirits while their families struggle to keep body and soul together. Times change and people must be willing to change with them." She sighed. "I suppose it was ever thus. Folks must have a doorstep at which to lay their troubles. And I am afraid around here that doorstep is Hunt's Mill." Having now disposed of that topic, Mrs. Willoughby moved quickly on. "But how long has your poor husband been dead? When last he visited our home he seemed the picture of health."

"It has been quite a long time," replied Diana evasively.

"We had no Christmas party," added Mathilde. "But we did have carolers."

Diana felt a guilty flush stealing up her cheeks. Next Mrs. Willoughby would be wanting to know exactly when she had laid her husband in the ground and if that came out it would be difficult to explain why she was already in half mourning. "His death was quite sudden. It is difficult to speak of," she added.

"Of course," murmured Mrs. Willoughby, the picture of sympathy. "To be widowed so young. It is a hard life."

Diana stole a look at her mother. Mrs. Brown's body visibly relaxed.

"Well, I must be going," announced Mrs. Willoughby. "Please don't hesitate to call on me if you should need anything," she said to Diana. To Mrs. Brown, she added, "I hope we shall meet again soon."

A few more pleasantries were exchanged and Mrs. Willoughby took her leave. "That was a close call," said Mrs. Brown.

"I thought it was a social call," said Mathilde, her brows puckering.

Both mother and sister ignored her.

"And how would you have explained yourself if she had asked exactly when your husband died?" continued Mrs. Brown.

"I would have thought of something," replied Diana. "At any rate, the subject will not come up now."

"If it does, everyone who is anyone will turn on you," predicted her mother.

"It sounds as if half the town is already against me," said Diana thoughtfully. "Whyever don't people wish to have a mill here?"

Her mother shook her head. "I don't know. But they will simply have to learn to accept it. It is your source of income."

Mr. Hughes, Diana learned, was the man who oversaw her husband's business interests in Yorkshire. She wrote him, requesting he call on her. Two weeks later, he sat across from Diana and her mother in their little drawing room, looking at Diana in puzzlement. "I have no idea whether or not your husband was well liked here in Heptonstall, Mrs. Hunt. I can, however, assure you that he was always a most excellent businessman. In addition to the mill, he also owns several wide looms for the knitting of stockings, all of which he is renting at a very good profit, I assure you."

"A woman called on me who talked of trouble and complaining," said Diana.

Mr. Hughes waved this aside. "There are always those who object to progress, Mrs. Hunt. A good businessman does not listen. These new looms, especially, are a most amazing invention. They make it possible to make twice the amount of stockings the old looms produced."

Diana wasn't interested in the details of her husband's business ventures. "It is most unpleasant living where I feel I am not liked," she said.

"Now, dear, I told you that you only feel this way because you are still in mourning," put in Mrs. Brown.

Mr. Hughes looked as though he didn't know what to say. He repeated himself. "Your husband's businesses are all doing well."

Diana sighed and thanked the man for coming.

"I have a friend," announced Mathilde after Hughes had left.

"I am glad you do," said Diana. "Perhaps you will share him with me," she added glumly.

"But he is your friend, too," said Mathilde. "He says you are very nice."

"Mathilde, who are you speaking of?" demanded her mama.

"Charles Gint."

"Charles Gint!" exclaimed Mrs. Brown. "Do you mean the gardener?"

Mathilde nodded. "He is very nice. His cat is going to have kittens and he has promised me one."

Diana rolled her eyes.

"We have been over this before," said Mrs. Brown sternly. "You know it isn't proper for you to be trailing the gardener about while he works. You are a young lady."

"I am bored," said Mathilde. "I miss my friends. I am sure Mr. Noodle and Miss Hammond would like us to come home."

"You will make new friends," said Mrs. Brown.

"Perhaps we should return to Tetbury," said Diana. "We could sell this house."

"How would it look if we returned home?" argued her mother. "You left to make a fine marriage to a wealthy man. We cannot simply go home and return to what we were."

Diana said nothing to this. What was there to say? Before

she left to marry Mr. Hunt, the whole town had heard of the Browns' good fortune. The lovely Diana was going to marry a rich man who would keep her and her family in style. And what would everyone think when the Browns returned home clasping but a few crumbs of that good fortune? What a laughing stock they should be!

Spring dragged on. Other than an occasional call from Mrs. Willoughby, the rest of the town seemed determined to ignore them.

"You are still in mourning," insisted Mrs. Brown.

"Is that why no one even talks to me after church, except the vicar's wife and Mr. and Mrs. Willoughby?"

"There is no one worth talking to except the vicar and his wife and the Willoughbys."

"I talk to everyone," said Mathilde.

The day after this conversation, Diana went in search of her gardener to speak with him about planting some apple trees. She thought he'd been at the front of the house, tending the roses, but now he was nowhere in sight. She hesitated on the front step, scanning the lawn for a glimpse of him. A giggle from the side of the house distracted her from her search. Mathilde. What was she up to?

Diana went around the house and came upon Mathilde and Charles Gint. Mathilde was fingering a rose in her hair and her cheeks were flushed pink. He leaned with one arm against the house, smiling down at her. For a fleeting second, Diana thought of Lord Woodham, then duty crowded the thought away. "Mathilde!"

Both Mathilde and Charles jumped.

"Charles gave me a flower," said Matilde.

"I see," said Diana. She smiled at her sister. The look she gave the gardener wasn't so cordial. "That was very nice of him. Now, go on inside. I want to speak with Charles."

"I hope you aren't behaving in an improper manner toward my sister," said Diana as soon as Mathilde had disappeared around the corner of the house.

The young man's face whitened. "No, Mrs. Hunt. I have great respect for your sister."

Diana couldn't think of anything more to say. "Well, see that you continue to do so," she said, and left, forgetting the reason she'd come looking for him in the first place.

She went back inside, assuring herself she wasn't jealous of her little sister, who had no cares and no enemies. This time next spring, she would be in London, purchasing new draperies and furniture for the house. Life would not remain this gray existence forever. Things would change, she'd make sure of that.

True to his word, Charles Gint gave Mathilde a kitten. Diana thought the whole thing highly improper, but Mrs. Brown never liked to deny Mathilde anything, so the kitten remained. "I shall name him Snowy," announced Mathilde, stroking the white fur.

Diana turned to hide a scowl. *Shame on you!* she scolded herself. *You wish you had someone giving you presents and so you are hard on Mathilde.* Her last conversation with Lord Woodham came to mind. Would he ever visit and bring her sweets from London?

In late spring, Mathilde developed a fondness for taking Williams and walking into town to buy treats from the bakery. Neither Diana nor Mrs. Brown objected. It gave Mathilde something to do. On each return trip she had some news to share. Mrs. White, the baker's wife, had a cold. She saw the vicar's wife, who asked to be remembered to Mama and Diana. The baker's son had given her an extra hot cross bun and not charged her. The baker's son was wondering how long her family would remain in mourning. How long before they could receive visitors?

"Does he plan to call?" asked Diana.

Mathilde nodded.

"Well, you may tell him that it will be some time before we are feeling up to having visitors," said Diana.

"I have seen the baker's son," said Mrs. Brown slowly. "He seems a very nice young man."

"I am sure he is, Mama," agreed Diana. "But a baker?"

Mrs. Brown shrugged. "I would be happy simply to have her settled."

"When I am out of mourning, I shall take Mathilde to London where she will have a chance to meet a proper suitor."

Mrs. Brown shook her head. "If wishes were horses, then every beggar would ride."

"Mama," said Diana in exasperation, "Was that not why you wanted me to marry well, so I could help Mathilde find a husband?"

Mrs. Brown stared at her daughter. "Diana, how could you think I would lay such a burden on you? I wanted you to marry well, simply because I needed to settle you. Of course, I had thought Mr. Hunt would wish to do something to help your sister, but . . ." Her voice trailed off. "My dear child. Is that why you took his offer?"

"You were so excited. Naturally, I thought. . . ." Diana left her sentence unfinished. What, exactly, had she thought at the time? Where had she gotten the idea that she was to be the savior of the family?"

"You were happy to be marrying Mr. Hunt," her mother was saying. Which of them was she trying to convince?

Diana said nothing to this. Just as she had said nothing when her mother first began to talk of Mr. Hunt as a prospective husband. So that was why she was now in half-mourning, only half-alive, all because she'd said nothing. She turned from the thought. It was too upsetting to dwell on. Her sister, at least, would fare well. "I don't think you should allow Mathilde to encourage the baker's son."

"My dear, in your sister's case, we cannot afford to be particular. If some nice man wishes to provide for her, we should be grateful."

"We mustn't push her into marrying anyone she doesn't wish to marry," said Diana fervently.

Her mother looked at her, puzzled. "Of course we won't. Why ever would you think such a thing?"

Diana merely shook her head and went back to sorting linens.

The following day, Mathilde came home from her trip to town crying, Williams visibly upset as well.

"What happened?" demanded Diana.

"Some young men standing outside the bakery called her stupid," said Williams.

"One of them took my hot cross bun," whimpered Mathilde.

"He said, 'Your sister is a rich leech'," added Williams in a low voice. "He told me to tell you that one of these days you and your family are going to get what's coming to you."

Diana felt the blood draining from her face, taking her strength with it. She looked at her mother and said to Mathilde, "I think your visits to the bakery had best stop for awhile, dearest."

This brought fresh tears, but Diana was adamant. "It isn't safe."

"But I want to go to the bakery," wailed Mathilde.

"You shall, when Mama or I are taking the carriage into town and can accompany you."

"It is for the best, lambkin," added Mrs. Brown. "Now, why don't you go out into the kitchen and see what Mrs. Appleby is making for our dinner?"

Mathilde's smile was the sun after the storm. "All right, Mama," she said cheerily, and hurried off down the hallway.

"What shall we do?" asked Diana, as soon as her sister was out of ear shot.

"We shall pay no mind to this, of course," replied her mother. "What is it, after all, but the grumblings of a lazy young man?"

"Perhaps," said Diana dubiously.

As summer dragged on, Diana's determination to move from Heptonstall grew stronger. This town was unfriendly to her. It would remain forever so. Come next spring she would sell the house and leave.

Eight

Christmas was as dull as the one before. Diana and her mother and sister exchanged presents, and there were gifts for the servants and a yule log, but no carolers came to their door and no one invited them out, and Mathilde moped about the house, making her sister feel very guilty.

"Next year will be different," Mrs. Brown predicted.

"It will," agreed Diana, remembering her resolution.

The day after boxing day, Addison came to the small drawing room to announce a visitor. "The Earl of Woodham."

Diana dropped her needlework and looked up in amazement. There he stood, large as life. She thought her memory had preserved him well, but memory had failed. He was taller, handsomer than she remembered. His strength and hardness of body seemed to call to the softness in her, and she felt a sudden longing to run her fingers along the sharp line of his jaw. She felt her cheeks warming. "Your lordship. What a surprise!"

The earl looked from Diana to Mrs. Brown, whose face registered an internal war between disapproval and amazement. "I hope I don't intrude," he said.

"Not at all," replied Diana. "Your company is most welcome. We have had a quiet Christmas and are all heartily tired of each other. I am sure you remember my mother."

The earl bowed over Mrs. Brown's hand as if she were a duchess.

And, indeed, she seemed to think she was one. Diana

watched her mother's haughty nod and frowned at her, then turned to Lord Woodham. "What brings you to Heptonstall?"

"I have been visiting friends in Yorkshire over the holiday. As I was nearby, I thought to come and see how you are faring in your new home. Oh, and I brought you something." He held out a beribboned box.

Diana saw the name *Gunthers*. "Sweets!"

"From London," he added, and the look he gave her spoke of kisses. She could almost taste them on her mouth.

"That was most kind. I am sure we will enjoy them," said Mrs. Brown, effectively breaking the spell.

The earl cleared his throat. "Are you happy in your new home, Mrs. Hunt?"

"People here dislike me," Diana blurted.

"Diana," scolded her mother.

"I cannot imagine such a thing," said the earl.

"I'm sure my daughter forgets that people naturally keep a polite distance from ladies who are recently bereaved," observed Mrs. Brown.

"Of course," agreed Woodham.

Diana's eyes flashed. "It is no such thing, Mama, and well you know it." She turned to the earl. "They despise me because I am Hunt's widow. They think I am tight and cruel like him."

"I am sure no one who meets you can think such a thing," said Woodham.

Diana shook her head. "I shall leave this place as soon as my mourning is over. I'm not welcome here."

"Nonsense," said Mrs. Brown. "You are imagining things."

"I suppose that man in the bakery was my imagination."

"Idle threats. How can a lazy loafer have the power to harm us?"

"What happened at the bakery?" asked the earl.

Diana related Mathilde's encounter there and he frowned. "Your husband owned the mill here?"

She nodded. "He had other business interests as well."

"And what are those?"

"Some sort of new looms, which he rented to several men about the shire."

Woodham nodded. "I believe there is some controversy revolving around the use of large looms. I don't suppose that means anything to you?" He raised an eyebrow.

Diana shook her head. "The same man who was Mr. Hunt's man of business sees to everything for me."

"I'm sure he is looking out for your best interests, then," said Woodham, and turned the subject.

Too soon, he left, and the grayness that hovered outside invaded the drawing room.

"I would like to know that man's intentions," said Mrs. Brown and popped one of Diana's precious sweets into her mouth.

Diana picked up the box. "He was a caller, and that is all I care."

"Well, you had best have a care," said her mother, "else you'll end up with no reputation."

"I can hardly end up with a worse one than I already have," Diana retorted.

January crawled by. The skies were constantly gray and dropping snow. Both Mathilde and Diana chafed at being confined indoors with little to distract them. Sometimes the sisters played at spillikins or worked their needlepoint, but just as often they squabbled. Then their mother scolded.

After one such scolding, Diana donned half boots and pulled on her new gray woolen cloak and fled the house to take a walk. She hadn't gotten far before she realized how late in the afternoon it was. Black already tinted the edges of the gray sky. Soon it would be dark and she was alone. The crunch of footsteps on the icy snow behind her made her start and she glanced back to see a man following her. There seemed to be something ominous about this figure appearing suddenly to shadow her. Like death, stalking his prey, he gave no greeting.

If she turned back to the house, she'd have to meet him face to face. She quickened her pace and hurried on. The footsteps behind her quickened as well. Panic urged her to run, but she dared not for fear of slipping on the ice. Her heart raced now, and urged her feet to follow suit. She tried to hurry faster, but the ice betrayed her, pushing her feet out from under her. With a screech, she went down. Now she could hear her pursuer running. She scrambled to get back on her feet, but it was too late. He was upon her. She screamed.

"Mrs. Hunt. It's me. Charles Gint."

"Charles!" Relief unleashed tears and rage. "Why didn't you say who you were?" she demanded. "You frightened me half to death."

"I'm sorry. I saw you leave the house and thought I'd follow to make sure nothing happened to you. It's not wise to be out alone like this, especially at this time of day. Are you all right?"

"No," snapped Diana. "I twisted my leg when I fell."

"Take my arm. I'll help you back."

Diana leaned on his arm and they began the slow progress back to the house. "When you said it wasn't wise to be out, did you mean for anyone or for me in particular?" asked Diana.

"Well, that is, no lady should be out when it's starting to get dark."

"Especially if her name is Hunt?"

Charles nodded. "You're not popular here."

"What have I ever done to these people?" demanded Diana.

"It is what your husband has done," said Charles. "But it's not just him. Times are hard all over the midlands. I hear in Nottinghamshire there's real trouble brewing."

Diana said nothing.

" 'Tis not that I wish to tell my betters what to do, but it would be best to take your coach when you go out," added Charles gently.

"You are right, of course. It was very foolish of me."

By the time Diana was back inside the house, she was shak-

ing. She tossed her cloak and bonnet on a chair in the hallway
and went into the drawing room to stand by the fire. Spring
is coming, she told herself.

In February, Williams reported to Diana that there was growing unrest in town. "The men cannot feed their families. They
lay the blame on the mill, and on those looms."

"What can I do?" demanded Diana.

"I don't know," replied Williams, "but I've been told you
should think about leaving before something bad happens."

"Who told you that?"

Williams shook her head. "We should leave."

"And where would we go?" countered Diana.

"Perhaps Mr. Barnes," began Williams in a timid voice.

"I shan't go crawling back to David Barnes," snapped Diana.

"Yes, Mrs. Hunt," said Williams meekly, and finished pin-
ning up her mistress' hair in silence.

Again, Diana sent for Mr. Hughes. "My servants tell me
there is increasing unrest in these parts. Is the mill in danger?"

"Of a few rabble rousers?" scoffed Hughes. He shook his
head. "Mrs. Hunt, if there were any real danger of harm to
your property I would be the first to tell you."

"I am not so worried about my property as I am my person,"
said Diana.

"Neither is in danger, I assure you."

"And you are sure of that?" pressed Diana.

"I'd stake my life on it."

Diana nodded. It was as she thought. Williams was jumping
at shadows.

Lady Woodham frowned. "Why would you wish to go haring off to Yorkshire when the season has just begun, Julian?"

"Because it promises to be infinitely more exciting than any affair to which you would drag me," Julian replied. "At any rate, you have Stephen to bear you company, and he is the one who needs to hang out for a rich wife."

"Ah, but I am not the Earl of Woodham," said Stephen, examining his fingernails. "I am not half so interesting to display." His mother gave him a disapproving look and he grinned impishly back at her. "Let him go, Mother. Perhaps some crazed Luddite will split his thick skull with an axe, then I shan't have to court this season's crop of squint-eyed heiresses."

Her ladyship saw no humor in this, but Julian chuckled. "Besides," he said, "I haven't felt at all well these past few weeks. I think a change of scene will do me good."

"Rather an unhealthy change, wouldn't you say?" observed his stepbrother.

"You are jealous," replied Julian.

Stephen shrugged. "You always have the fun. First the war, now Yorkshire and those mad frame-wreckers. I should like to see that first hand."

"You are welcome to tag along."

"He is going to do no such thing," interrupted her ladyship. "I cannot stop you from such foolishness, Julian, but I certainly can prevent Stephen from being equally foolish." Stephen scowled at this, and Lady Woodham softened her voice. "Come now. Would you really have me set off for London alone?"

"Of course not," said Stephen. "And truth to tell, I'll take the gaming tables over a handful of bumpkins any day."

"As you wish," said Julian. It was just as well his stepbrother didn't really want to accompany him, for after he'd visited his friend in Yorkshire, he planned to go to Heptonstall to see how the huntress fared. The talk of growing unrest and violence made him uneasy. God only knew what sort of dangerous situation the foolish female would get herself into there. She seemed to attract danger as easily as she attracted men.

* * *

The sound of shattering glass made all three ladies jump and scream. Mrs. Brown gathered Mathilde to her and drew her to the far side of the drawing room while Diana crept to the window to investigate. At her feet she saw the rock with the paper still half wrapped around it. Hands shaking, she plucked it from the rock and picked it up.

"What does it say?" asked Mrs. Brown.

Diana read the childlike printing. *gredy biTch*. Greedy bitch. Without answering, she let the paper fall from her hand. Like a dove, it floated down to rest next to the rock.

Mrs. Brown left Mathilde and came to retrieve it. She picked the paper up and scanned it, then sucked in her breath.

"What is it, Mama?" asked Mathilde. "What does it say?"

"Nothing," said Mrs. Brown sharply. "Just a prank, that is all it was. Just a prank. Now, go find Addison. Tell him we have a mess to clean in the drawing room."

"Yes, Mama," said Mathilde, and left.

"We cannot stay here," said Mrs. Brown. "You must go back and ask Mr. Barnes. . . ."

"No!"

"Diana, we need their help. And we need only stay until we can sell this house."

"Surely we have enough money left from your sale of the house in Tetbury."

"You know we had debts to pay with that money," said Mrs. Brown.

Diana remembered. What was left, Mama was saving for a dowry for Mathilde. "There must be some other way. I shall send for Mr. Hughes."

"Much good he will do you," scoffed her mother.

"I shall write him, nonetheless."

A week passed and Diana had no word from her man of business. "I suppose you heard the news," said Mrs. Appleby one day after Diana finished conferring with her about the week's menus.

"What news is that?"

"Frame-breakers got into Mr. Willis's place. Shot him in the shoulder, smashed his frame to bits. It was one old Hunt had rented to him. Rumor has it the mill is next." Mrs. Appleby gave Diana a smug smile. "This may be the last week you can afford to pay for food."

"If that is so, this may be your last week of employment," retorted Diana, and left the kitchen.

What to do? Why hadn't she heard from Mr. Hughes yet? She went to write him another letter.

It was the following day that Addison and Williams went to town to shop and came back with the news. Mr. Hughes was dead.

"Dead?" stammered Diana. "How did this happen?"

"His home was burned to the ground," said Addison.

"Who could have done such a thing?"

"No one knows for sure. Word has it that the constable cannot get any information at all."

"Who do people say did it?" asked Diana.

Addison shook his head. "No one is discussing who is responsible, madam. But general opinion seems to be that the man deserved his fate."

Diana felt dread wash over her. If people thought poor Mr. Hughes deserved what happened to him, what fate did they think she deserved?

The next few days crawled by. Mr. Hughes' attackers still went undiscovered, and Diana felt like a woman in a castle under siege, waiting for the enemy to scale the walls and drag them out to their deaths.

It was shortly after dinner on Saturday evening when Addison informed Diana that Charles Gint was at the kitchen door, asking for a word with her. She found Gint still standing outside the door when she got there, and looked at him questioningly, but he cast his glance beyond her toward the little scullery maid, laboring over the dirty pots and shook his head.

"Come with me," said Diana, and led the way to her study.

"What is it?" she asked as soon as he had shut the door behind them.

"Your family is in grave danger," said Charles.

"What do you mean?"

"A group of men plan to burn the mill tonight."

Diana sank onto a chair. "What shall I do? I must inform the constable!"

Gint shook his head. "It will do no good. And besides, you have a more immediate problem. The mill isn't the only thing they mean to burn."

Diana felt her heart catch and stumble on to a faster pace. "What do you mean?"

"After they've set the mill on fire they will come here. You must leave Heptonstall tonight."

"But I cannot possibly be ready to leave by tonight. We must pack."

"There's no time. Even as we speak, your driver is putting the horses in harness."

Her house, her furniture; it wasn't much, but it was all she had.

"You must be ready to leave in half an hour. We don't dare wait any longer."

"Half an hour?" repeated Diana.

Charles took her arm and urged her from the room. "Hurry. You must be ready when I come back for you."

The urgency in his voice spurred her into action, and she ran to the drawing room.

Her mother and sister were sitting in front of the fire, Mrs. Brown reading to Mathilde. Mrs. Brown's smile melted at the sight of Diana's pale face. "What is wrong?" she demanded, her voice trembling.

"We must leave."

"What?"

"Now. Tonight!" cried Diana, giving in to the hysteria growing in her.

The book fell from Mrs. Brown's hands. "They are coming for us, aren't they," she whispered.

"Yes, but they shan't find us. We leave Heptonstall in half an hour."

"Half an hour!" echoed Mrs. Brown. "I cannot possibly pack in half an hour."

"It is all the time we have," Diana called over her shoulder as she hurried from the room. She rushed into the dining room to grab the two things of value in the house; a set of silver candlesticks and a silver epergne. She set them on the hall table, then ran upstairs to her room and gave the bellpull a jerk. Without waiting for Williams, she pulled open the wardrobe and began to take out her small supply of gowns and toss them on the bed.

Five minutes later, Williams came to the room. "Oh, my," she whispered.

"We leave in half an hour," said Diana briskly. "Tell Addison. If you wish to come with us you must both be packed and ready."

A wide-eyed Williams pulled out Diana's valise from the wardrobe.

Diana took it from her. "Time is too short. I'll pack for myself. Go see to your own needs."

Williams gave her a grateful look and dashed from the room.

Diana stuffed what gowns would fit in the valise, then ran down the corridor to see how her mother and sister fared. She could hear her mother's agitated voice floating out from Mathilde's room.

Once inside, she saw Mrs. Brown, standing next to the bed furiously folding a gown. Before her rose a fluffy mountain of clothes, and Mathilde sat next to it, picking about its contents. "I don't see why I cannot take the jonquil afternoon gown," she said.

"I shan't discuss it further," snapped Mrs. Brown. "Now, hand me the blue sarsenet."

"Here, Mama. I'll help Mathilde finish packing," offered Diana, joining her mother.

"She is being most difficult," said Mrs. Brown.

"I am not," said Mathilde.

Mrs. Brown ignored her. "Take what you think will serve best," she said to Diana, then left.

"May I take Snowy?" asked Mathilde.

Diana had little desire to haul a cat across England in a closed carriage, but what would happen to the poor thing if they left it? "I suppose we must. You had best go find him immediately."

"All right," said Mathilde, and left with no further thought for her gowns.

Diana had them packed in five minutes. She had just gotten downstairs when Charles Gint returned.

"Good," he said. "I see you are ready. Where's Addison?"

"I don't know. I haven't seen him."

As if on cue, Addison made his entrance, coming down the hallway from the kitchen, a well-worn valise in his hand.

"We must leave now," Charles told him.

Addison silently bent to pick up the two valises sitting next to Diana, then followed Charles out the front door.

Diana ran back upstairs, calling for her mother. When she got to Mrs. Brown's room, she saw her mother was still furiously packing. "Mama, we must go."

"I am nearly done," said Mrs. Brown firmly.

"We must leave now," urged Diana.

"Take those two valises down and I shall be right behind you," said Mrs. Brown, rummaging about under the bed.

"Mama!"

"I said I will be right behind you," snapped the disembodied voice.

Diana scooped up the valises and stomped off. When she got belowstairs, she found Williams already there. "Where is Mathilde?"

"I don't know, Madam. I last saw her on her way to the kitchen, looking for the cat."

"Here," said Diana, giving her the silver pieces. "Take these to the carriage."

Williams hurried out and Diana went to the kitchen. No one was there. She noticed the small collection of still unscrubbed pots. Even the scullery maid knew danger was blowing their direction and had fled. Diana ran to the back door and called for Mathilde.

"I cannot find Snowy."

Mathilde's voice seemed far off. There would be no coaxing her back. "I have found him," called Diana.

A moment later, Mathilde was at the door. "Oh, I am so glad," she panted. "I looked everywhere. Where is he?"

"In the carriage," lied Diana, and promised herself she would get her sister another cat as soon as they were settled in a new home. "Now, hurry. We must be leaving."

Diana rushed Mathilde down the hallway and out the front door. Charles was hovering there and took her elbow, urging her to move faster still. "Mama," she began.

"She is already in the carriage," replied Charles, "and so are her things."

Diana stopped. Why was the sky unnaturally light? Then she saw the huge tower of flame, rising into the darkness like a giant genie, released from his bottle. And what was that she heard? Voices? She turned to Charles. "Are they on their way here?"

"There's no time to lose," he said, sweeping her on to the carriage.

"Snowy!" cried Mathilde from inside the carriage. "Where is Snowy?"

"Mathilde! Sit down!" cried Mrs. Brown.

Mathilde appeared in the door of the carriage, glaring at Diana. "He's not here. You lied." She began to descend the carriage steps.

Diana reached up to turn her around. "No, Mathilde. There is no time left. We must leave now."

"I want Snowy," ground out Mathilde, straining against her sister's hands.

"Snowy is with me," said Charles. Mathilde stopped and stared at him with her pale blue eyes.

"He doesn't like carriage travel. It makes him ill. So I will keep him at my house."

Mathilde's brows lowered. "But he's mine."

"So I told him. But he said he would really rather stay on here. He asked me to beg your forgiveness for his lack of loyalty." Mathilde still hesitated on the carriage steps. "I will take good care of him," Charles added.

Mathilde blinked, swiped at her eyes and went back inside the carriage.

Blessing Charles Gint, Diana followed her. She stopped at the door. "Will you suffer for having helped us?"

He smiled and shook his head. "I think not."

Diana held out her hand. "Thank you, Charles Gint."

Instead of taking it, he merely stooped to let up the steps. Diana moved back and let him shut her in the carriage. Like God, she thought, shutting Noah in the ark. She heard the crack of the whip, then the carriage lurched forward and rolled off down the road as the babble of voices came closer, like a great wave.

Woodham had meant to make the journey to Heptonstall in easy stages, but an unsettled feeling pushed him on. He rode in the near darkness of a quarter moon, heedless of the cold and the grumblings of his empty stomach.

When he was still several miles away, he saw the conflagration. Hunt's mill! It could be nothing else. Dear God, what had they done to Diana?

As he rode through town he noted the groups of men, rushing by him, some sober and carrying buckets, others foxed and laughing. Shades of what he'd seen in Yorkshire. Hungry men, angry men, men turned mean by deprivation. One group eyed him suspiciously, and he rode over to them. "I thought to find an inn for the night," he said to the largest man, who was gripping an iron bar. "What's toward?"

"Revenge," replied the man.

The earl nodded his head the direction he'd come. "I saw the fire. No one cares to put it out?"

The man nodded slowly and drawled, "That be right. No one cares."

"Who started it?"

"No one knows. And if I were you, I'd push on."

"Perhaps I will," said Woodham, and reined his horse away. He could feel the mens' suspicious gaze boring into his back and forced himself to keep the animal to a walk. The smaller fire he saw further ahead screamed for him to gallop through town, but he dared not. He was a stranger passing through. He couldn't help Diana if he didn't remain just that.

Every man in the town seemed to be out. Activity eddied and swirled about him. Hatred seemed to float on the air like a scent, mixing with the smell of burning wood and sweaty bodies.

At the edge of town he stopped his horse across from what had been Diana Hunt's house. Flames lapped up the wood while a handful of men made a feeble attempt to douse them. *Oh God . . .*

Woodham didn't realize he'd spoken the words until a man touched his arm.

"You knew her?" asked the man.

"Where is she?" demanded Woodham.

"She is gone."

Relief rushed through the earl's veins, leaving him weak. "She has gotten safely away, then?"

The other man nodded. "And now I suggest you keep travelling. This town is not a safe place for any friend of Diana Hunt."

"Where did she go?"

The man shook his head. "I don't know," he sighed. "I only hope it was far from here."

Nine

The men stopped the carriage just outside of town. They hauled Mathilde out and a dozen of them carried her off, raised high above their heads like a helpless animal being taken to the altar of sacrifice. She screamed and held out a pleading hand to Diana, but Diana was, herself, surrounded by men whose eyes glowed fire red in the light of their torches. They pulled her from the carriage next and set her in the midst of them. One man stepped forward and set his torch to the hem of her skirt. She screamed.

The scream woke her. Panting, she pulled her damp hair back and looked around the room. There was nothing but cheery sunlight and the same familiar furniture of her old room at Spinney Hall. A dream, that was all it was. She was safely away from Heptonstall. The last year and its culminating horror was behind her now, and nothing more to her than the dream she'd just had. She took a deep breath and rang for Williams.

An hour later, she was seated in the drawing room, giving David Barnes and his mother a more full account of her adventures than the short two sentence version they'd gotten the night before.

"Terrible," shuddered Mary Barnes. "You poor child. I cannot imagine how you endured it. What will you do now?"

"I am not sure," said Diana. She didn't look at David, but she felt his gaze on her.

"Well, you must remain with us for a while, until you have found your feet," said Mary.

"Thank you," said Diana politely, and thought how galling it was to be accepting hospitality from her husband's murderer.

Mary Barnes certainly was enjoying her status as mistress of her brother's house. Diana noted the new carpet and draperies.

Mary smiled, and as if having read her guest's mind, said, "We have made some changes. Poor Charles let the house go shamelessly, but I think it looks quite nice now." Mary looked around the room. "Yes, it is much improved. Of course, the dining room is completely redone as well."

Diana merely nodded, unsure what to say.

At that moment her mother joined them.

"Ah, and here is Mrs. Brown," said Mary, still using her grand lady tone of voice, "I trust you slept well."

"As well as can be expected after the horrible experience we endured," replied Mrs. Brown. "Mathilde is still sleeping."

"Such an awful thing to suffer," said Mary. "And to think you lost everything."

"We are thankful to be alive," said Mrs. Brown. "They tried to stop the carriage on our way out of town. If our driver hadn't sprung the horses and galloped full speed at the crowd of ruffians I am sure we would all be dead today."

Diana felt suddenly cold and pulled her shawl more tightly about her shoulders.

"Come sit by the fire," said David gently. "You look chilled to the bone."

She left her seat for one closer to the fire and he came to stand by her. "It is just the memory of the whole thing," she said. "I can hardly bear to think of it."

"Then don't. Think to the future instead."

The future was a giant gaping blackness. Diana shivered again, and David tossed another log on the fire.

He left her in peace for the first week. In fact, he was the perfect host.

"We are so happy to have you back among us again," Mrs. Bellows told her after church on Sunday, and smiled at David, standing next to Diana. "How fortunate you had Mr. Barnes and his good mother to take you in."

"Yes, wasn't it?" replied Diana, and wondered when she would be presented with the bill for David's kindness.

It came later that night. Mary retired almost immediately after supper, Mrs. Brown following suit, and taking a reluctant Mathilde with her. Diana was about to go upstairs also when David said, "It is not so very late. Stay a while, aunt, and let us talk of your future."

Diana shot a quick look to her mother, who was halfway up the stairs, hoping she would insist her daughter come to bed. But Mrs. Brown was busy lecturing Mathilde for talking too much at dinner. Well, perhaps it was better to have the dreaded conversation now and be done with it. She went back into the drawing room with David and stood before the fire.

He settled easily onto the sofa. "What will you do now, Diana?"

She stared into the fire, remembering the conflagration in Heptonstall and shrugged listlessly.

"You cannot go on indefinitely like this."

"Like what?"

"With no plans for your future. No one can remain a guest forever."

"I don't know what to do," said Diana.

"I can take care of you."

Diana turned to face him. "Do you offer marriage, David?"

"How would that look? Marriage to my uncle's widow? Most improper."

"Nothing like what you are proposing," Diana observed.

He leaned back against the sofa cushions. "What I have proposed is security. Come now, Diana. What alternatives do you have? You have a mother and sister to keep. Your house is nothing but ashes. Of course, you could have it rebuilt. I am sure the townspeople would welcome you back." Diana scowled at this and he grinned.

"I have a jointure," she reminded him.

He chuckled. "Ah, yes. My generous uncle has left you well provided for, hasn't he?"

"I am not destitute," insisted Diana.

"Neither are you rich. The mill was your main source of income. It will be a while before that is running again. By now, I'll wager, all of your looms have been smashed. But by all means, try and find yourself a little cottage somewhere. You can take in mending. I am sure you and your mother and sister are used to economizing."

Diana's face showed what she thought of economizing.

"Just as I thought," crowed David, and she determined afresh that she would never come to him.

But instinct told her not to anger him. Not here, in his house. She needed his hospitality and his help. "I need time," she said. "Before I can make any decisions about my future I must go to London and find myself a new man of business." *And a new husband.* Why wait any longer? She could take a house in London for the spring. By summer she could be engaged again and all her financial worries would be at an end.

"I shall be happy to accompany you," David offered.

Diana shook her head. "I need only have you make arrangements for a place for me to stay with Mama and Mathilde, and take us to Croyden where we may take the coach for London."

"A woman alone in London? How will you manage?" protested David.

By my wits, thought Diana.

London was huge. And noisey. And chock full of rich noblemen and shops and theatres. Diana smiled as she looked out the window of her room at Grilon's Hotel in Albemarle Street. She was here at last, and she intended to make the most of it. To think they would soon be moving into a townhouse in Berkley Square! It wouldn't be long before she was attending balls and routs and Venetian breakfasts. Would she see the Earl of Woodham at any of those affairs?

"And how do you think you will pay for all this?" demanded Mrs. Brown, bringing Diana back to the present.

Diana smiled at the memory of her conversation with the man of business she'd hired regarding just that. "I want a house in the best part of London," she'd said.

"That would be Mayfair." He'd looked at her inferior gown and pelisse and added, "I'm afraid it is very expensive, Mrs. Hunt."

"That is of no consequence," said Diana, thinking fast. "My nephew, David Barnes, will pay for it. I shall write down his direction for you."

"Well?" Again, her mother's voice recalled her wandering thoughts.

Diana turned from the window. "I am going to find a rich husband."

"It has not yet been two years," protested Mrs. Brown.

"No one I meet in London need know how long I've been widowed," said Diana. Her mother looked dubious. Diana crossed the room and eagerly caught her mother's hands. "Oh, Mama, think of it. There are all manner of rich and titled gentlemen here in London, and there is no telling who I may find to marry."

"I just don't know," sighed Mrs. Brown. "I think we should simply be content with what we have."

"With both the mill and the house in ashes, what have we?" Diana argued. "You know my jointure was to be paid out of profits from the mill. And most of the looms have been smashed, too."

Mrs. Brown now looked as though she might cry.

"Don't worry, Mama. All will be well. You'll see."

"And how do you intend to attract this wealthy husband?"

"I have heard it said that wealth attracts wealth. I will let it be known that the late Mr. Hunt was a very rich man. No one need know that he neglected to leave his riches to me. And if I am living in a fine house and wearing fine clothes, who will suspect?"

"And how do you intend to pay for that fine house and those fine clothes."

"I have that all worked out as well," replied Diana mysteriously, "so you needn't worry. We shall be fine. You'll see."

"I cannot like this," said Mrs. Brown.

"I cannot help it," said her daughter, ending the conversation.

That was on a Tuesday. On Wednesday, the ladies went shopping. Diana purchased three new bonnets, six pairs of gloves and four pairs of evening slippers. At the modiste's, she was fitted for two morning gowns, a walking gown, and six ball gowns. "Please be so good as to send the bill to Mr. David Barnes," Diana instructed before they left the shop. "Here is the direction."

As she handed the Frenchwoman the slip of paper with David's address, she heard a moan behind her, a rustle of silk and then a thud and turned to see her mother on the floor in a dead faint.

The day they moved into their townhouse, she thought her mother would faint again. Mrs. Brown looked around her with ever widening eyes. "Oh, dear," she said at last.

Addison, however, was grinning broadly. "Very nice," he approved.

"Will it do, Addison?" asked Diana.

He nodded. "It will do very well."

"For what will it do very well?" asked Mathilde.

"For sending us to the poor house," snapped Mrs. Brown.

"Mama, we shall be fine," said Diana.

Mrs. Brown lowered her voice. "And how fine shall we be when David Barnes receives this mountain of bills you have been creating?"

"By the time David receives the bills I will be engaged to

a wealthy man who will be more than happy to reimburse him," replied Diana calmly.

"I hope for all our sakes you are right," said Mrs. Brown.

Diana had doubts about a great many things, but her power over men was not one of them. Aside from the expense involved, hunting for a husband was no different in London than in Bath. She had the house and soon she would have the clothes. And then she would begin in earnest.

Meanwhile, she had a townhouse to staff. She interviewed and hired a housekeeper, a spare woman with gray hair and a manner of quiet confidence, then set the woman and Addison to the task of hiring the other necessary servants. They, in turn, hired a footman, an upstairs maid, a new cook and a scullery maid.

Mrs. Brown watched their number of servants grow in size and made more dire predictions of financial disaster. But Diana plugged doggedly on, and after two weeks she had a well-staffed, elegantly appointed townhouse and a new wardrobe, and was ready to make her assault on polite society.

None of her Mayfair neighbors had yet come to call. Most likely, they were giving her time to settle in. Well, she was settled. She would let them know by calling on them.

It was a fine spring morning when she knocked on the first neighbor's door. A middle-aged butler opened it. He blinked at the sight of her.

"I should like to see your mistress," she said, trying to give no outward show of the butterflies suddenly swooping about inside her.

"I shall see whether Lady St. Clair is at home," he replied. "If Madam would be so good as to give me her card?"

"Card?" repeated Diana stupidly.

"Did you have a calling card?" asked the butler.

None of Diana's neighbors had used such tools in Tetbury. But then, none of them had been nobility. She decided to brazen it out. "I am afraid that I quite came away without them, but you may tell Lady St. Clair that Mrs. Hunt, her neighbor, is here to pay her respects."

The barely disguised expression on the man's face told what he thought of her and her excuse for having no calling card. "I am afraid that Lady St. Clair is not at home," he replied, and shut the door on Diana.

She felt the warmth on her cheeks and knew her face was red. Was this the reception she was going to get in London, then? Turned away with no one giving her so much as a chance? She bit her lip to stem the tears and went back down the front steps. What if Mama had been right and she'd spent all this money for naught? What would she do if London society rejected her?

She would have to return to David Barnes. But that was unthinkable. Mary Barnes had murdered her husband. How could she have any association with such a pair!

She'd have to think of some way to beat down the door to polite society. But how? Who could she turn to for help? There was only one person. Diana hurried down the walk and turned back to her own home to pen a letter.

"The Earl of Woodham," intoned Addison from the drawing room door.

The earl strode into the room and took Diana's hands in his. "I thought I'd lost you," he said. "And here I find you in London."

"You looked for me, then?"

He nodded and seated himself next to her on the sofa. "I had seen how things were in Yorkshire. I came to Heptonstall, fearful for your safety, but I was too late to find you."

She bit her lip and nodded. "They burned us out. We were lucky to escape with our lives. I am left with nothing."

The earl looked around him and observed, "You have done very well with nothing."

She shook her head and lowered her eyes. "I am in grave trouble. The mill was my living."

"I see," said Woodham slowly. "You are out of mourning?"

Diana felt a guilty flush on her cheek but raised her chin and said, "I cannot afford to mourn any longer."

"So the huntress has changed her mind."

"What do you mean?"

"You once told me that you would have both love and marriage or neither."

"Love is a luxury for the rich, your lordship," replied Diana. "But I will, at least, have honor. I will have marriage."

"And money," added the earl.

"And money," agreed Diana. "I have others to consider besides myself."

"I see," said the earl slowly. "And what, exactly, is it you wish of me?"

"I need your advice. I am afraid I attempted to pay a social call earlier and failed miserably."

"How so?"

Diana related her experience calling on Lady St. Clair and he listened and shook his head.

"The butler would not even relay my message."

"Of course not, for you told him there on the doorstep you were no one worthy of her ladyship's attention. You came to the door yourself, rather than remaining in your carriage and sending your footman."

"How ridiculous," scoffed Diana. "Why should I want my carriage to go only a few steps?"

"You should want your carriage so that you would have something to remain in while your footman was at the door of Lady St. Clair's townhouse. It is not a matter of convenience, but of consequence. And you had no card to present. What was the man to think?"

Diana sighed. "Yes, I see," she said at last. She studied the earl. Would he help her? "I must gain acceptance into polite society here in London," she said, and looked steadily at him.

He had been sitting with one booted leg crossed over the other, lazily swinging it. He stopped and the easy smile fell from his face.

For the first time, Diana truly saw the great chasm between them. Desperately, she tried to jump it. "I am not wholly without breeding. My mother is a lady."

"And your father?"

Diana found herself suddenly unable to look at the Earl of Woodham. "He was a soldier," she said quietly.

"It is a noble calling," said the earl kindly.

"But it does not make him nobility," whispered Diana.

"Mrs. Hunt," said Woodham gently, "the people you seek to befriend are a tightly closed circle. They won't readily welcome . . ." Here he paused.

"Nobodies?" supplied Diana, cocking an eyebrow.

"It is the way of things."

"How can they know I am a nobody?"

"If you were someone, you would have no need to ask such a question," replied Woodham.

Diana looked at her lap. "I am ruined, then."

The earl sat, studying her. "Would you and your mother care to attend the opera this Thursday night?" he asked suddenly.

Diana looked at him in amazement. Perhaps it was not a chasm that separated them after all. "That is most kind, your lordship. We should love to."

Woodham smiled at her. "This is no entree into society, I assure you. But while you are in London, you may as well enjoy yourself."

As soon as the words were out of his mouth Julian had regretted them. Taking the woman he planned to make his mistress to the opera and letting her sit in his box as if she had a social right to be there was madness. What would his friends say? Well, there was no going back on his promise. Besides, she'd looked so thrilled at the prospect, and he flattered himself that it was his company she was most excited about, rather than the visit to opera itself. Still, why ever had he committed to such folly!

When he arrived at her townhouse to fetch her, she nearly took his breath away. She was dressed in a gown of peacock blue, its low decolletage presenting a good deal of creamy breasts for his inspection. Around her neck hung a necklace of what passed quite successfully for sapphires.

"This is most kind of you, your lordship," said Mrs. Brown, distracting him from his study of her daughter.

"It is my pleasure," said the earl. "Shall we go?"

The cadaverous old butler helped the ladies on with their cloaks and opened the door for them, smiling on his employer more like a doting father than a servant. Very curious, thought Julian.

Once in the carriage, Diana chatted easily about what she had seen of London so far. Her mother, the earl noticed, said little, only sat regarding him suspiciously.

He found it made him most uncomfortable. The woman was no gypsy. How could she know his plans for her daughter. She didn't. He was merely being fanciful. And anyway, what matter if she did? Diana Hunt could do far worse than to be kept by the Earl of Woodham. Her mama would do well to remember that.

As they settled themselves in his opera box, Julian felt as if the eyes of all London were upon them. His stepmother would hear of this, he supposed, and wonder why he had felt unable to escort her to the very same opera the week before. Then would come a cold, dignified lecture on the importance of behaving in a manner worthy of one's station in life.

He took his seat behind his beautiful guest, pulled out his opera glasses and scanned the crowd. In the box directly opposite sat a fine featured woman with dark chestnut curls, her glasses trained on him. She lowered the glasses but remained looking in his direction, giving him a small nod and a sly smile. Curse it all! Of all the nights one might attend the opera, why had Louisa picked this particular one? Julian nodded in her direction, then passed the opera glasses up to his guests. He folded his arms, slouched down in his chair and feigned interest as the curtain went up.

But as the night went on he found it difficult to keep his eyes directed toward the stage. Rebelliously, his gaze continued to drift to the delicate neck and shoulders in front of him. The first thing he'd do after Diana Hunt had consented to be his mistress would be to buy her a necklace of real sapphires. And diamonds. Such a lovely throat demanded diamonds as well.

The next morning a footman arrived at Lord Woodham's townhouse with a summons from Lady Dalton. It came as no surprise to the earl. He'd been planning to call on Louisa anyway, and so he would tell her.

Her butler let him into her drawing room at precisely two o'clock. He found her perched on a sofa, a pug dog curled up against her. The dog awakened at his entrance, jumped down and ran, yapping, to his feet. Woodham bent to scratch the animal's rump, then went to take the hand her ladyship held out to him. "And what do you think of my new sofa?" she greeted him.

He regarded the sphinx shaped legs. "Egyptian. You will tire of it."

She frowned. "Thank you, cousin, for doing your best to rob me of my pleasure."

"Then I should say we are even," replied Woodham lightly, "for I know that is what you intended to do last night at the opera."

"I intended no such thing!" she cried. "What a vile thing to say!"

The earl grinned. "Come now, Louisa, there is no sense playing the wounded saint with me. I remember how you looked at me, and I have seen that particular look before. It always precedes some trick or other."

"Well, I shan't serve you any tricks if you tell me who the woman is. She's terribly beautiful."

Julian nodded. "She is."

"Well, then," prompted Lady Dalton, "who is she?"

"No one of social importance. She is a neighbor of mine. A widow."

"A widow," mused her ladyship. "A wealthy one?"

"Hardly," he replied.

"I should like to meet this woman," said Lady Dalton suddenly.

"She is not accustomed to moving in the first circles," hedged Julian.

Her ladyship raised an eyebrow. "She isn't a cit, is she?"

"No," said Woodham. "Shabby genteel, more like."

"What is your interest in her?" asked Lady Dalton.

"Really, Louisa. You're not my mother."

"Thank God," said her ladyship heartily. "Do you court her?"

"I am merely sorry for her," said Julian. "She married that pinch purse, Hunt, and was immediately widowed."

"I should not pity her because of that," said Louisa. "I saw the man once."

The earl shook his head. "Bad fortune has dogged her ever since."

"And so you have become her knight in shining armour," guessed her ladyship.

Julian tried to meet her gaze with a look of innocence. "I was simply being kind," he said.

"I see," drawled her ladyship.

"Do you?"

She leaned back against the sofa cushions and regarded him with that same sly smile. "Oh, I do. I should like to practice a little kindness, myself. I think I shall call on her tomorrow. Would you care to drop by as well?"

Julian scowled at his mischievous cousin. "Louisa, why are you so determined to act perversely?"

"I am bored," she replied. "Now, don't worry, Julian. You may as easily dally with her if she is socially acceptable."

"To take her up will do your reputation no good," he cautioned.

"Is she an impure?" guessed his cousin.

"Really, Louisa, someone should take soap to your mouth."

"Well, is she?" persisted her ladyship.

"No, she is not," snapped Julian.

"Yet," murmured his cousin.

"What was that?" he demanded.

"Nothing," she replied lightly. "I have not yet offered you refreshment. Would you care for burgundy?"

"Yes," replied the earl. He definitely needed a drink.

Ten

Diana turned the calling card over in her hand. Lady Dalton. Who was that? She looked questioningly at Addison.

"I shall be happy to tell your ladyship you are at home to visitors," he said.

Taking his cue, she nodded and the butler left to fetch the mysterious caller.

He returned with a pretty woman with dark curls and a very fashionable gown. She entered the room with the ease of one who knew her social standing and so could be confident anywhere. "Mrs. Hunt, I am Lady Dalton. I understand from my cousin, Lord Woodham, that you know few people in London, so I took the liberty of calling on you."

"That is very kind," said Diana and blessed the earl for the good samaritan he was. "Would you care for tea?"

Lady Dalton shook her head. "No, I think not. But I imagine my cousin will join us, and he likes a bit of sherry in the morning."

"Of course," said Diana, trying to hide her astonishment.

"Meanwhile, before he arrives we can have a comfortable coze, just the two of us. I am sure you are wondering why I am calling on you."

"I imagine it is because Lord Woodham told you I am newly arrived and know no one."

"It is because I wish to see the woman who has so captivated my slippery cousin. You know that every matchmaking mama in London has thrown her daughter at him."

"I am afraid you are mistaken if you think the earl has intentions of any serious kind toward me," said Diana.

"Oh, I know his intentions are quite the opposite. Or so he believes."

Diana's brows knit. "I am afraid I don't understand."

"My cousin *thinks* he wishes only to dally with you." Diana blushed and Lady Dalton said, "Please forgive me for being so blunt, but I am sure Julian will arrive at any moment, and I wished to speak to you first. You see, it is my belief Julian *really* wishes something entirely different. Unfortunately, he is not only very high in the instep, but very cynical as well, and I am afraid he wouldn't recognize love if it came up and bit him on the ear."

Diana could barely find her voice. "You think he loves me?"

"Save his stepmama, no woman has ever before shared his opera box. I think he either loves you or he has gone daft. Which is it?"

Diana shook her head. "I don't know."

"Well, I do," said Lady Dalton. "And I intend to make sure Julian knows as well."

"I am not nobility," said Diana softly.

Lady Dalton nodded. "I am well aware of that. But you are gently bred. And you are the woman he loves. And you love him?"

Diana bit her lip and looked at her lap. "He saved me from a highwayman."

Lady Dalton sighed. "How romantic. It is the stuff of which dreams are made."

Diana thought of the nightmares that had haunted her after the experience and said nothing.

"So you do love him?" her ladyship persisted.

She met Lady Dalton's curious gaze. "I do, but I won't be his mistress."

"Gracious, no!" agreed her ladyship. "You must marry. Julian must know what it is to have a woman's love. That is something which has been sadly lacking in his life these many years."

"His stepmother," began Diana.

"Is as cold a harpy as you'd ever wish to meet," finished Lady Dalton. "She has only love enough for her own son. No, Julian is a man who has been starved of affection for a long time. His father, I believe, cared for him. But the old earl was a stern man. When Julian insisted on playing at soldier it caused a great rift between them. The earl died before Julian could return home to heal it. So, you see? He has been greatly deprived."

Greatly deprived? Someone with money and position greatly deprived. No, Diana didn't see, but she nodded her head anyway.

"Good," said Lady Dalton. "Now, we simply need to make Julian realize he needs to marry you."

"How do you propose to do that?"

"Why, by moving you into his circle and introducing you to other eligible men, of course. You see, what Julian needs is a little competition."

Diana looked at Lady Dalton in new amazement. "You don't know me. Why would you wish to help me?"

Lady Dalton smiled. "I am bored," she confessed.

At that moment, Mrs. Brown entered the room. "Addison told me we had a caller," she said in an awed voice.

Diana made the introductions, and Mrs. Brown found a chair. "It is very good of your ladyship to call on us," she said. "Such an honor."

"And how are you enjoying London thus far?" asked Lady Dalton politely.

Diana half listened to her mother's words as she went back over her conversation with Lady Dalton. She knew she hadn't been entirely honest with her ladyship. If Lord Woodham offered matrimony, she would accept him in a heartbeat. But she couldn't afford to wait indefinitely for him. She needed a wealthy husband. Of course, whoever she married this time would, most likely, be more long-lived than Mr. Hunt, so she would have to make sure he was a kinder, handsomer man. But if he wasn't so kind and handsome as Lord Woodham she would have to settle. Her collection of creditors was growing daily.

Lord Woodham, perversely, never made his appearance in Diana's drawing room that morning, and it left her wondering afresh what, exactly, his feelings were toward her.

Lady Dalton, however, had no doubts whatsoever. The fact that her handsome cousin didn't call surprised her not in the least. Men were like horses. They didn't take naturally to the saddle. Julian was merely bucking to show he had spirit. But he would come around. Like horses, men could be trained.

He encountered her that night at a rout and casually inquired about her visit to Mrs. Hunt.

"It was most enjoyable," replied her ladyship. "I found her charming."

"Did she tell you why she has come to London?" asked Woodham, sounding like a man with a secret.

"No, I don't believe she did."

"She has come to seek a rich husband."

"Really?" replied Lady Dalton in a bored voice.

"Now do you still wish to foist her upon the ton?"

"And why shouldn't I?" countered her ladyship.

"I have just told you why," said Woodham.

"Because she seeks a husband? What woman does not?"

The earl shook his head. "You are all a mercenary lot, Louisa."

"And how, pray, would we survive if we weren't, dear cousin? If we are mercenary, it is men who have forced us to be so."

"Bah," said the earl. "Such radical talk. I think I shall tell Dalton."

She pouted. "I suppose you would, too, you vile man."

Woodham grinned. "I might if you don't behave."

"I always behave," she said lightly.

"Vixen," he said.

"And in Mrs. Hunt's case, I intend to behave very nobly and see if I cannot procure vouchers to Almacks for her and her mother."

"I should like to see that," muttered the earl.

"You doubt my power? Fie, Julian. You know very well I have always gotten whatever I set my mind to."

"You have had a very long run of luck," agreed the earl. "It has been my experience that every lucky streak must come to an end sooner or later."

"My luck will hold long enough to help Mrs. Hunt, I'll warrant," predicted her ladyship.

And it seemed she was right, for a week later, Woodham received a scrawled note from her crowing over her success. She would be at Almacks that Wednesday evening with Mrs. Hunt and her mother. Would they, by any chance, encounter him there?

Why not? he thought.

His stepmother seemed surprised when he announced his intention to accompany her and Stephen there.

"I am sure he doesn't go for the pleasure of our company," said Stephen.

Lady Woodham studied her stepson. "Julian, never tell me one of this season's crop of beauties has captured your fancy."

"I merely wish to see what is available," he replied evasively.

His stepbrother eyed him speculatively, but before Stephen could say anything, he changed the subject.

Almacks was a veritable crush of people. The important mingled with the self-important. Young men in evening breeches and slippers looked over clumps of excited young women who, in turn, regarded them from behind fidgeting fans. Diana took in the expensive gowns and jewels and nervously fingered her paste ones.

"You look incomparable," said Lady Dalton, as if reading her mind.

"I don't belong here," she said nervously. "I should never have come to London."

"Nonsense," said her ladyship. "The only difference between most of these people and you is that they give themselves airs and you don't."

"At any rate, there is no sense in leaving now we are here," put in Mrs. Brown. She looked around. "I must admit, this place is not half so grand as I'd imagined."

"It is not the building that makes Almacks what it is," said Lady Dalton. "It is the people inside it. Ah, Sir Harold." She smiled at the man approaching them.

He bowed over her hand and begged her to introduce him to her friend.

Lady Dalton made the introductions and Diana sized up her first potential suitor. Sir Harold Blaine was not so old as Mr. Hunt had been, and in much better physical condition. The skin at his neck was becoming slack, and when he bowed over her hand, she noticed his hair was thinning.

"And from where have you ladies come?" he asked after he had properly greeted each woman.

"Heptonstall," Diana replied. "My late husband owned the mill there."

"A mill. Very good investment these days, from what I hear. If we can get these crazed Luddites to settle down and stop wrecking things, that is."

Diana thought of the mill and her house, and of poor Mr. Hughes. "These are difficult times," she said.

"It would appear that Sir Harold has discovered an oasis in the desert," said another man, joining them. He turned to Lady Dalton. "Have pity on a weary pilgrim and introduce me."

"Mrs. Hunt, allow me to present the Earl of Ferndale," said Lady Dalton.

The earl seemed to be close in age to Sir Harold, but he was a much handsomer man. In fact, Diana concluded, this

new arrival boasted looks that could almost rival Lord Woodham. Time had salted Lord Ferndale's hair with gray, but that
seemed to be the only part of his body it had conquered. His
skin still clung firmly to his jaw. The shoulders under his coat
were broad and no protruding belly pushed against his coat,
nor did any creaking betray the presence of a corset as he
bowed over Diana's hand. If he had money he would do admirably.

"Do you dance, Mrs. Hunt?" he asked.

"I haven't for some time," Diana confessed. "I am only
recently out of mourning."

"Allow me to reintroduce you to the joys of the dance floor,"
he said.

"Here now," protested Sir Harold. "I was just about to ask
Mrs. Hunt to dance myself."

"The race is to the swift, Blaine," replied Lord Ferndale
with a smile.

"Well," huffed Sir Harold. He turned to Mrs. Brown. "Perhaps this kind woman will take pity on me and give me a
dance."

Mrs. Brown simpered and took his arm.

Lady Dalton watched both mother and daughter take their
places on the dance floor and smiled. She was joined by Lady
Woodham, looking like a marble statue with her white skin
and cream-colored gown. The diamonds at her throat winked
like ice in the sun. "Louisa, Julian tells me you are responsible
for that woman's presence here tonight."

"Yes, I am," replied Lady Dalton.

Lady Woodham observed Diana as she moved down the
floor. "I wonder why you stir yourself on behalf of a cheap
little adventuress."

"Why, because it amuses me to do so," replied Lady Dalton,
looking at the older woman as if she were terribly obtuse.
"Why should I not?"

"Because she is not one of us," replied Lady Woodham.
"She is a climber."

"She seems pleasant enough to me," said Lady Dalton. She grinned slyly at the older woman. "Your son appears quite fond of her."

"Neither of my sons are well acquainted with the woman," said her ladyship frostily. "Nor have any of us the desire to become better so."

With that she moved off, leaving Lady Dalton smiling behind her fan.

Lord Woodham came to Diana halfway through the evening. "Are you enjoying yourself, Mrs. Hunt?"

"I am enjoying myself greatly," she replied. "Your cousin, Lady Dalton, has been most kind to me."

"It would appear your social success is guaranteed," said Woodham.

"Thanks to your lordship," said Diana.

"I have done nothing to help you here," said the earl. "Your success is entirely my cousin's doing." He cocked his head to survey her. "Well, not entirely."

She blushed and lowered her gaze. "Your lordship is too kind."

"Ah, there you are, Mrs. Hunt," warbled Lady Dalton, coming up behind them. "You must allow me to present Sir Anthony, who has been dying to meet you this past hour."

Lord Woodham bowed and made his exit, and Diana watched him go, wishing he had asked her to dance.

The following day, flowers arrived for Diana from both Sir Harold and Lord Ferndale. "Oh, my," gushed her mother. "Two suitors already. My dear, you were absolutely right about coming to London. In fact, that is what we should have done in the first place. Of course, we had no connections then, so maybe it is all for the best. For if you hadn't met and married Mr. Hunt, you'd never have met Lord Woodham. Or Lady Dalton. Only think of it! Two noblemen! Of course, my uncle was a knight, you remember, so it is not as though we are entirely out of our element, so we shouldn't be at all surprised that you are taking so well." Addsion entered the room at that moment, bearing an envelope. "Oh, and what is that?" cried Mrs. Brown as if it were Christmas and she had just been given yet another present.

"Lady Dalton's footman has just now brought it," said the butler, handing it to Diana.

She tore it open and read. "It is an invitation. Lady Dalton is giving a dinner party next Thursday night."

Mrs. Brown beamed on her daughter, and Diana noticed that Addison, too, smiled as he left the drawing room. It had, indeed, been an excellent idea to come to London.

Diana's first impression when she entered Lady Dalton's drawing room was of a miniature crowd. All were finely dressed, expensive jewels glittering on the ladies' necks and in their hair. The men's coats were of the finest cloth and clung to their shoulders in a haughty display of superior tailoring. The scent of orange blossoms and Hungary Water sat heavy on the air.

At first the crowd seemed to be one giant monster gazing at her. Then it separated into individual faces and she was able to pick out familiar ones. There was Sir Harold, with his slightly jowly chin and thinning hair, and hovering behind Lady Dalton, who was approaching her with outstretched arms, was Lord Ferndale. And there, at the edge of the gathering, stood Lord Woodham. Diana's jittery spirits settled.

"My dear Mrs. Hunt," said Lady Dalton, taking Diana's hands in hers. "How glad I am you could join us. I have a great many people dying to make your acquaintance."

Diana took in the bored faces. "They all appear quite hale and hearty to me," she observed.

Her ladyship laughed. "Come," she said. "Let me present you."

Remembering her mother's advice, Diana was gracious, but

revealed as little of her background as possible. "The less you say the less you can betray," her mother had warned. She was not so sure of this, for it seemed to her that even as the other guests murmured polite greetings they stripped her naked and knew her for a nobody. The women were cooler to her than the men, and while that was no new experience, here in this small room, where all of society seemed boiled down to these eleven people, she found it disconcerting.

Never mind, she told herself. Lady Dalton is your friend. And Lord Woodham. He had smiled at her and told her she looked breathtakingly beautiful, and if Lord Woodham thought she looked beautiful, what did it matter what the rest of the company thought?

Once Lady Dalton had finished taking her around the room and introducing her to the other guests, both Lord Ferndale and Sir Harold came to her side. She smiled on them. "You are making me feel so very much at home. I must confess, I was not at all sure I would like it here in London."

"And why is that?" inquired Lord Ferndale.

"It is a very big city. And coming to such a place, a woman alone, can be terrifying."

"But you are not alone now," said Ferndale.

"Certainly not," agreed Sir Harold.

"A woman unmarried must always feel alone," said Diana, lowering her eyes.

"Such a lovely woman cannot remain unmarried long," said Lord Ferndale.

Sir Harold looked across Diana at his rival and said, "Certainly not."

She stole a look across the dining room to see if Lord Woodham was observing her triumph. He lounged against the mantelpiece, arms folded across his chest and grinned at her. It was a cynical grin, a superior grin, and it tarnished her pleasure.

In spite of the fact that she sat between her two admirers and had them both eating from her hand before the twelve courses were through, she was never able to put the sparkle back into the evening. The gentlemen joined the ladies in the drawing room after drinking their port. The guests settled themselves to listen to the more accomplished among them play the pianoforte, but the earl made no move to vie for a seat near Diana. Instead, he sat across the room watching her and her admirers with a mocking smile.

It is of no consequence, she reminded herself. You have come to London to make a fine marriage. Lord Woodham has not and will not offer marriage. Get on about your business and ignore him. And following her advice, she flashed a brilliant smile at Lord Ferndale.

Eleven

The following day, Lord Woodham called, offering to take Diana driving in Hyde Park. "Unless, of course, you are expecting callers?"

"I am not expecting callers today," she said in a tone which implied that tomorrow was another story. "I'll go put on my bonnet."

"It is kind of your lordship to call," said Mrs. Brown stiffly after Diana had left.

He bowed.

"I am sure your lordship has many other demands on your time. I hope you feel under no obligation to us simply because my daughter was your neighbor."

"Since the war there is little I feel obliged to do, Mrs. Brown," he said. "I enjoy your daughter's company."

Mrs. Brown's eyes narrowed suspiciously.

"I should like to go driving, too," piped Mathilde.

Mrs. Brown looked at her in exasperation. "As you were not invited, you may stay at home and bear me company."

"Why can we not go to the park, too, Mama?" begged Mathilde.

"We shall go for a drive later on today," promised Mrs. Brown, "if you don't tease me further. Now, you have said quite enough. I am sure you are boring Lord Woodham to death with your prattle."

Julian was spared from the need for any polite answer by Diana's return.

Once in his curricle and bowling down the street, he said, "I don't believe your mother cares for me."

"I cannot imagine why your lordship should think such a thing," said Diana.

"Possibly it is because every time she looks at me I feel like a rat who has been caught raiding the pantry."

Diana smiled but made no reply to this. "Your lordship honors me greatly today."

"And what thought lurks behind that innocent statement?"

"Oh, nothing. It seems rather odd that you should call, after barely saying two words to me last night."

So his ignoring her had irritated her. Julian grinned. "Last night you seemed to have more than your fair share of masculine attention. I hardly deemed mine necessary. And as to why I called today, my cousin informs me that it will do you great good to be seen with me."

"And that is the only reason you are taking me driving, because Louisa commands it?"

"Louisa, is it? Are you already such bosom beaux?"

"I like your cousin very much," said Diana softly. "She has been kind to me."

"You seem to stir that feeling in people," observed Julian.

"Your lordship is teasing me," said Diana.

"Not in the least. There is something about you, my dear Mrs. Hunt, that makes one want to help you. What stirs the gentlemen, I can well imagine. What drives my cousin to champion you I have no idea," he finished honestly.

This made her bristle. "It cannot be that she values my friendship?"

"She was your champion long before you were friends," said Julian, unrepentant. He shook his head. "Strange. I cannot fathom her motives."

* * *

Diana suddenly found herself wondering about Lady Dalton's motives also. Her ladyship was at home to visitors the following day, and Diana decided to pay her a call.

She was ushered into her friend's drawing room to find her ladyship already had two other visitors. Diana had hardly been introduced when one woman, a beauty showing the first signs of aging, announced stiffly that she really must be going and took her leave.

"How very odd," said Lady Dalton after the woman had left. "It is not like Lady St. Clair to run off so quickly."

Diana tried to will away the blush she felt on her cheeks, but she knew it still sat betrayingly there when Lady Dalton looked her way.

The other woman, a young matron, shrugged her shoulders. "Ah, well. Now she is gone we may talk about her."

Lady Dalton smiled. "There is little enough to say about Lady St. Clair, I'm afraid. She is, truly, the most boring woman in London. Let's talk instead about your upcoming ball."

Lady Bonneyfield smiled and obliged. "We shall have a running supper, and I have hired the same musicians who played for the countess Lieven's ball last year."

"It sounds perfectly wonderful," sighed Diana. "I haven't been to a ball since my husband died."

"Well, then, you shall come to mine!" declared the other woman.

"Oh, but I couldn't," protested Diana, suddenly feeling self-conscious.

"Nonsense," said the other woman. "I insist. I want my ball to be a terrible crush, the most well attended affair this season. So you see, you would be doing me a favor by coming."

"You must," agreed Lady Dalton, "for when it comes to giving balls no one can rival Lady Bonneyfield."

"I should very much like to," said Diana shyly.

"Then it is settled. I shall have my footman bring you an invitation first thing tomorrow."

Lady Bonneyfield stayed a little longer, then she, too, left.

"Now," said Lady Dalton, "before anyone else arrives you must tell me what on earth you have done to Lady St. Clair."

"I have done nothing other than to be so foolish as to call on her without a card," said Diana, and spilled the whole, embarrassing story.

Lady Dalton shook her head. "She is a stickler, and I must admit, it was bad ton."

"There is no nobility among our friends in Tetbury, and we all made free to call on each other there without leaving cards."

"This is not Tetbury," said Lady Dalton. "But never mind. Perhaps after Lady Bonneyfield's ball it will be Lady St. Clair who will come calling on you, for I assure you she likes to be forward with whatever is *a la mode* in London. And after the ball everyone who is anyone will be calling on you."

"You are too kind," murmured Diana. "Do you know? I have given much thought to the matter lately, and I cannot imagine why you should be so kind to me."

Lady Dalton sat back and regarded her. "That is a difficult question to answer, for there have been many reasons. I first helped you because I was bored, and intrigued with the idea of presenting someone new to the ton. Julian's interest in you also made me wish to help you, for I dearly want to see him happy. Of course, he thinks himself happy now. But men really know so little of what is good for them, don't they? And now I help you simply because I have come to value your friendship."

Diana felt tears springing to her eyes. This had to be the kindest thing anyone had ever said to her. The only response she was able to come up with was a simple, "Thank you." It was truly amazing how her luck had changed.

Lord Woodham called the following week, and brought sugarplums.

"I like sugarplums a great deal," said Mathilde.

"I thought, perhaps, you might," he said.

Mathilde turned to Diana. "If you marry Lord Woodham we can have sugarplums as often as we wish."

Diana blushed.

Her mama, too, was looking extremely red-faced. "Come, Mathilde," she said. "I think, perhaps this would be a good time for you to work your needlepoint. It is in the sitting room."

"But I want to stay and talk with Lord Woodham."

"Mathilde."

The tone in her mother's voice brooked no argument. "Yes, Mama," she said, and began to dawdle her way across the room. "It's not fair," she muttered as she went. "Diana gets all the suitors. And she is to go to the ball. When may I go to balls?"

"Soon," said her mother, taking her arm and shepherding her out the door. "Now, come along. I shall get you started."

Lord Woodham grinned at Diana and came to join her on the sofa. "So you are to go to a ball?"

She nodded. "I have been invited to Lady Bonneyfield's ball."

"Lady Bonneyfield, eh?"

"I met her at your cousin's."

"You are becoming the rage of London."

"Thanks to your lordship."

"I have done nothing," he reminded her.

"If you hadn't taken me to the opera I'd never have met your cousin."

"And I'd have had you to myself. What a fool I was to do such a thing. Will you save me a dance?"

"Will you be at the ball, then?"

"Watching for you," he said, and raised her hand to his lips. Diana smiled at him and he moved closer to her. The sound of a throat being cleared made him turn, and at the sight of Mrs. Brown standing in the doorway, the picture of disapproval, he moved away, and straightened his cravat. "Well," he said. "I suppose I should be leaving. I look forward to seeing you at the ball, Mrs. Hunt." He rose. She gave him her hand and he bowed over it.

He bowed over Mrs. Brown's hand as well, but the stern look on her face refused to soften. "I don't trust that one," she said after he'd gone. "His intentions aren't honorable. You'd do well not to encourage him."

Of course, her mother was right, but Diana had dreamed of the Earl of Woodham for so long it seemed impossible to stop now. She would make her practical plans, but she would still nurse the secret hope that her knight in shining armor would, in the end, rescue her from marriage to a lesser man.

Two weeks later, at Lady Bonneyfield's ball, Sir Harold led Diana out for the first dance. Lord Ferndale fetched her lobster patties and tiny cakes from the supper table and asked to take her driving the following week. Lord Woodham was nowhere in sight, so she danced with Lord Ferndale.

They had finished their dance and stood chatting at the edge of the dance floor when Woodham appeared at her side. "Mrs. Hunt, I hope you have the next dance free."

"I do," she said. But before walking off on the earl's arm, she made sure to smile at Lord Ferndale as if she hated to leave his company.

Lord Ferndale looked coldly on the younger man, then bowed to Diana.

The musicians started a waltz and the couples began to glide and twirl like so many music box dancers brought to life. The earl said nothing until they had circled the floor. "It would appear that the hunt goes well for you in London," he observed at last.

"I am afraid I don't understand your lordship," she replied, the pink in her cheeks contradicting her.

He grinned. "You might be able to bring Ferndale up to scratch. I suppose you have mentioned the fact that your first husband was very rich."

"I had rather not talk of my first husband," said Diana primly.

"An excellent plan," he agreed, and waltzed them out of the twirling crowd. French doors stood before them, and he opened them and motioned her out onto the balcony. "You look warm, Mrs. Hunt. Would you care for a breath of fresh air?" Diana hesitated. "Never fear," he said. "You are a married woman. Your reputation doesn't wound so easily as that of a green girl."

The air outside wasn't fresh. It smelled of thousands of coal fires, and it nipped Diana's flesh with cold fingers and made her shiver.

The earl came to stand behind her. "You are cold," he said, putting his hands on her shoulders. Without another word, he turned her to face him, then circled his arms around her and pulled her close. Now every part of her trembled and she knew it had nothing to do with the cold. His lips touched hers and million sparks ignited in her body. Not content with her lips, he ran his mouth along her chin. "Diana," he breathed into her ear. "I don't know if I can bear to share you with anyone."

"Your lordship," she managed, "I. . . ."

His lips covered hers, cutting off all speech. What had she meant to say? She couldn't remember. She reached up and circled his neck with her hands and pressed closer to him.

Inside, Lady Woodham watched her stepson follow Mrs. Hunt out onto the balcony and frowned. "Something must be done about that woman."

"I suppose this is where I am obliged to say that I shall be happy to be of service," drawled Stephen.

"It is in your best interests as well as my own to prevent the creature from luring Julian into offering marriage."

"He will make her an offer, I am sure," predicted Stephen, "but not the sort which worries you."

"I am not so sure," said Lady Woodham. "I should certainly hate to suddenly find myself related to such a creature."

Stephen shrugged. "I should not mind a close association with her."

His mother scowled at him and said, "I don't wish to pry her fingers from one son only to have her sink them into another."

"Never fear, dearest, I shan't allow the Medusa to turn me to stone," said Stephen, and sauntered off in the direction of the balcony.

He lounged about nearby until a bemused looking Mrs. Hunt re-entered the room, followed by his brother, who, he noticed was wearing a very smug smile. Stephen frowned.

Diana tried to reorient herself. She was at a ball and not in some secluded spinney; she must look as if she'd just been doing nothing more than taking a breath of cool air. She pressed her lips together to recapture for her memory the feel of Lord Woodham's kiss, and smoothed her hair, unknowingly betraying herself as surely as if she'd made an announcement of her activities on the balcony.

"Mrs. Hunt, is it not?"

She turned to see the earl's stepbrother.

He bowed and said, "My brother is monopolizing you most unfairly. Perhaps you would care to take a stroll about the room?"

Diana looked to the earl, who merely nodded.

"Of course," she said, and took the proferred arm.

"Are you enjoying your stay in London, Mrs. Hunt?" asked Stephen as they walked among the guests.

"Yes, I am," she said.

"How quickly time flies. It seems only little more than a year since your husband passed away."

"It has been a great deal longer than that," said Diana quickly.

"Of course," he murmured. "And now that you are barely recovered from one heartache, here comes my wicked stepbrother to offer you yet another."

"I am afraid I don't understand you."

"Julian is a selfish man. He thinks only of himself. I am afraid pretty women are only toys to him."

"Perhaps you misjudge your brother," said Diana.

"Perhaps," agreed Stephen. "For your sake, Mrs. Hunt, I would hope so. But you must ask Julian some time about Mrs. Mellancamp."

"Mrs. Mellancamp?"

"The woman who put a period to her existence because he wouldn't marry her. And then there is that lovely lady with the discreet house in the less fashionable part of town. You must remember to ask Julian sometime who pays the rent on it."

Diana blinked. "I don't believe we should be speaking of such things."

"Of course, we shouldn't," he agreed. "But I had rather broach an indelicate matter than see an innocent woman suffer."

"That is kind of you," said Diana stiffly. "Now you have done your duty and your conscience may rest easy. If you will excuse me, I think I would like to say good evening to Lady Dalton."

"Of course," he murmured, and led her to where her friend sat.

Lady Dalton welcomed Diana to her side even as she shooed her step-cousin away. "What odious things has Stephen the Martyr been saying to you?" she demanded. "I saw your face fall clear from across the room."

"Stephen the Martyr?"

Lady Dalton shrugged. "It is Julian's pet name for him. Now out with it, what did he say?"

"He warned me away from Lord Woodham."

Lady Dalton frowned. "You must pay him no mind. He's just a jealous boy. His mother raised him to be an earl, and alas, he's only a second son."

"Did you know a Mrs. Mellancamp?"

Lady Dalton rolled her eyes. "Oh, leave it to Stephen to

drag that skeleton from the closet. That was several years ago, when the old earl was alive, and before Julian got it in his head to be a soldier. He had a mad affair with the woman, was sure he was in love with her. His father threatened to disinherit him if he married her. The silly creature had the consideration to get herself run down by a carriage while Julian and his papa were still arguing over her."

"His stepbrother told me she killed herself."

"That would be just like the wicked boy to say such a thing."

Diana wanted to ask whether Lady Dalton knew if the earl kept a mistress, but held her tongue. Sadly, he most likely did.

"You should not take Stephen's behavior to heart," continued Lady Dalton. "Both he and his mama have no desire to see Julian marry and set up his nursery. They would discourage even a duchess from having him."

Diana sat, turning all this over in her mind. Had that been the purpose of Stephen's talk, to discourage her from marrying his brother? "Your cousin has been very kind to me," she said. "Why do you think he takes such an interest?"

"Who can know for certain?" replied her ladyship. "Perhaps he thinks himself Pygmalion and you Galatea. All I can tell you, is such determined pursuit is most unusual, which leads me to think he cares for you more than he wishes to admit. Ah, here comes Jonathan. I see he has had enough of the card room, which means he will drag me away soon." She patted Diana's hand. "Don't let the wicked stepbrother ruin your evening. And tomorrow you must call on me and tell me of all the men who swooned at your feet and of all the jealous looks my cousin cast in your direction." With that she was gone, flitting off to her husband.

Diana watched her and felt suddenly envious. How she'd love to be a Lady Dalton, with a titled husband and a secure future, and with nothing to do but enjoy the trials and tribulations of others as if it were a play produced for her entertainment. For a few moments, she watched the crowd, waiting to see if anyone would come to sit with her and visit. But everyone was engaged with their own circle of friends.

Suddenly, Diana felt very alone. She took her leave of her hostess and told the footman to order her carriage brought around.

While she waited, the Earl of Ferndale came up to her. "Are you at home to callers tomorrow Mrs. Hunt?"

Diana quickly pulled a curtain across her dark thoughts. "I am promised to Lady Dalton tomorrow, but if you would care to call on me the day after I shall be home."

"I shall call then," he said, and bowed over her hand.

Diana rode home absorbed in thought. Why was Lord Woodham's stepbrother warning her away from him? There could be only one reason. He must believe the earl was interested in her to the point of offering matrimony. Why else would he tell her such tall tales? Perhaps just a little nudge was all it would take to make the earl declare himself. If he thought her about to marry again, about to accept another man . . . But, of course, he knew she meant to marry again. He wasn't able to leave off teasing her about her quest for a wealthy husband. Perhaps he still thought she'd have him as a lover after she married. She frowned. He must be made to understand that she would have him only as a husband.

Remembering their encounter on the balcony, she frowned. That had hardly been the way to convince him that she was beyond dalliance. She pressed her lips firmly together. There would be no more kisses for the Earl of Woodham. Not until he was her husband.

The following day, Diana called on Lady Dalton. It seemed half of London had also been invited to call on her ladyship, for the drawing room was full. Diana saw that Lord Woodham had been commanded to attend as well.

"This is a ridiculous crush," he greeted her.

"It is rather a crowd," she agreed.

"I am surprised to see you here, Mrs. Hunt. I had thought

one of your new admirers would be worshipping at your feet today."

"Services are tomorrow," she replied.

He grinned. "I shall bear that in mind."

Diana was in the drawing room with her mother when Lord Ferndale was announced.

"How good to see you again, Mrs. Brown," he said politely, and bowed over her mother's hand.

Mrs. Brown simpered and blushed like a schoolgirl, and Diana found her own cheeks blushing as well. She felt a sudden wild desire to explain to Lord Ferndale that her mother rarely acted so silly, that really, she was a woman of great good sense.

Lord Ferndale didn't seem bothered by her mother's silliness. Instead, he settled on a seat and inquired how Diana had enjoyed the ball.

Diana didn't get a chance to reply, for at that moment Mathilde made her entrance.

"Mathilde, I thought you were in the kitchen," said Mrs. Brown in tones which plainly proclaimed her wish that her daughter was still there.

"We have a visitor?" asked Mathilde, venturing further into the room. Diana saw she had a dusting of flour on her chin. Matilde, however, seemed unaware of it. She curtseyed to the earl, then found herself a seat. "Have you, perhaps, brought sugar plums?" she asked.

"No, I'm afraid I haven't," he said.

"That is a pity. I am very fond of sugar plums." She studied Ferndale a moment. "You are not so very wrinkled. Why is your hair gray?"

The polite smile on Lord Ferndale's face frosted over.

"Mathilde!" gasped her mother. "Now, that is enough. You will come with me this moment." She grabbed her daughter by the arm and yanked her from the chair.

"But Mama," cried Mathilde, as her mother forced her from

the room. "I only wanted to know why the gentleman's hair was so gray."

Diana felt sick inside. Never had Mathilde embarrassed her so thoroughly before. Of course, in Tetbury, everyone knew Mathilde. Everyone understood. But here, to talk so to a stranger? What could she say? "I do beg your lordship's pardon."

"It is perfectly all right," he said stiffly, and she knew it wasn't at all right.

"I am afraid my sister is rather simple."

Now a wary look crept into Lord Ferndale's eyes. "Simple?"

Diana nodded and rushed on, sure that a torrent of words would explain everything. "She is quite sweet, and I can assure you she meant no harm."

"She has always been this way?"

Of course. What man would wish to marry into a family that suffered a simple-minded child. Perhaps he would think it catching. For a wild moment, she thought of lying, telling Lord Ferndale her sister had been perfectly normal until she was kicked in the head by a horse.

"I am afraid I must be going," said the earl.

"Surely there is no need to rush off," pleaded Diana.

"I had forgotten. I have an important appointment this afternoon. I hope you will forgive me and allow me to call another time?" The earl was already on his feet and edging for the door.

Diana swallowed back the tears. "Of course," she managed.

"I don't know how I could have come to forget it." He was babbling now, backing away as if she were a leper.

"Good day, your lordship," she said, and turned her back on him.

Twelve

Diana was able to control herself only until she heard the door shut behind Lord Ferndale, then she collapsed on the sofa in tears. All her fine connections would do her no good at all at this rate. By now David Barnes had a good-sized collection of bills, and he could descend on her at any moment, demanding an explanation. What would she tell him if she couldn't produce a rich future husband? How could she repay him? How would they live?

A gentle tapping on the door and the muffled sound of Addison's voice made her sit and swipe away the tears. "Yes?" she called.

The door opened. "The Earl of Woodham is here to see you, madam. Are you feeling up to visitors, or shall I ask him to come back?"

She should not receive him. It would make him all the more anxious to see her. Somehow, however, Diana found herself not feeling up to romantic strategy. "I shall see him," she said, and pulled out her handkerchief to quickly blow her nose.

She was just stuffing it in the pocket of her morning gown when the earl entered the room. He came and stood in front of her and put a hand under her chin, lifting her face for his inspection. She pressed her lips together and tried to regard him calmly.

"You have been crying."

"Ladies do that," she said, and turned her face away.

He sat down next to her. "Would you care to tell me what happened?"

She shook her head and stared at her lap. Fresh tears gathered in her eyes.

"Lord Ferndale did not offer marriage?" persisted the earl.

"I am afraid that after meeting my sister. . . ." Diana's throat closed and made further speech impossible. She pressed a hand to her eyes.

The earl took her hand and sat with her in silence for several moments while she tried to compose herself. "You didn't really care for the fellow, anyway, did you?" he said at last.

"He would have made a much better husband than Mr. Hunt."

"There are few men who would not." Woodham patted her hand. "Don't despair. You still have one suitor left. And I suspect old Blaine will make a much more tolerant husband than Ferndale."

"What do you mean?"

He raised her hand to his lips. "Why, only that he would be much more understanding if you were to have . . . friends."

Understanding dawned. "Such as yourself?"

The earl smiled. "Such as myself."

Diana snatched her hand away. "From what I hear you already have a friend," she retorted scornfully.

"Where did you hear such a thing?" he demanded.

"From your brother."

Woodham rolled his eyes. "Stephen the Martyr."

"It is true, is it not?"

"My dear Mrs. Hunt, we should not even be speaking of such things."

"But I wish to speak of them. That woman. . . ."

"It means nothing," insisted the earl.

"To you, perhaps," said Diana. "To a woman the attentions of the man she loves always mean something."

"Love?" he scoffed. "If you are speaking of the woman my stepbrother mentioned, I can assure you, love does not even enter into our arrangement. The lady seeks fine jewels, a park phaeton, servants. She has no particular love for me, only my pocketbook. It is much like the arrangement you had with Hunt."

Diana gasped and drew away from Woodham as if he'd slapped her. "How dare you! How dare you compare me to some cheap woman who . . ." She found herself unable to complete her sentence. Instead, she rose from the sofa and commanded, "Leave my house."

The earl didn't obey. His face showed exasperation. "Diana."

She turned her back to him.

She heard him rise, but his steps didn't move away. Instead, he came to stand behind her. He placed his hands on her arms and she shook them off, turning on him.

"I am no cheap adventuress," she said. "I came to Mr. Hunt to be a wife. I asked no fine jewels in exchange, no park phaeton. Only the keep of myself and my family. And I would have earned that keep. All I seek now is someone to be kind to me."

"Diana," he began, his voice pleading, but she held up a silencing hand.

"Your kindness, my lord, comes with a high price. I shan't pay it. In fact, I am weary of your constant assault upon my principles. I don't wish to see you any more." She turned again.

This time he left.

She stood, a statue of flesh and blood, and listened to the sound of his retreating footsteps, of the opening and closing of the door. There went her happiness. She remained standing, looking at the flames in the hearth through a curtain of tears.

The door opened again. "Diana? Where is Lord Ferndale? What has happened?"

Diana covered her face and wept.

* * *

Sir Harold was a specimen far inferior to both the earls, but now he was Diana's only hope, and she encouraged him with a falseness that sickened her. Every time she flattered him he seemed to puff up like a giant bullfrog, and she found herself wondering if he was any better than Mr. Hunt. No, she corrected herself, looking at the hothouse orchids he had sent. There was one big difference between Sir Harold and Mr. Hunt. Sir Harold was not clutch-fisted.

So he would do. She would give him her body and her undivided attention when he wished it, and she would give him her smiles. The only thing he'd lack was her heart. And what fashionable marriage ever worried about the lack of such a small thing as a heart?

She was driving beside Sir Harold in Hyde Park when she saw the Earl of Woodham again. He tipped his hat to her from across a crowd of carriages and she gave him the smallest nod that manners would permit.

Sir Harold followed her gaze. "I thought you and young Woodham were great friends."

"We are acquaintances. That is all," said Diana.

"Well," said Sir Harold, and smiled broadly. "Well."

When they arrived back at the house, she invited him in for a glass of sherry and he accepted. Mathilde was in the drawing room, and Diana braced herself for another horrible scene such as the one she'd experienced with Lord Ferndale.

Mathilde cocked her head to one side and studied him. "Are you one of Diana's suitors?"

Sir Harold chuckled and winked at a blushing Diana. "I am. And you are?"

"This is my sister, Miss Brown."

Mathilde held out her hand in the manner of a grand lady and Sir Harold took it and bowed over it. "I am very fond of sweets," she informed him.

"I shall have to remember that," he said soberly.

At that moment Mrs. Brown rushed into the drawing room.

"Mathilde," she scolded. "I thought I instructed you to do your needlepoint in the sitting room."

"I heard the carriage," said Mathilde, "and wanted to meet Diana's suitor."

"Well, now you have met him," said Mrs. Brown sharply. "Come along."

"Let your charming daughter stay," said Sir Harold heartily. "And yourself as well. Then I will have three lovely ladies to bear me company."

Mrs. Brown looked nervously at Diana and took a seat.

"So you are fond of sweets, Miss Brown?"

Mathilde nodded eagerly.

"Well, then, we shall have to take you to Gunther's sometime. Should you like that?"

"I should if I knew what it was," replied Mathilde.

"It is a confection shop with the most delicious treats you could ever imagine. You may get all manner of sugarplums there, and ices as well."

"I should like to go," said Mathilde. "When will you take us?"

"Mathilde!" cried both her mother and sister.

Sir Harold seemed not at all bothered. "Don't scold the child on my account," he said.

Both women looked at him as if he were mad.

He shrugged. "Your little sister, Mrs. Hunt, reminds me very much of a cousin of mine. Sweet little thing. Not much in the brain box, but a kinder heart you couldn't find in all of England."

Diana looked at Sir Harold in amazement. Perhaps, she could, with time, give this man her heart.

Addison came, carrying sherry and ratafia and small crystal goblets on a silver tray. Sir Harold drank some sherry and pronounced it first rate.

It should be, thought Diana. It cost my nephew a pretty sum.

After Sir Harold left, her mother turned to her with tears in her eyes. "My child, here is a man to whom you can truly entrust your heart."

Diana had to agree. He wasn't the dashing Lord Woodham. No, indeed. He was a man of kindness, who would respect a woman's principles. Sir Harold was a treasure, and she was well rid of the Earl of Woodham. She was. Truly.

After that day, Sir Harold was a regular visitor. He took Diana and her mother and sister to the opera, and making good on his promise, took them all to Gunther's as well, where they feasted on ices and biscuits. And at Almacks, he hardly left Diana's side.

"Should you care to go driving with me tomorrow, Mrs. Hunt?" he asked her, as he strolled with her to her carriage.

"I should like it above all things," she replied.

"Well," he said heartily. "Until tomorrow, then."

"Until tomorrow," she repeated, and allowed him to hand her up into the carriage.

She amused herself on the drive home by wondering how long it would be before Sir Harold offered for her. Surely now it was only a matter of days.

The following day as they tooled down the streets of Mayfair, he regaled her with descriptions of both his townhouse and his country estate. There could be only one reason a man would tick off his worldly possessions to a lady. As soon as they returned she would invite him to step in and drink some sherry. And she would make sure they had the drawing room to themselves.

But when they got home, an unfamiliar carriage was parked in front of the house. Foreboding made the skin at the back of Diana's neck prickle, and it was all she could do to walk up the front walk and enter the house.

"I am afraid you have company, madam," said Addison, as soon as she and Sir Harold had come through the door.

Diana didn't need to ask who it was. She knew. She knew even before he came out of the drawing room, her protesting mother trailing him, and moved to stand before her in the hallway.

"I will see you alone," said David Barnes.

"Here now, sir. I don't care for the tone of your voice," said Sir Harold. "I'll ask you to apologize to the lady."

"Lady!" echoed David. "Oh, that is rich. This woman is no lady, I assure you. She is merely a cheap fortune hunter, and it would appear you are her next victim."

"Mr. Barnes!" cried Mrs. Brown.

Sir Harold looked at Diana questioningly. "What is this about?"

"She married my uncle less than two years ago," answered David. "And now here she is in London, hunting for her next victim. And she does her hunting at my expense," he finished.

"You must not believe this man," said Diana.

"By all means, don't take my word," said David. "Feel free to talk to my man of business, who can show you the pile of bills sitting on my desk—bills for this woman's London adventure."

Diana looked anxiously at Sir Harold. His face was pale, and he appeared about to cry. So did her mother.

"You didn't think she was a wealthy widow, did you?" David continued. Sir Harold said nothing and David nodded. "Well, dear aunt," he said to Diana. "I see you have deceived this good man quite as thoroughly as you did my poor uncle. Does he know of your close attachment to the Earl of Woodham as well?"

"Woodham!" exclaimed Sir Harold. He looked at Diana, all kindness erased from his face.

David smirked. "Ah, so you are acquainted with the Earl of Woodham. So is my aunt. Intimately."

Diana's head began to tingle, the hallway and all the people started to circle her, then came the darkness and the stars, and she was conscious of her body being carried, and of voices. But she wasn't in her body. She was somewhere above it, somewhere in the darkness with the tiny bells.

"See what you have done, you wicked man," she heard her mother cry.

Then she heard Mathilde. "What is wrong with Diana?"

"Never mind," said her mother. "Go to your room at once."

"I want to help Diana," cried Mathilde.

You cannot find me, thought Diana. I am caught here somewhere in the darkness.

"Attend to your daughter," said David from somewhere far off. "I shall take care of Diana. We have business to discuss."

Now Sir Harold's voice seemed miles and miles away. "I shall leave you to settle your family matters, Mrs. Brown."

"Don't leave," she tried to cry. But nothing came out.

Then the darkness began to curl away like so much smoke and she was aware of something slapping against her cheek. It hit again, and she realized it hurt. She was being slapped. Her eyelids lifted and she saw David's face hovering above her. She searched the room. No one else was there. She struggled to sit up.

"Thank you for rejoining us," said David politely. His lips smiled, but his face was granite. "Your little trick didn't work, for your friend has fled."

"You must let me explain," she said weakly. "A glass of water, please."

He looked around. "I see sherry. After your shock I am sure you could use it." He went to the small table where the tray with the decanter and delicate goblet sat. "You are greatly in my debt, you realize," he said over his shoulder.

Diana swallowed. "I was going to pay you back. Every farthing."

David didn't appear to be listening. He stood before her, examining the cut glass goblet. "I remember seeing the bill for these. Two dozen, I believe it was." His eyes narrowed. "When, exactly, were you going to pay me?"

Diana gulped the sherry, then coughed. "If you hadn't created that scene in the hallway, I'd have had the means to repay you before the month was out."

He snatched the glass away. "Do you have any idea the amount of money you have spent? Any idea at all?" He ended on a roar and threw the goblet across the room, shattering it against the wall."

Diana jumped and stared at the pile of glittering shards on the Aubusson carpet.

"I should do that with you," said David, his voice a growl. "When I think how you've ruined me, what a fool you made of me. . . ."

She only had time to cry, "David, no!" before he was kneeling on the sofa, his hands pressing on her neck, making her terrified cry only a gurgle.

He regarded her neck as if it were an interesting object of art. He loosened his hold a little.

"Please," she panted.

"How she pleads, how she begs. Now that she has nearly ruined my life she begs for hers, for her worthless life." He let the fingers of one hand slide caressingly down her neck and along the edge of her bodice, sending yet a new fear racing through her veins and making her shiver. "You will pay me back, Diana. Starting now. This very moment. You will wrap those lovely arms around me, and you will whisper dearest and darling in my ears the way you did in Woodham's. Then tomorrow we will go and make arrangements to see all the pretties you have bought sold at auction. And then, my dear, you will return with me to Spinney Hall. You may be my . . . housekeeper." One side of his mouth stretched into a teasing smile. "And don't worry. I won't forget your dear mama. She may be my cook. And your sister, would she like to be my housekeeper also?"

Anger mixed with terror and exploded in words. "You worthless leech! If you so much as touch my sister I shall tell the world that your mother is a murderess!"

The words were barely out of her mouth when David slapped her hard, bringing fresh ringing to her ears and the taste of blood to her mouth. "Don't you ever say such a thing again, or I'll see to it the magistrate hears about the kippers his bride served him on his wedding day, the bride who thought to become a rich widow, the bride who went to London on her nephew's funds!" He fell on her, his mouth biting into hers as if he would suck the life from her.

She heard knocking on the drawing room door and her mother's voice calling her name. The drawing room door. He had locked it. She struggled to free herself. He let up the pressure of his lips for a moment and she pulled her face away to let out a shriek.

"Tell your mother to leave us in peace," commanded David.

"Mother!" cried Diana, trying to rise.

He pushed her back down and called over his shoulder, "Leave us alone!"

Diana heard the sound of a key in the door, then a deep voice saying, "I think not."

Thirteen

"You have an odd way of paying a social call, sir," observed Woodham, strolling into the room.

David Barnes released his hold on Diana and turned to face the earl. "This woman deserves no social call from anyone. She is a common adventuress, and she has done her adventuring at my expense. I have a mountain of bills on my desk courtesy of her, and how I shall pay them all God alone knows."

"You may send them to me," said the earl curtly. "And now you may leave before I break your neck."

David looked down at Diana, quietly crying on the sofa, and gave a contemptuous snort. "She is more trouble than she's worth. You are welcome to her." Without another word, he strode from the room and brushed past the earl.

Woodham turned to Mrs. Brown, who was standing in the doorway, wringing her hands. "Would you allow me a few moments alone with your daughter?"

She bit her lip and looked at Diana, then nodded and left the room, closing the door behind her.

Woodham went to the sofa and took Diana in his arms, and she gave herself up to gusty sobs. His chest was hard against her cheek, a strong rock, and she could hear the rumbling of his voice as he said "It's all right now. You are safe." He caressed her hair with his hand and kissed the top of her head and she snuggled closer against him.

They sat that way for some time. Diana was the first to

speak. "I thought he was going to kill me." The words came out in a croak.

The earl ran his hand along her neck, where David's hands had pressed so hard. "I really should have broken his neck."

"My throat hurts," she whimpered.

"Then don't speak," he murmured, and kissed her again.

Disregarding his advice, she lifted her face to his. "Why had you come?"

"Your butler sent the footman for me when Barnes first showed up. He was afraid there would be trouble."

Fresh tears welled up in Diana's eyes, produced by a mixture of gratitude to her loyal butler and regret that only chivalry had brought the earl to her door.

"Now, why the tears?" he whispered.

"I thought you had come to see me," she choked.

"If I remember correctly, you told me you never wished to see me again."

She hid her face in his shoulder and said nothing.

"You are sadly in need of protection, my dear."

She stiffened in his arms. "So it comes again to that."

"You have run out of suitors," said the earl gently. "I saw Blaine leaving here as if the demons of hell pursued him."

Diana pulled out of his embrace and gave a jagged sigh. "I may be out of suitors here in London, but I am not out of choices. I shall return to Tetbury."

"And marry a shopkeeper? How delightful that will be for you," murmured Woodham.

"It may not prove delightful, but it will at least be honorable," retorted Diana. "I am not sure I can ever fully repay you. I shall, naturally, try."

"Little fool," said the earl, and drew her back to him. He touched her ravaged cheek with his hand. "And speaking of fools, you realize that is exactly what I shall look when word gets out," he said. "Woodham caught by a pretty face."

"I don't understand," said Diana.

"Nor do I. But I shall marry you, nonetheless."

"Marry me?" she parroted.

"Yes, marry you. How else am I to have you when you refuse to be sensible?" He caught her to him and kissed her ravenously.

She was painfully aware of the soreness in her mouth and jaw and exquisitely aware of his hard body pressing against hers. She closed her eyes and savored the delirious torture of his mouth moving down her neck, of his hot breath on her collarbone, of his hands possessively claiming her body for his own. "Are you sure?" she whispered.

"God help me," he moaned. "I am sure of only one thing. I must have you."

A gentle tapping on the drawing room door brought the earl and Diana back up to sitting position. He adjusted his coat and cravat while she straightened her skirt and called, "Come in."

The door opened and her mother hesitantly entered.

The earl stood and Diana rose also. He took her hand and she suddenly remembered her papa holding her hand as a child and walking with her down the flagway. The warm, safe memory enveloped her like a blanket and she smiled.

Mrs. Brown smiled, too.

"I wish to marry your daughter," said the earl.

Diana half expected her mother to crow with triumph and rush to her and hug her, but Mrs. Brown received the news with all the stately calm of a duchess. "You have my blessing," she said with a regal nod.

Diana looked to the earl and he turned his head and smiled at her and squeezed her hand.

Mrs. Brown rang the bellpull. "I'll have Addison bring wine and biscuits and we shall celebrate." The three seated themselves and Mrs. Brown, all business, said, "Your lordship realizes that my daughter has no income, can bring nothing to this marriage?"

The earl nodded. "I am sure you are concerned about your other daughter as well. I have a cottage at Ottershaw Park which will serve admirably as a home for the two of you."

Mrs. Brown blinked, then shook her head and burst into tears, and Diana ran to hug her. "Your lordship is too kind," Mrs. Brown said, fishing for a handkerchief.

Addison arrived, and Diana gave orders for refreshments. "And Addison?"

He turned at the door. "Yes, madam?"

"Thank you."

"It is my pleasure to serve you, madam," he replied.

She smiled at him. "I believe it is."

"Naturally, you will wish to take him with you," the earl said to Mrs. Brown. "You may also feel free to take with you or hire any other servants you deem necessary. The cottage is not large, so I doubt you'll need more than a cook and a maid."

"I must thank your lordship for his generous offer," said Mrs. Brown, "but I think, perhaps, it would be best if Mathilde and I returned to Tetbury."

"Mama," protested Diana.

Mrs. Brown shook her head. "It is where we are most comfortable, child."

The earl nodded. "I understand. I will be only too happy to help you with the purchase of a new house there."

Mrs. Brown beamed on him and, looking at the two of them, Diana wanted to laugh out loud. How the earl had suddenly risen in her mother's estimation!

"I don't wish to wait," he said, giving Diana a look that melted her bones. "I'll get a special license. Can you be ready in three days?"

"I could be ready in three hours," she said. Three days and Lord Woodham would be hers!

He stayed half an hour longer before saying, "I suppose I should leave and allow you to do whatever it is females do to get ready to marry."

Mrs. Brown bid the earl farewell, then slipped away and left the betrothed couple alone.

The earl touched Diana's cheek. "Tell your maid to fetch a slab of beefsteak and lay it on that bruise," he said.

She touched his hand with hers and smiled up at him. Was this a dream? Was she really going to be marrying this man? He kissed her gently, then put an arm around her and they walked from the room together. At the front door, he kissed her once more, heedless of Addison, standing patiently by with his hat and gloves and sword stick. "Goodbye, my huntress," he whispered. "I'll come to fetch you tomorrow and we'll visit Rundell and Bridge and buy you a necklace that isn't paste."

Diana went upstairs in a fog to change, the throbbing of her cheek only a minor irritation.

Williams, however, was shocked by the sight of it. "Oh, madam, your poor face!"

"It will be fine," said Diana. Now everything would be fine.

The Earl of Woodham was shown up to Lady Dalton's sitting room, where he found her reading Mrs. Edgeworth's *Vivian.* "I am at a most exciting part," she said, "and I hate to lay it down."

"You may find my news worth the interruption," he said, settling into a wing chair.

She tossed the book aside and looked at him expectantly.

"I am to marry Diana Hunt in three days."

She stared at him. "Gracious, Julian! You quite take my breath away. How terribly romantic! So you at last realize your need to possess the lady's heart."

"I assure you," said Julian, "it is not her heart which I am longing to possess. That she may keep for herself."

"I don't believe it. There are a good many pretty ladies with more to offer than Diana Hunt. And you've offered marriage to none of them."

He shrugged. "None of them interest me." He slouched

down in the chair and stretched his legs. "How the tabbies will talk over this one."

"I can think of one particular tabby who won't be amused," said Lady Dalton, and Julian's smile turned down.

"It is high time my stepmother repaired to the dower house and let me lead my life in peace."

"If you think you will have peace by bringing Diana Hunt into your house you are very much mistaken," cautioned her ladyship.

Julian's scowl deepened. "I thought you, of all people, would wish me joy, Louisa."

"I do, dearest," she replied earnestly. "Indeed, I do. God knows you've had little enough of it since your father married that woman."

Julian stared into the fire. "Marriage is a curse," he muttered.

"To the right woman, it can be a blessing," said her ladyship softly. "I think, in the long run, you'll have no regrets."

No regrets, he thought as he drove away. Was Louisa right? He had to admit, for a man who was marrying beneath him socially, and a poor woman at that, he was very happy. Perhaps he had run mad. Madmen were often irrationally happy, weren't they?

Well, no matter. It was a fine madness and he was in love with all the world. But not with Diana Hunt, he reminded himself. A man didn't marry for love. He married so he'd have someone to see his house ran smoothly and to produce fine heirs.

Diana would do both admirably. She was determined and beautiful and clever. Very clever. The bloodlines were there. She would give him a fine heir. And how he would enjoy getting it!

The following day he took her to Rundell and Bridge and bought her an intricate necklace of diamonds and pearls, and matching earrings. She sparkled brighter than the diamonds, flashing him looks which promised of rich rewards for his generosity. She was like a spun sugar treat, waiting to be devoured and the thought of doing just that literally made his mouth water.

Stephen idly sifted through the day's mail, which had been deposited on the silver salver on the downstairs hall table. A large packet directed to his stepbrother caught his eye. David Barnes. Wasn't that the man who'd inherited old Hunt's place? Stephen turned it over curiously. "Why would Barnes be writing to Julian?" he mused.

Hearing the rattle of carriage wheels outside, he slipped the packet into his coat pocket.

Julian returned to his townhouse in high spirits.

"You look like the cat who got into the cream," observed his stepbrother, stepping away from the hall table where the salver with the day's mail reposed.

Julian said nothing to this. "Checking to see how many ton hostesses are desperate for an available male for their dinner parties?"

Stephen gave him an unamused smile. "Forgive me if I don't stay to enjoy any more of your banter."

"Going out?"

"Just thought I'd pop 'round to White's."

Julian nodded. "Then you won't be here when I make my announcement to Mother."

"And what announcement is that?"

"Why, that I intend to marry."

Stephen's eyes widened. "No. You haven't seemed particularly partial to anyone, except of course, Hunt's little strumpet."

Julian bared his teeth in a menacing smile. "This once I'll forgive you, but if you ever refer to my future wife in those terms again, I'll have to put a bullet through you."

Stephen let out a low whistle. "You have done some foolish things, dear brother, but this one tops them all."

"Did you think I would never marry, Stephen?" asked Julian softly.

"Oh, I knew you would," replied Stephen genially. "It is mother who hoped you'd remain a bachelor all your days."

Julian nodded.

"She'll take this hard," said Stephen.

"And you? How will you take it?"

"As a great jest. Now, don't scowl at me, brother. You must admit, it is rather funny, the Earl of Woodham marrying a complete nobody."

"She is not without breeding," said Julian stiffly.

"No, only without position or wealth." He shook his head. "If I were you, I shouldn't tell mother until it is a *fait accompli.*"

He sauntered out the door and Julian watched him go with a scowl. His brother had the gift for souring things. Well, it was his own fault, Julian concluded. He'd held out the sweet cream of happy experience for Stephen to squeeze lemons on. Stephen was right about one thing, though. Julian would be a fool to tell their mother. If he thought Stephen had put in him in a foul mood, her reaction to his news would fall on his happiness like locusts and devour it.

Julian dined at his club that night to avoid seeing his stepmother, and the day of his nuptials, he left the house before she came down from her bedroom. He bought an armful of tulips to take to Diana, and sugarplums for Matilde. For Mrs. Brown, he had in his coat pocket a small box from Rundell and Bridge containing a locket with an inscription which read, "From your son." He knew she would take great joy in showing it to all her old friends in Tetbury, and bragging on her daughter's great success.

She'd had no fondness for him at first. He knew that. And

he also knew that it was nothing personal. It was the threat he'd presented she disliked, not his person. Ever since he'd saved Diana from that snake Barnes, she'd looked on him as if he were Saint George, slayer of dragons. He supposed he had slain all the family's dragons for them. He smiled. And tonight he'd have his reward.

Addison let him in, the smile on his face making him look less cadaverous than usual. "Good day, your lordship," he said, taking the flowers and sweets and assisting the earl out of his driving coat.

"Good day, Addison. Where are my ladies?" asked Julian, feeling like king of the world.

"They are all awaiting you in the drawing room, your lordship."

"Good," said Julian, taking back his presents. "I hope Mrs. Hunt is ready."

"She is, your lordship."

At that moment the door opened and Diana herself stood framed in it. She wore a cream colored gown with some sort of flower embroidered on its hem and her hair was pulled to the side and spun into curls. The flush of excitement stained her cheeks pink and her eyes sparkled like blue gems. She looked at him as if he were a god.

"Julian."

She made his name sound like a caress, and as he put the tulips in her arms he wished he'd brought her something more. Mere flowers weren't a worthy enough offering for such a perfect creature.

"Oh, Julian. They are lovely."

"Like you."

She blushed and smiled up at him, then gave the flowers to Addison and led Julian into the room.

"I wish someone would bring me flowers," said Matilde wistfully.

"I thought you had rather have these," said Julian, producing the box of sugarplums.

Matilde's eyes grew round. "Oh, yes. Thank you."

Mrs. Brown nodded approvingly and said, "Your lordship is too kind."

"Not nearly kind enough," he replied, and fished the beribboned little box from his pocket. "When Diana and I were at Rundell and Bridge she helped me select this for you. I hope you will like it."

"Your lordship." Mrs. Brown sounded almost shocked. She opened the box and took out the locket. The earl watched her press her lips together and knew she was trying not to cry. She looked at him, damp eyed. "Thank you. You are truly a most generous man."

What an odd and wonderful feeling to see women touched, not so much by his gifts as by the fact that he'd thought enough to give them. He remembered the avaricious look in his mistress's eyes when he'd given her his farewell present. Her gaze had never left the jewel box, never looked into his face. He remembered her gleeful triumph as she pulled the necklace from the box, and how she held it up for inspection, assessing its worth.

"Julian?"

He recalled his wandering thoughts. "Yes?"

Diana was smiling at him.

That smile. He couldn't see enough of it. "Are you ready, then?" She nodded and he gave her his arm. "Then let's be off to St. James. The Reverend is waiting."

Diana listened in a daze as the Earl Woodham gave her his vows.

"With my body, I thee worship. With all my worldly goods, I thee endow."

With my body, I thee worship. She shivered in nervous anticipation.

Lady Woodham, she thought as Julian, at last, led her out of the church. She still could barely believe her good fortune.

In the carriage, he took her immediately into his arms and

kissed her. He pulled away and scowled at her bonnet. "That thing is a hindrance," he objected.

"Then I shall remove it," she offered.

"Allow me." He undid the ribbon and gently lifted the bonnet from her head. "Your hair is like gold," he whispered, catching a curl and brushing it against his lips. "I feel like a pirate who's found hidden treasure."

Diana found herself feeling suddenly self-conscious, and was aware of her face growing warm. She caught her lower lip between her teeth and looked at her lap.

"Come now, I cannot be embarrassing you," he teased. "Not after all I have said and done to you."

This caused Diana's face to flush hotter still. "I feel so. . . ." Her voice trailed off. She wasn't exactly sure what she felt.

"Happy?" he prompted.

"Oh, yes. Most definitely happy."

"Don't be nervous, little huntress," he said. "I shall take good care of you." He pulled her onto his lap, then said, "Now, then. Where would you like to go for our wedding trip?"

"Wedding trip? We will go on a wedding trip?"

"Is that not the customary thing to do?"

"I wouldn't know," said Diana. "Mr. Hunt certainly planned no wedding trip."

Julian shook his head. "What a jest of a groom you had, poor thing." He began to unbutton her pelisse.

"Julian," she said nervously, "what are you doing?"

"I thought, perhaps, you might be warm," he replied. "It's rather stuffy in here."

"It is," she agreed, and allowed him to set her free of the pelisse.

He shut the curtain at the carriage window, leaving them in an early twilight. Then he smiled at her and placed a kiss at the base of her neck. She closed her eyes to savor the feel of warm lips on skin. Now she could feel him tugging at the ribbons of her gown. "Julian!" she protested, sure that some way, somehow, someone must catch her in an embarrassingly immodest condition.

"Ssh," he commanded, and slid the bodice of her gown off her shoulder. He kissed the bared shoulder, then tasted the exposed skin of her upper chest. "I take my wedding vows very seriously," he said between kisses. "With my body I thee worship."

She repeated it like a litany. "With my body, I thee worship."

His mouth moved lower, shooting exquisite sensations from her chest to her toes. "Diana," he murmured.

The carriage came to a halt and Diana gave a start, then scrambled off his lap, terrified of being caught in her present unmodest state.

Her husband merely chuckled. "It would appear we are home, and will have to conclude the services later." She slid her gown back in place and he tied the ribbons for her. He was assisting her with the bonnet when the footman knocked discreetly on the door and asked if his lordship would care to have the steps let down.

"Yes," called the earl, and Diana, taking note of the proceedings, wondered if this sort of carriage seduction had been a regular occurrence in the past.

It didn't signify. She was now Lady Woodham, and from this day on, she would be the only female Lord Woodham kissed in the warm dusk world of his carriage.

He descended the steps before her, then helped her out. Lacing her hand through his arm, he led her up the front walk. "Welcome to your new home, Lady Woodham," he said, as they reached the front door.

The butler ushered them in and Julian asked where his stepmother was.

"I believe her ladyship is in the drawing room," he replied.

"Excellent," said Julian. "Shall we?"

"Perhaps you should go in and speak to her," said Diana nervously.

"We'll do it together," he replied. He patted her hand. "Don't be afraid. She can't eat you."

"She can try," replied Diana.

He shook his head at her and led her into the drawing room, where she saw Lady Woodham was not alone. Julian's stepbrother sat with her.

Her ladyship raised a cold, questioning eyebrow at Diana, then turned to her stepson. "Julian?"

"Mother, I should like to present you to my wife."

Lady Woodham blinked, then looked again at Diana as if she'd been hopeful that she was seeing things. "Surely you are jesting."

"It is no jest. We were married today by special license."

"You have married this. . . . ?" Lady Woodham's eyes rolled up and she slumped in her chair in a faint.

"I tried to prepare her," said Stephen, jumping up.

"I can imagine," said Julian, and Diana heard the sarcasm heavy in his voice. He moved to the bellpull and jerked it, and the butler appeared so quickly Diana felt sure he'd been eavesdropping at the door. "I am afraid my mother has fainted. Send James and Andrew to come carry her to her room."

Diana sank onto the nearest chair. Not exactly a warm welcome from her future mother-in-law. She should never have married Julian. His mother would never forgive him.

Two tall footmen in scarlet livery came and bore away the dowager Lady Woodham.

"Perhaps I should," began Diana, moving to follow.

Her husband put a hand on her arm and shook his head. "Her maid will attend to her."

"Well," said Stephen. "I'm still here, so on behalf of my mother, welcome." He came forward and kissed her on the cheek. "Allow me to wish you happy."

Diana felt relieved someone, at least, was going to be gracious enough to bid her welcome. "Thank you," she murmured.

"Let me show you to your room," said Julian, taking her by the arm and removing her from Stephen's grasp.

She smiled tentatively at Stephen, who wore an enigmatic look, then nodded and let Julian lead her away.

"Your brother, at least, was friendly," she commented as they walked up thickly carpeted steps.

"Wasn't he, though?" replied Julian. Again, the sarcasm.

He said no more until he reached the door to her room. "I think you will like it," he said. "It is quite the nicest room in the house."

He opened the door and she walked in. Rose brocade draperies hung at the window and her feet sank into thick dusky rose colored carpet. The fireplace mantel was marble, and a small vase of hothouse rosebuds sat on it. A larger bouquet of roses in various stages of bloom sat on the table beside the bed, and their fragrance danced about the room. She went to the bedside table and touched a velvety, red petal. "Did you order these placed here?" she asked shyly.

"I did," he said. "Are you pleased?"

"How could I not be?" She eyed the bed.

As if following her thoughts, he came to stand behind her. "We have adjoining rooms, with a dressing room in between. When you are angry with me you may lock me out."

"I could never be angry with you," she said.

"You have been before. I feel confident you will be so again."

"There was only one reason to be angry with you before. It is gone."

He gave a snort and shook his head. "I have come to heel like a well trained dog."

"You can refer to saving me and offering me the protection of your name in such terms?" she said, stung.

"Ah, see?" he teased. "I am already well on my way to making you angry. Forgive me. May we remove this bonnet once and for all? I would dearly like to kiss you without having to dodge the brim."

Diana complied and tossed the bonnet on the bed.

"That's much better," he approved, and pulled her to him. He was just about to kiss her when the sound of approaching voices made him frown and turn her loose. "Fresh interruptions," he grumbled. "Now you can see why newly married couples leave the country."

They parted and the housekeeper arrived, followed by Williams. "Williams!" cried Diana happily. "You have just now arrived?"

"Yes, er, your ladyship," stumbled Williams. She dropped a wobbly curtsey to the earl, keeping her gaze firmly on the carpet in front of her.

"I suppose you would like to freshen up and fix your hair and any number of things for which I'm not wanted," grumbled Julian.

"Yes, I think perhaps I would," agreed Diana.

"Very well. I shall await you in the drawing room, and we'll find some way to idle away the time until dinner. I have some books on Italy which I'd like you to look at."

"I shall be down shortly," promised Diana.

As soon as he was gone she said, "Do hurry, Williams. I wish to speak to Lady Woodham before I join my husband."

Williams helped Diana change her gown, and repinned her hair, then Diana went down the hallway, looking for Lady Woodham's bedchamber. At one door near the end of the hall she heard the sound of muffled voices. She raised her hand to knock, but hesitated. Should she be here? Perhaps she'd do more harm than good if she tried to talk to her new mother-in-law.

She already dislikes me, Diana finally reasoned. So I've nothing to lose, really. Perhaps, when she knows I truly love Julian she'll feel a little more kindly disposed toward me. Even after assuring herself, it took all Diana's strength of will to rap her knuckles on the hard wood.

A moment later the door was opened by Stephen, and Diana

heard Lady Woodham's voice from inside the room call, "Who is it?"

He turned his head and said, "It is your new daughter."

"I don't wish to see anyone now. I am unwell." Lady Woodham's voice sounded petulant.

"Please, your ladyship. Won't you see me for just a moment?" called Diana. "I promise I won't stay long. I have something important to tell you."

Stephen watched for a sign of assent or refusal, then nodded his head to Diana and opened the door, and Diana stepped into what she saw was Lady Woodham's sitting room.

"You may leave us, Stephen," said her ladyship.

"As you wish, Mother," he replied, and after making a half bow to Diana, left.

Diana stood looking at the older woman. Her ladyship reclined in a soft chair, her hands cupped over the ends of the arms. For some reason Diana thought of a picture she'd once seen of the Great Sphinx in a book. It had been an unnerving sight, with its great lion's head and its huge paws, and she'd always wondered how she'd react if she'd seen the thing firsthand. Now she knew. She was terrified.

The Sphinx spoke. "Why are you here?"

Diana cleared her throat nervously. "I had to speak with you. I felt you should know that I didn't marry your son for position or wealth."

Lady Woodham raised a delicate dark eyebrow.

Diana plunged doggedly on. "I truly do care for him. He has been so good to me."

"Please," interrupted Lady Woodham in an incensed voice, "don't embarrass us both by going into detail."

Diana shook her head, not understanding.

"I am well aware of the fact that my stepson has promised to pay all your bills. I am also aware of the fact that your family suspects you of being a murderess."

Diana reeled with the shock of this revelation. "What are you saying?"

"It is useless to pretend innocence. I've had your measure from the first time I laid eyes on you, and I can assure you that I will be sending for my solicitor first thing in the morning. If you won't leave voluntarily, then I shall find a way to legally break this marriage—before Julian winds up suddenly dead like your first husband."

Diana backed away, hardly believing her ears.

"Yes, leave," taunted Lady Woodham, "for I don't wish to even be in the same room with you."

Diana jerked the door open and ran straight into Stephen. "Here now," he began, but she shook her head and ran down the hall, back to her room, tears choking all speech from her.

It took her some time to compose herself, but finally, after Williams had bathed her forehead with lavender water, she felt enough restored to search out her husband. The butler pointed her to the drawing room, where he sat on the sofa, all manner of books and maps spread about him.

The sight was homey, yet foreign, and exciting, and realizing he was planning their future comforted her enough to enable her to mask her worry. "What is this?"

"I'm planning our wedding trip," he said, clearing a space for her next to him. "Would you like to visit Rome?"

"I would like to visit any place with fine food and comfortable beds," she replied.

"You would love the Italian Alps in the summer," continued Julian.

I would love any spot on earth as long as you were there, thought Diana, and smiled at him.

He grinned back at her and then returned his attention to the maps.

Stephen joined them. "Such conjugal bliss. I think I will most definitely have to offer for Miss Nettle. I can picture us now, seated before the fire in the drawing room of Thorne Hall."

"Thorne Hall?" repeated Diana incredulously. "Is that truly the name of the place?"

Stephen held up his hands in a gesture of helplessness. "I

know it sounds terribly ridiculous. Nettles and thorns. But one cannot help one's name, after all."

"Where is Mother?" asked Julian.

"She begged to be excused from joining us. She is feeling quite unwell."

Julian frowned, and Diana felt both guilty for causing the present uncomfortable situation and relief that she wouldn't have to suffer seeing her ladyship's stony face across the dinner table.

As they went in to dinner, she said, "Julian, I am sorry."

He shrugged. "It is of no matter, I assure you."

They had finished dinner and were seated in the drawing room, Stephen making an awkward third and seeming not in the least bothered by it, when Lady Woodham's abigail came, asking to speak to the earl.

Diana saw Julian's smile stiffen. "What is it?"

"Her ladyship is feeling very ill, your lordship. She asks that you send for the doctor."

Diana felt stricken afresh and looked to Julian.

"I am sure she will recover," he said. "I have yet to hear of someone dying of ill humor."

"Begging your lordship's pardon, but she's truly not at all well. I'm worried."

Julian sighed. "I'll come see her." Diana rose to join him, but he motioned for her to stay. "I'll be back shortly," he promised.

"I'd best come, too," said Stephen, and went with Julian.

Diana sat alone in the grand drawing room of her husband's townhouse and suddenly pined for her own drawing room and her own close family circle. It had been a mistake to marry him. She was bringing division in his family. Just having her in the same house was making her mother-in-law ill. The minutes dawdled by. What was taking so long?

At last she heard the sound of footsteps outside the drawing room door, and voices. She ran to the door and opened it to see a footman leaving and Julian turning toward her. "Are you sending for the doctor?"

He nodded and went with Diana back into the drawing room.

"Oh, dear," she fretted as soon as the door was closed. "What can be wrong? She was in perfect health when I saw her this afternoon."

"You saw her?" asked Julian.

Diana blushed. "I went to speak with her. I thought, perhaps. . . ." What had she thought, that simply by begging Lady Woodham to do so she could make her mother-in-law accept her? It had been a foolish plan, and she hated to reveal such naivete to her husband. She shook her head. "It is of no consequence."

"I'm sure it is nothing serious," said Julian. "I am sorry this had to happen on our wedding day. All brides cherish that day, don't they?"

Diana thought of Mr. Hunt. "Not all brides."

Stephen joined them at that moment. "I cannot like this, Julian. It looks serious."

"Let's save the prognosis for Doctor Stone," said Julian.

Stephen said nothing more. He took a chair in front of the fire and sat staring at it as if its flames held the answers of the universe.

When the doctor came, both men again left Diana to her own devices. *Well,* she told herself, *the doctor will give Lady Woodham medicine and she will feel better, then we may pick up our happiness like dropped stitches. I was only being morbid earlier. All is not black and horrible. My mother-in-law is ill. That is all. People become ill all the time and the world does not end.*

Doctor Stone finished with his patient and went with Julian to his study. "I think she will be all right, but it was a near call. Rest and fresh country air would be a good thing. And, if I were you, your lordship, I should watch her carefully. She has lovely skin, but she is paying dearly for it."

"What do you mean?" asked Woodham.

"I believe this to be a case of arsenic poisoning," said the doctor. "I suspect your mother doses herself with arsenic thinking to improve her complexion. Many women either ingest it or use creams containing it—a dangerous but popular beauty treatment. It could be she accidentally took a stronger dose than she normally would. If she is taking the stuff, she should be discouraged from such a foolish practice."

"But she's never been ill like this before that I recall," said Julian.

The doctor frowned. "Then I repeat what I just said. Watch her carefully. Good evening, your lordship."

Julian hardly heard the doctor. He sat down heavily on the seat at his desk, feeling suddenly ill himself. Watch her carefully. The underlying message in the doctor's words was impossible to miss. But who would want to poison his stepmother?

The door opened and Stephen entered the room. "What did the doctor say?"

"He thinks she was poisoned."

"Poisoned! My God, that's preposterous." Stephen went to stand by the window. "And while he was at it, did he happen to tell you which of the two of us he thinks did it?"

Julian continued as if his brother hadn't spoken. "He also said she could have overdosed herself. She takes arsenic for her complexion, doesn't she?"

Stephen shrugged. "She has for years. Odd she would pick today of all days to try and give herself a fatal dose."

Odd, indeed, mused Julian.

"There's a full moon tonight," observed Stephen.

"This is no matter for jest," snapped Julian.

"I wasn't jesting." Stephen pulled a packet out of his coat pocket. He came and tossed it on the desk. "This came for you the other day. I must confess, I was curious and opened it. I wish now I hadn't."

Julian looked at the packet and said, "I know what this is."

"I think you had better open it. There is a letter with it."

Julian pulled out the thick wad of merchants' bills. Lord, but Diana had been busy. He turned to the enclosed letter and read:

Dear Lord Woodham:

I am appreciative of your willingness to cover Mrs. Hunt's bills. As you can see, they are many. I assume this means your lordship is contemplating offering matrimony to the lady, and, as you are helping me out of a difficult financial position, I feel it only fair to warn you, she comes to you with a cloud of suspicion over her head. Did your lordship know that my uncle, Charles Hunt, died on his wedding day? We suspect that his bride poisoned him. I would strongly caution you, if you want to live to enjoy your wedding night, beware what you eat at your wedding breakfast.

Your servant,
David Barnes

Fourteen

Julian crumpled the letter and threw it across the room. Vicious lies! That's all they were. Diana might be an adventuress, but she wasn't a murderess. Such calumny seemed beyond even a man like Barnes.

"You don't believe it," observed Stephen.

"The man is mad."

Stephen shrugged. "Of course, it is all coincidence."

"It is," insisted Julian. Which of them was he trying to convince? "You need tell no one of that letter," he added.

"My lips are sealed. Now."

"What do you mean by that?"

"I mean that I already told Mother." A charged silence hung on the air, and Stephen hurried to fill it. "Well, what would you have had me do? You come home looking moonstruck and speaking of marrying, then I read that the very woman you want to marry is suspected of poisoning her husband."

"So good little mama's boy that you are, you rushed to tattle."

"I thought, perhaps, she might talk sense into you."

Julian gave a cynical snort. "I can handle my own problems, little brother. And I can handle them much easier when I am allowed to see my own mail."

Even in the candlelight, the flush on Stephen's face was plainly visible. "Well," he said quickly, "you need have no fear of me spreading tales."

"You had best not," said Julian grimly.

"There's no need for veiled threats," said Stephen lightly. "After all, it's in my best interest to keep this a secret. Imagine what such unpleasant conjecture would do to my chances of securing Miss Nettle's hand, and all the rich property that goes with it."

"Yes, imagine," said Julian sourly.

"If I were you, brother, I would be careful what I ate."

With that parting shot, Stephen strolled out of the room, and watching him go, Julian remembered what a puling little mama's boy he'd been as a child. As a man, he was no improvement. His lovely face and fine manners were the mask he showed to the polite world. Beneath it, he was sneaky and cowardly and spoilt. How Julian pitied poor little Miss Nettle.

Was Stephen the only one wearing a mask? The contents of David Barnes' letter haunted Julian's thoughts. He shook his mind free. Such a thing was simply too preposterous to believe. He knew the woman, knew her better than she knew herself. She was no murderess.

"Julian?"

A soft voice from the doorway made him start. He looked up to see Diana coming toward him. Only a few hours earlier, he would have rushed to take her in his arms. Suddenly, his legs seemed made of lead.

"Is your mother all right?"

The doctor said she was poisoned. The words refused to come out. Instead, Julian said, "The doctor thinks she will be fine."

She nodded. "That is good news."

"He suggests fresh air for her." Julian hesitated. Diana was looking at him expectantly. "We might need to postpone our trip."

"I shan't mind," she said and came to the desk. There she saw the bills.

She picked one up and Julian's eyes darted to the crumpled note across the room. That must be thrown on the fire tonight.

"It is a very great amount, isn't it?" she said in a small voice.

"It shan't ruin me, if that's what you're worried about. And don't worry, I won't strangle you."

She looked at him soberly. "I'd rather not remember that incident."

"Of course," he said, and took the bill from her hand. "Let's go to the drawing room."

Stephen was nowhere in sight and Julian was glad. Coming back from his dimly lit study to the bright, cheery drawing room pulled the cobweb of doubt from his mind. He was being womanish. "I think we should toast to our future," he said.

"Yes, let's," she agreed.

"There's some fine Madeira in the dining room. I'll just fetch it, myself, then we won't have to be disturbed." He went to the dining room, where the butler was still overseeing the clearing of the table.

"Your lordship wished something?" asked the butler.

"Yes," replied Julian with a grin. "I wish not to be disturbed." He got two glasses and poured the wine from the decanter on the side table. Shutting the door firmly behind him, he went back to the drawing room, and seated himself next to Diana. He handed her a glass and said, "To our future."

"To our future," she repeated and watched Julian take a hearty gulp.

He noticed she didn't drink.

Seeing his eyes on her full glass, she said, "I am afraid I stuffed myself at dinner in rather an unladylike fashion. I honestly couldn't manage so much as a thimbleful of wine.

"No matter," he said, taking her glass from her.

"Please. Finish yours," she urged.

He smiled at her and raised the glass to his lips. Did the wine taste off? Impossible. It was the same wine he'd drunk earlier. He sipped again. No, there was no mistaking it. Something was wrong with this wine.

"What is it, Julian?" asked Diana, watching him curiously. "Is something wrong with the wine?"

He tried to rein his galloping thoughts and appear normal. "No, no. I just. . . ." His voice trickled off as the wild thoughts spun around his mind. He couldn't quite seem to catch any of them. His stepmother, she'd never been sick like this before. David Barnes' letter, it was sour grapes. Why did the wine taste off? Was it his imagination? There was a full moon tonight. He put his hand to his forehead.

"Julian, what is it?"

Her voice sounded anxious. Had she asked her first husband those same words. *Don't be ridiculous,* he told himself. *She loves me. She's always loved me.*

She's always wanted your title.

"No!"

"Julian?"

He blinked and stared at his wife. "I'm sorry. I'm afraid I'm feeling rather unwell, myself."

She took his arm. "You must go to bed. Perhaps what your stepmother had was catching."

"Yes," he said, trying to sound calm and rational. "I think, perhaps I shall see you to your room and then go lie down."

She was still looking at him with concern. "Don't worry about me. I can find my bed." She stood, looking down at him and he found himself suddenly unable to look her in the face. "Perhaps, if you were to lie here on the sofa, by the fire," she suggested, and he nodded and turned his head to the flame. "Would you care for a cup of tea?"

"No." The word sounded short and panic laden even to his own ears. He forced his voice to soften. "I'm sure I'll be fine by morning."

"Then I'll bid you goodnight," she said softly.

He didn't turn to look at her. "Goodnight, Diana. I hope you sleep well."

She said nothing, only turned and left, and he cursed his stepmother and his stepbrother, and that fool Barnes. Then he cursed himself for being easily frightened. He remembered what he'd thought when he first met Diana en route to her old husband. *She needs someone young, with fire in his loins.* Some wedding night his bride would have, and all because her husband had let others peck away his happiness like so many crows. His stomach cramped up and he grabbed it. This was some imagination he was developing.

Julian's illness worsened with the night. He experienced vomiting and diarrhea which left him weak and sweating, and then dizziness. When the illness reached its apex he thought he was indeed dying. But the strong constitution that had served him so well in the Peninsular wars saved him yet again, and he managed to drag himself down to the kitchen, where, remembering a remedy he'd once heard, he mixed himself a mug of saltwater. He remained in the kitchen, alternately vomiting and drinking saltwater. Later he found some milk and drank that. By dawn he knew he'd been spared, and he crawled off to his bedroom to sleep.

It was late afternoon when he woke, and after his valet had shaved him and dressed him, he went to see how his stepmother fared.

She was in her sitting room, still in her wrapper and lying on the sofa. Her lovely pale skin looked jaundiced this morning and there were dark circles under her eyes. "Julian, you don't look at all well," she greeted him.

"I am fine," he said.

"Were you ill?" she persisted.

He turned her question aside. "A mild stomach disorder. I am fine now. But how are you?"

"It appears I will live," she said.

"The doctor suggests fresh air. Should you like to return to Ottershaw Park?"

"Yes, I think perhaps I would. Will you go also?"
Julian nodded.

"I suppose you plan to bring your bride."

"I had thought to, yes," replied Julian sarcastically.

Her ladyship frowned. "If you have any sense at all you will seek an annulment. When did you begin to feel ill?"

"I merely had a stomach upset," insisted Julian.

"The same night your new bride came to the house. I became ill shortly after she visited me in my room."

"Coincidence," said Julian firmly.

"A very odd coincidence, considering the fact that David Barnes thinks she poisoned her first husband," observed her ladyship.

"I am not even remotely concerned about what an unprincipled man like Barnes might think. For all we know, he could have poisoned the old man himself."

"Oh, really Julian," said Lady Woodham in disgust.

Julian ended the discussion, rising and saying, "If you are feeling up to it, we may leave London by the end of the week."

Her ladyship nodded.

"And Julian."

"Yes?"

"I don't wish to see that creature."

"I am sure that can be arranged. If you wish, you may take your meals in your room. And I'll send word to the Park to have the dower house opened."

"Really, Julian, don't be ridiculous. That child has no more idea how an earl's house should be run than a chimney sweep."

"Then I suppose you will have to teach her," said Julian sweetly.

Lady Woodham scowled at this and he left her, sure he'd hear no more from his stepmother on that head. She'd never willingly give over the reins to a usurper.

He knew he should behave like a proper groom and go find his bride, but his desire to be with her had ebbed away. He went, instead, to his club and hid there for the day.

He returned in the early evening, and forced his steps to her room. He knocked on the door and her abigail opened it. If he'd been in the mood to be amused, he would have found the maid's round-eyed look and stuttered greeting amusing. He passed the curtseying girl and went to stand by his wife. She was in the process of readying herself for dinner and sat before her dressing table, her hair half pinned. For a moment the old desire flickered, like the last leap of a dying flame.

She watched him in the mirror's reflection, a look of concern on her face. "I knocked on your door earlier today, but there was no answer. Are you feeling better?"

He nodded. "Yes." He found himself unable to think of anything else to say. Not since he was twelve had he been at a loss for words in the presence of a female.

She dropped her gaze and plucked at her wrapper, the perfect picture of hurt and confusion. Was it real or was she pretending? Oh, God. He hated this. They were like two people in an arranged marriage, strangers watching each other from opposite banks of a river, and he had no idea how to cross it. Perhaps, it couldn't be crossed. "I'll await you in the drawing room," he said.

She nodded and he left, wondering if this was how the rest of his married life would be. If it was just a simple matter of having no common ground, no tender feelings, he could cope. Hadn't his life been full enough of that over the years? But to live each day wondering if it would be his last, could he stand that? Perhaps his stepmother was right, and he should bring the curtain down on this farce before it turned to tragedy.

Stephen was already in the drawing room, lounging in a chair before the fire. He tossed a casual glance at Julian and said, "Ah, I see the dutiful groom has returned. Your bride was asking me earlier where you were."

"I had business," said Julian shortly. His stepbrother's snide smile begged for a fist and he had to clench his hands at his sides to refrain from obliging.

"Mother appears to be recovering," said Stephen. "So I suppose you will dump us at the Park and tool off to Italy."

Italy. Was it only yesterday he'd talked so enthusiastically with Diana of going there? "We shall remain at the Park for a while," he said. "Until I know Mother is well."

"Ever the dutiful son," said Stephen.

Julian's first impulse was to warn his stepbrother not to push him too far. Of course, that would be exactly what Stephen wanted, to get a rise out of him. He took the chair opposite and said, "And since I am going to see our mother back to the Park, you may feel free to remain here and court your rich Miss Nettle."

"I think Miss Nettle will wait," said Stephen coldly.

"You may suit yourself," said Julian.

Diana joined them, and an onlooker might have guessed Stephen to be her husband rather than Julian. It was Stephen who first jumped up and offered her his chair, Stephen who told her how very beautiful she looked. Julian managed to add that he had never seen Diana when she did not look beautiful, but he knew it wasn't enough to overshadow the fact that his stepbrother had spoken the first compliment.

Throughout dinner Stephen carried the conversation, both bride and groom lapsing into uncomfortable silence. After dinner, Julian forced himself to sit next to Diana. He even dredged up a smile for her. And she returned it, but her eyes told him she knew it had been forced and she was hurt.

Stephen produced a deck of cards. "Since we are trapped at home for a cozy evening *en famille,* we can at least amuse ourselves."

"Perhaps Diana doesn't wish to play," said Julian. Yet, what else was there to do? Only yesterday he'd have had no trouble answering that question.

"I don't mind playing cards," she said quickly.

The three of them sat down at the marble inlaid card table. I should have taken her to the opera tonight, thought Julian, or to a ball. Anything, something.

But if he'd taken her anywhere it would have meant a carriage ride, and he had no desire to ride alone with his bride in a carriage. His bride. The irony of the whole thing struck him. No one save his family even knew him married. And here he'd been wed over twenty-four hours and had yet to consummate his marriage.

"What we need is some port," announced Stephen. He turned to Diana. "Would you care for ratafia?"

"Yes, but there is no need to ring. I can as quickly step into the dining room," she offered.

"Allow me," said Stephen.

"No. I insist." She rose and was gone even before Stephen was halfway out of his chair.

He sat back down and smiled at his brother. "You were thirsty, weren't you? I hope it does not make you nervous having your wife serve you."

Julian pressed his lips together, refusing to be baited.

"So quick to serve her husband," murmured Stephen. "I should think it reflects a generosity of heart rather than a lack of breeding, although I daresay she is not used to having servants at her beck and call."

"You shall have to ask her," replied Julian, his voice smooth as glass.

Diana returned with two goblets of wine.

"You are not drinking?" asked Julian.

She shook her head. "I saw only the wine."

"I shall ring for Hansen to bring ratafia," said Julian.

"Pray don't. I really am not thirsty."

Stephen took his goblet and drank deeply, all the while watching Julian over the crystal brim.

His goblet sat next to him, like an asp, waiting. He forced his fingers to curl around the stem, forced the goblet of dark, red liquid to his lips. Odd he'd never noticed before how very like the color of blood it was. He closed his eyes and drank until the goblet was drained. Then he set it down and smiled at his stepbrother. "A very good year," he said. "I understand we have almost drunk it up. Pity."

Stephen's smile had faded. "Pity," he agreed and began to deal out the cards.

The supper cart made its appearance at 10:30.

"I wish your mother felt well enough to join us," said Diana.

"Perhaps next week, when we are back at Ottershaw Park," said Julian.

"Are you going to try some of the oysters, Julian?" asked Stephen innocently.

Julian felt his face flushing. He was sure Diana had no idea what his stepbrother was talking about, but he knew. Oysters gave a man stamina in bed. Stephen was obviously very sure that Julian was staying away from his wife's bed, and was enjoying the fact. "I'll take some oysters," he told the butler.

"Give him a large helping," added Stephen, and grinned.

Diana looked from one to the other. "I'm afraid I don't understand. Is there some jest here?"

"None at all," said Julian. "Would you care for some?"

"Yes, please," she said.

Stephen consumed his supper, then announced his intention to go out. "Now that Mother is recovering nicely I think I may safely leave. If you should have sudden need of me, you may send Andrew 'round to Boodles."

He sauntered out of the room, leaving Julian alone with his wife.

"Are you tired?" asked Julian.

She blushed and nodded her head.

He rose and escorted her to the door. "Why don't you go on up?"

"You aren't coming?"

"Not yet. I need to let my food settle."

"I can stay with you," she offered.

He shook his head. "You are tired. Go on up to bed. I'll be up later."

She seemed to take a sudden interest in his boots. "I'll wait for you."

He kissed the top of her head. "Goodnight, Diana."

She raised her face and again he saw the confusion in her eyes. What kind of fool was he? He'd let a poison far worse than arsenic seep into his mind. He had but to hold Diana and it would be cured. He took her into his arms and waited.

"Julian," she whispered.

It was no use. Her very breath felt like the breath of the grave. He released his hold and stepped back. "Goodnight, my dear," he said, and went to shut himself in his study.

He hid there a good two hours, turning the circumstances of the past two days over and over in his mind. At last, weary from the effort, he went to his room and rang for his valet.

Julian had stripped down to just his breeches when he heard the gentle tapping on the dressing room door. With lead in his belly, he dismissed his valet and went to open the door. There stood Diana in the night glow of moonlight mixed with candlelight, a gossamer white nightgown clinging to her body. Her hair was down and hung in a waving, golden curtain past her shoulders. The look she gave him cried of yearning and unfulfilled desire. She looked like a ghost. He took a step back, and she glided into the room.

Once inside, she didn't seem to know what to do. She nibbled a fingernail and regarded him, childlike. Then she spoke. "I heard you talking with your valet."

"Did we wake you?" he asked solicitously.

She shook her head, and blushed. "I . . ."

He knew she wanted him to help her, say something, take control, but he couldn't. He was frozen, a statue.

She stepped up to him and touched her fingers to his shoulder. "I was remembering our wedding vows," she whispered. "With my body I thee worship."

"With all my earthly goods I thee endow," he added. His voice sounded harsh even in his own ears.

She pressed her lips together so hard he could see the skin turn white around the edges. Then she said, "I have no worldly goods left, Julian. All I have is my body."

The words tore at his heart. He would bleed to death right here before her, but he couldn't touch her. There was no healing in that. He'd tried it downstairs and he knew. There was no longer sweetness in touching her, instead it was vinegar to the teeth. He shook his head. "Diana."

He didn't need to say any more. She looked at him as if he'd struck her. "I see you are tired," she said. "I'll trouble you no more."

For an instant something deep inside begged him to cry out to her and call her back, but he slapped it firmly down. He wouldn't take her into his bed until he had some answers. More than that, he wouldn't even take her into his arms.

Diana shut the door behind her and ran to her bed. She buried her face in her pillow and set loose the tears. She'd wanted Julian from the moment she saw him. But now she'd won her prize and it had turned to ashes in her hand. What had happened?

Her mother-in-law, that was what had happened. The reigning Lady Woodham rejected the usurper, and her son had done what any dutiful son would do. He rejected her as well.

What would happen now? Would they send her away, buy her off with money? As if that alone could heal her broken heart and give her back her pride. And what if she didn't wish to be sent away? What if she wished to keep her prize?

But he doesn't want me. The plain truth stood firmly before her eyes, refusing to be banished, and all she could do was ask, "Why? Why?"

Fifteen

Diana sat across from her mother-in-law, who had not acknowledged her presence, either by look or word, since they entered the carriage in London. Lady Woodham sat in cold, marble splendor, acknowledging the existence of her sons with an occasional word, but Diana, simply, was not. Julian gave his wife no touch or loving look to warm her cold soul, either. Stephen, alone, had tossed her an occasional encouraging smile, and like weak sun on a winter's day, it hadn't been enough. The journey had been misery on wheels.

Now they were nearly to Ottershaw Park, and still Diana hadn't succeeded in unraveling the mystery of her husband's sudden change toward her. It couldn't be, as she'd thought the night before, simple loyalty to the dowager countess, for surely he'd known of his stepmother's disapproval before he'd offered marriage. What, then, had happened?

They passed the drive that led to Spinney Hall, and looking at that drive and remembering past events, Diana had her first clue. David Barnes. She suddenly saw again the pile of bills on her husband's desk. What vitriol had David sent along with them? He had to be, somehow, responsible for coating her husband's passion with ice. She would ask Julian first chance she got.

They passed the spinney where Julian had kissed her and Diana swallowed the lump in her throat and blinked back tears. She stole a glance at Julian. He was looking out the window, also. Did he remember, too? As if hearing her unspoken question, he looked at her and smiled. It was the polite smile of a stranger, and it shattered her heart into a thousand crying pieces.

Lady Woodham seemed to grow in strength and energy as the carriage rolled up the drive of the Park, like some giant genie rising from a bottle, looming larger and larger, and Diana felt as though she were shrinking. She stirred down the panic bubbling in her. She had to be brave and fight for her marriage. Only in saving that could she save her life, for without Julian she had no life.

The carriage rolled to a stop, and the footman opened the door and let down the steps. The men descended first, then handed out the ladies, Stephen helping his mother and Julian giving Diana his hand. He dropped it as soon as she was on the ground, and she determined to talk with him that very afternoon.

"It's good to be home," said Lady Woodham, and for the first time Diana noticed warmth in her voice.

She followed her mother-in-law inside the house, and stood by while the dowager gave instructions to the household staff. She watched the servants carrying her trunks up the stairs to the room her mother-in-law had assigned her and knew there could be only one mistress here, and Lady Woodham had, by her actions, already claimed the title. When they drove by the dower house no one mentioned her ladyship taking up residence there, and Diana realized that while this strange distance hung between herself and her husband, the dowager countess would reign supreme. Here was another reason to talk with her husband as soon as possible.

The personal maids and valets had already arrived, and Diana entered her room to find Williams hanging her gowns in the wardrobe. This room, she noticed, was all done in blues, and although the spring sun flooded it, she found it cold.

Williams hurried to help her out of her traveling clothes, and she changed into a muslin gown, which left her shivering.

"There is still a bit of bite in the air, isn't there?" said Williams, producing a Norwich shawl to drape over her shoulders.

Diana still found herself cold. "I'll never be warm in this room," she said.

"I'll make sure a fire is laid before you come up tonight, and have a warm brick in the bed," promised Williams. She looked around. "It is a pretty room." She laid the words before her mistress as an offering, but Diana scorned it.

"It is a cold room," she said. Williams looked perplexed, but Diana didn't bother to explain. Instead she left and went in search of her husband.

She'd heard no voices from the room adjoining hers, so she reasoned he must be in the study. The groom of chambers showed her where it was, but it, too, proved empty. She went to the drawing room. Memories swarmed her. She could still see Lady Woodham looking at her with those hard, assessing eyes, and Julian, sitting next to her, smiling. She remembered the circumstances of their meeting, felt again the terror the highwayman had brought her, then the wash of relief when Julian stood by her side, the savior who'd bought her with another man's blood. Memory of that first encounter, and all the following ones in the spinney marched through her mind, then their post nuptial carriage ride where Julian had teased her with the appetizer for what lay ahead. But something had killed her husband's appetite, and she had to find out what.

She went to the French doors and looked out. Directly before her was a terrace, fringed with flowers. Steps led down to a formal garden with a fountain, its beds planted with dahlias, yuccas, and a variety of edgings. Beyond it, like the background in a painting, sprawled the landscaped park. She saw a figure walking just beyond the garden toward the park. It had to be Julian.

She hurried to join him, and was halfway to him before she realized that his hair wasn't black but brown, and it was really Stephen she'd been pursuing. He saw her before she could turn back and came to join her. "Exploring your new home?"

"Actually, I was looking for Julian. Have you seen him?"

"I believe he went to the stables to speak with the groom. When one is lord of the manor one's work is never done."

Was there the smallest note of bitterness in his voice? "And you have no work to do?" asked Diana.

"I am only a second son. My job is simple."

"And what, pray, is that?"

"Why, to see that the new countess enjoys her first day in her new home." He offered her his arm. "Come. I shall show you the park."

She hesitated. "I think, perhaps, I should find Julian."

"Even if you find him, I assure you, he won't have a thought for you until dinner. There is always so much to see to when one has been gone for some time."

"Of course," agreed Diana listlessly. Not wishing to make a scene, she took his arm and let him lead her off, wondering how much she'd enjoy a walk with the man who'd tried so hard to discourage her interest in Julian.

He seemed to read her thoughts, for he said, "I hope I can be forgiven for my damping skepticism during our conversation at Lady Bonneyfield's ball. Behold me, all contrition and humble apologies. How could I know a heart as hard as Julian's could actually be pierced by Cupid's arrow?"

"How, indeed?" replied Diana politely.

"I am forgiven, then?"

"Of course," she said. The way her marriage was beginning, she needed every ally she could get.

Julian watched from the drawing room window as his stepbrother led his wife into the park. Yet another conquest. How wonderful for her, he thought bitterly. What a fool he'd been. His stepmother was right. This woman cared not the least bit for him. Ever since their first conversation she'd been the angler and he'd been the fish. And, oh, how cleverly she'd played the line, too. He'd send to London for his solicitor first thing tomorrow.

Stephen had been right. Diana didn't see her husband until dinner. Throughout the meal, and late into the evening he sat, hedged by family. Would she ever find an opportunity to speak with him? Even after the supper cart had come and gone, Lady Woodham and Stephen remained in the drawing room as if part of a conspiracy to protect Julian from his wife.

At last, however, Lady Woodham yawned and announced her intention to find her bed. Stephen followed suit, and the newlywed couple found themselves alone.

"Well," said Julian stiffly, "I imagine you, too, are tired, my dear. It was a long journey and you cannot have slept well in that inn."

Alone, added Diana mentally, for her husband had never left the private room they'd ordered for their dinner. Indeed, she hadn't slept well. She'd wakened at every heavy-booted footstep outside her door, hoping to hear a knock and a request for admittance. "I am tired," she admitted, "but before I retire I wish a word with you." He seemed to stiffen and she had to force herself to continue. "I am wondering if, perhaps, David Barnes wrote you about me."

He raised an eyebrow. "Wrote me? What might he have written, Diana?"

"I'm not sure," she said. "I only know that something is terribly wrong."

"Why do you say that?"

She looked him squarely in the eye. "Because my touch has become unpleasant to you."

"Nonsense," he said. "You are imagining things."

"Am I? Then will you come and kiss me?"

The look on his face was a slap. "Diana, I am tired. It's been a long day."

She couldn't look at that cold face any longer. She dropped

her gaze and said in defeat, "Of course. Forgive me." Then she turned and walked away as quickly as she could, her one goal now to gain her room before she burst into tears.

Julian watched her go and bit his lip. He should have thrown Barnes' accusations at her and demanded she explain how her first husband died. And, of course, she'd have fallen at his feet and confessed all, he concluded cynically. Then, what could he do? Already, he was having doubts about seeking an annulment and shipping Diana off to the continent. Granted, that would rid him of his beautiful, treacherous wife, but if he turned her loose she'd surely find a new victim. Victims, more like. No. He couldn't be so irresponsible. Like it or not, he had to prove his wife a murderess.

He'd learn nothing treating her like a leper. Tomorrow he would take her for a drive. He still didn't think he could bring himself to bed her, but he could, perhaps, manage a kiss or two. That would loosen her tongue, he concluded, and smiled grimly at the pun.

Julian found only his stepbrother when he entered the breakfast room the following morning. Stephen was enjoying a hearty breakfast of kippers and eggs and hailed him with his fork.

"Where is Mother?" asked Julian.

"In her room, most like, avoiding your bride. And speaking of your bride, how do you intend to amuse her today?" he asked, going to the sideboard to add more to his plate.

Julian watched him. In spite of the fact he had no title, Stephen lived well. Julian wondered if he planned to stay forever at Ottershaw Park. If his stepmother had her way, of course, he would. Julian recalled his wandering thoughts. "I shall take her for a drive."

"Charming," said Stephen.

"And what will you do all day?"

"I shall compose a sonnet of undying devotion to send Miss Nettle."

"You should have offered for her before we left London. It will serve you right if someone else is before you with an offer."

Stephen shrugged. "My dear Miss Nettle will hold out for me, I assure you."

"If your dear Miss Nettle doesn't hold out for you and settles for some fat baronet, you will have to bear the consequences and decide whether you prefer a uniform or the life of the cloth," said Julian.

His stepbrother's smile disappeared. "Are you tossing me out, brother?"

"You're becoming far too big a bird to remain in the nest," said Julian. "Wouldn't you agree?"

Stephen studied him and said slowly, "I suppose you'll be turning Mother out, too."

"Turning her out? She has the dower house. You could always share that with her, couldn't you?"

Stephen scowled and arose. "I had best begin my sonnet."

Julian smiled at the plate with its uneaten second helping as his brother stalked from the room. He hadn't baited Stephen like that since they were cubs. He'd forgotten what fun it was.

He poured himself a cup of the bitter hot chocolate he loved and finished his ham, then went to knock on his wife's door. Her abigail answered and gave him the same nervous curtsey she always did, and he wondered idly when she'd ever lose her fear of him. Diana was dressed for the day in a muslin gown with little roses embroidered around the neck of the bodice. Her maid had threaded a pink ribbon through her hair and he had the odd impulse to run his hand along the ribbon and feel its smoothness. Instead, he kissed her hand and asked her if she'd care to go for a drive.

The sober mask fell from her face and she smiled pure sunshine at him. "I should like that very much. Let me just put on my pelisse and bonnet and I shall be down directly."

He left her room feeling like a child on Christmas morning, and was halfway down the stairs before he remembered this was no pleasure outing. By the time Diana joined him, the knowledge of his circumstances and the purpose of their morning drive had turned his heart cold again and made his smile stiff.

She seemed to sense it, for the one she gave him in return was guarded.

This would never do. He'd get nothing out of her this way. He forced the stiffness from his face. "Have I told you yet this morning how lovely you look?"

She shook her head. "No, you haven't."

"It seems to me I've seen that bonnet before," he continued.

She blushed. "I wore it on our wedding day."

Julian could feel the warmth of embarrassment on his cheeks as well. "How could I have forgotten? But the same bonnet in one week? Unthinkable. You will have to order some new clothes."

"I believe I have cost you enough already," she said primly.

"A husband is supposed to spend a great deal of money on his wife," Julian replied.

They were at the stable now, and seeing the phaeton ready-harnessed and the groom standing at the horses' heads, Julian realized he'd made a mistake. How could his wife confess anything to him in an open carriage with a groom up on the seat? "I have a sudden desire to sit in the sun," he said. "Would you mind a stroll in the garden instead?"

She looked perplexed, but said, "Of course not."

"Unhitch the horses," he said to the groom, and turned Diana back toward the house. "Where were we? Oh, yes. Husbands. You know, I've always wondered what sort of husband old Hunt would have turned into had he lived. Would having such a lovely wife have loosened those tight fists of his?"

A cloud seemed to pass over Diana's face. "I suppose we'll never know," she said in a quiet voice.

"No," Julian agreed. "We shan't. There was a great deal of talk after he died, you know."

"What sort of talk?" she asked sharply.

"People thought it odd that he should expire so suddenly."

"The doctor said he died of gastric fever," said Diana in the voice of a sleepwalker. She suddenly awoke and turned her head with a quick, jerky movement to look him in the face. "Why do you bring this up now? Why do you ask how my husband died?" Her voice was tainted with hysteria.

"Diana, I was only making conversation," he replied, sounding every bit the concerned husband.

"To speak of something which you must know I find horrible, this is your idea of making conversation?" she continued wildly.

"Why should this upset you so?" he countered. "It is not as if you were in love with the man. God knows you barely mourned him."

"I barely *knew* him!" she cried. "Oh, God." She broke from Julian and ran off into the house.

"Well," he murmured with grim satisfaction, "I see you still have a bit of conscience left."

The memory of that terrifying time pursued Diana all the way to her room. Again, she could see the corpse of her husband lying among the tangled bedclothes, smell the putrid smell of death, and feel the terror grabbing at her heart. She shut the bedroom door and leaned against it, panting.

Williams, who was inspecting the hem of a gown, took one look at her face and cried, "Oh, dear, what has happened?"

"Why would he want to talk of Mr. Hunt's death?" She covered her mouth with her hand and tried to calm herself.

"The earl wanted to talk about Mr. Hunt?" asked Williams, confused.

Diana nodded. "It brought it all back. I . . ." She rubbed

her forehead, as if by doing so she could rub out the horror still clinging to her mind.

"Oh, dear," fussed Williams. "You come lie down and I'll bathe your forehead with lavender water."

Diana complied. "I cannot imagine why he would want to talk of Mr. Hunt's death after all this time."

"It's very odd, isn't it?" agreed Williams, dousing a handkerchief.

Amorphous bits of idea and image pulled together into solid thought and Diana suddenly knew why her husband wanted to speak of her first husband's death. Of course! How could she have been so stupid? David Barnes had taken his revenge on her after all. She pulled off the scented handkerchief and sat up.

"My lady, your headache," protested Williams.

Diana didn't hear her. "Here, fix my hair. I must find Julian straight away."

Diana descended the staircase she'd so admired when she first set foot in the house and headed straight for her husband's study. The groom of chambers opened the door and she entered to see Julian standing at the window. He turned as she entered, surprise evident on his face. "Are you feeling better?"

"Did David Barnes tell you I poisoned Mr. Hunt?"

He blinked as if she'd moved too fast for him.

"That is why you wanted to speak of my husband's death, isn't it? You think I murdered my husband and you hoped I might, somehow, betray myself."

The half embarrassed look on his face and his temporary lack of words told her all. "You believed a man like David Barnes?"

Julian stood before her with his jaw locked.

She shook her head. "No wonder you had no desire to come near me. Were you afraid I'd stab you in your sleep?" She nearly choked on the last words. Angry tears stung the back of her eyes.

"Diana," he began.

She turned her back to him. "You shan't worry that I'll bother you in the future," she said coldly. "For I have no more desire to sleep with a man who chooses to believe the worst of people than you have to sleep with a murderess."

"Diana!"

His voice was demanding now, insisting she turn around. Instead, she left the room and returned to her bedroom. Once in her room, she said to Williams, "If my husband wishes to see me, I am indisposed."

Julian didn't follow her. He wasn't sure what to say, what to think. Her scent of lavender lingered to haunt him, and he poured himself some wine from the decanter on his desk to banish it. He sat for some time mulling over what she'd said. Was it possible Barnes had lied? The man had wanted Diana for himself, and maybe since he couldn't have her, he'd thought to play spoilsport. God knew, she'd made his life difficult. Perhaps this was his way of seeking revenge. The more Julian considered this the more probable it seemed. He needed to talk with Diana.

He had no sooner determined to do so than the same pain grabbed his gut that he'd felt on his wedding day. Oh, God. He'd taken poison again, no doubt about it. But when? Where? He wrapped his arms tightly about his middle in a futile effort to press out the pain and stumbled from his desk. He closed his eyes and doubled up, the half drained glass of wine on his desk standing sentry. It could have been the wine. It could have been the hot chocolate he'd had at breakfast. How long did arsenic take to do its job? Fresh agony grabbed him in an iron grip and he let out a cry and stumbled from the room. He'd have to get to the kitchen.

In the hallway, the groom of chambers found him and rushed to hold him up. "Your lordship."

"Get me to the kitchen," panted Julian. "I need saltwater."

In the kitchen, the butler jumped up from where he sat polishing the silver and the cook, seeing the master of the house entering her domain half dragged and half carried, let out a shriek and commanded the doctor be sent for.

"No doctor," croaked Julian. "Mix me some saltwater."

"Oh, Lord, oh Lord," cried the woman, and waddled off to do his bidding.

Julian sat, hunched over, sure this time he would die. The cook placed the mug of saltwater in his hand and he drank it and retched on the kitchen floor.

"What is this?" demanded a voice from the door.

Julian was only vaguely aware of his stepmother entering the room.

The groom of chambers acted as spokesman for the group in the kitchen. "His lordship was taken suddenly ill."

"Send for the doctor," commanded Lady Woodham.

"No!" cried Julian, then grabbed his stomach. "No doctor."

"You need a doctor."

"I tell you I don't," he moaned. "Leave me." She turned and marched from the kitchen and Julian said to the cook, "More saltwater, and be quick."

At last he knew he'd done all he could. The groom of chambers fetched two footmen to assist him to his room, and, once there, his valet removed his boots and coat and loosened his cravat. "That is enough," he panted. "Let me rest now." The man bowed and left, and Julian fell into an exhausted sleep.

At one point he dreamed Diana came to stand by his bed and lay a cool hand on his forehead. "Murderess," he said, and had the satisfaction of seeing her draw away her hand.

When he awoke, long shadows covered the bedroom carpet. The waning twilight seemed symbolic of his life. His window was partly open and he could hear a robin, finishing its dusk-time concert. As a small boy, he'd loved to lie in bed and listen to the robins sing. The world had been a simple place, then, with a nanny who fussed over him and a mother who always came to kiss him goodnight. Sudden tears welled up and the sob he'd stuffed down deep in his gut since he was six at last escaped. He thought of his mother's tender caresses and another sob found its way to freedom. He pressed his lips firmly together and wiped the tears away, telling himself it was his weakened condition that was turning him sentimental and womanish.

"Julian?"

He jumped at the sound of the soft voice. How long had she been standing there? What had she seen? What had she heard? He turned his head away, ashamed of the wet stains on his cheeks, angry that he'd been caught in this condition.

Diana came further into the room. "You were poisoned, weren't you?"

Feeling at a disadvantage on his back, he sat up a little. What should he say to this question? If only he knew for sure who his poisoner was. If only he knew for sure it wasn't her. He saw the mug in her hand. "What makes you think that?" he hedged.

"I suppose I have become cynical," she said. "I see poisoners everywhere." She bit her lip and set the mug on his nightstand. "I have heard milk is good." She stepped back and stood regarding him.

"Thank you," he said, and left the mug where she'd set it.

She seemed to be debating something within herself. At last she said, "Perhaps I am a jinx."

"Why do you say that?"

Again, there was a hesitation. At last she plunged into speech. "My first husband was poisoned. I know the symptoms."

A million thoughts whirled through Julian's mind. He grabbed at one. "You told me your husband died of gastric fever."

"I told everyone my husband died of gastric fever. It is what the doctor said. But he was poisoned."

"By whom?"

"By his sister, Mary Barnes."

Julian sat completely up. "Why would she want to do such a thing?"

"She did it for her son. I heard them talking, after Mr. Hunt's death. She felt David deserved Mr. Hunt's money. She talked with the lawyer to make sure of the wording in the will, then killed Mr. Hunt on our wedding day before we could possibly conceive a son." By the end of her speech, Diana's face was flushing cherry red, but she didn't drop her gaze.

"Why are you telling me this now?"

"Because you need to know I am no poisoner."

"I have only your word for that," pointed out Julian.

"It is all I can give you. Mary Barnes certainly won't oblige me with a confession, nor will her son, who now hates me." She nodded to the glass. "The milk will make you feel better."

"It was kind of you to bring it," he said.

Her chin raised a fraction. "But you won't drink it?"

He shook his head. "I think not."

She looked at him sadly. "Oh, Julian, why can you not trust me?"

His heart whimpered for tenderness even as he tightened its stone casing. He turned his gaze to the window and said, "Because you are a woman."

"I cannot help that I was born a woman," she said.

Of course, she was right. And he couldn't help being unable to trust her. His life was at stake. He sighed.

She took a step closer to the bed. "I suppose there is nothing I can say to convince you that you can trust me. But I realize I need to confess something to you."

Julian quickly sorted through a number of possible confessions. She'd just lied, and she really had been the one who'd poisoned her husband. She'd been David Barnes's mistress. She'd married Julian for his money.

"You used to tease me about being a huntress."

So, he was to hear that she'd married him for his money.

Of course, she would add that with his wealth he had bought her undying loyalty.

"But I am afraid I married you with no practical reason in mind."

His brows knit and he stared at her. "What do you mean?"

She half smiled and shook her head and her cheeks turned pink. "I mean that I married you simply because I wanted you. I'm afraid I always wanted you, which was very wrong, I know, and I would have been a good wife to Mr. Hunt. I would have honored my marriage vows. But. . . ."

He knew he was looking at her dumbfounded. She hung her head, as if ashamed.

"You rescued me from the highwayman, and then from David Barnes."

And I'd have rescued you from the mob in Heptonstall, too, if need be, thought Julian. *God help me, I've been obsessed. And blind.*

"At any rate, I've come to care for you very deeply. And even if you don't—can't—return my regard, I felt you should know I didn't marry you for any reason save love."

Very prettily said. And here was where he was supposed to take her into his arms and make passionate love to her. Then afterwards she'd say, "Now, have a drink of milk." And perhaps there was nothing in the milk. Perhaps, she truly was his ally and not his enemy. He found himself suddenly wishing that was so, but he knew he couldn't risk trusting her. Not yet. In fact, he wasn't sure he could trust any member of his family. "Diana," he said gently.

She looked at him, hope plain in her eyes.

"I want to trust you, but you must give me time. Can you understand that?"

She pressed her lips together and nodded. Without a word, she went to the door connecting their rooms. At the door she found her voice. "I am willing to give you time, but there is someone in this house who isn't, and I mean to find who."

Julian continued to stare at the door long after Diana had

gone through it. Either she was a greater actress than Sarah Siddons or she was telling the truth. There was really only one sure way to find out which it was. He steeled himself and reached for the glass of milk.

Julian didn't come down to dinner that night, but Stephen and Lady Woodham both joined Diana in the drawing room before the meal.

"I stopped to see Julian on my way down," Lady Woodham informed Diana. "He is doing better, but is still weak. I suggest you leave him alone the next few days and allow him to rest."

Diana blinked in astonishment and found herself at a loss for a reply.

Her ladyship didn't seem to expect one, however, for she turned her back on Diana and went to take a seat before the fire.

Diana scowled at her back and turned to see Stephen observing her with a grin on his face. She tried for an air of dignity by lifting her chin, but she knew her reddened face made the effort useless.

At that moment, Hansen opened the door leading to the dining room and announced that dinner was served.

Lady Woodham glanced at the ormolu clock on the mantel. "Fifteen minutes late," she informed him. "Tell Cook she is getting sloppy, and I'll not have it."

"She did have a bit of an interruption in her schedule earlier today," pointed out Stephen.

"That is no excuse, Stephen, and well you know it," retorted Lady Woodham.

"Of course," he murmured, and offered his mother his arm.

Diana sat through seven courses of torture. At last the syllabub had been consumed and it was time to leave Stephen to enjoy his port in after-dinner grandeur. Before Diana could rise, her stepmother stole the privilege and led the way to the drawing room. She may think to lead me from the dining room, but she cannot force me to attend her there, thought Diana, and said, "If you will excuse me, I think I shall retire to my room."

Lady Woodham gave her a condescending smile which told whom she thought to be the victor in this particular battle. "As you wish."

Diana nodded regally and left. But she didn't go to her room. She'd been thinking throughout dinner, remembering Mary Barnes' resentment of her brother and her determination to get Spinney Hall for her son at any cost. Ottershaw Park was a far bigger prize than Spinney Hall, and if anyone could commit murder it was Lady Woodham. And Diana had a strong suspicion that her ladyship was an arsenic eater. Even in Tetbury, ladies knew about the supposed benefits of a pinch of arsenic for white skin. Lady Woodham was vain. To what lengths would she go to maintain that creamy complexion? And, more to the point, to what lengths would she go to gain Ottershaw Park and the title for her son?

This was the best time to search her mother-in-law's dressing table, while her abigail was dining in the servants' hall. Diana took a brace of candles from the hall table and slipped into Lady Woodham's bedroom. The quiet emptiness of the room and the eerie shadows cast by the candlelight made Diana feel as if spiders were crawling up and down her skin, but she forced herself to the dressing table. The assortment of bottles, rougepots and pillboxes was amazing. She picked up a cut crystal bottle and opened the stopper.

"What," said a sepulchral voice behind her, "are you doing?"

Sixteen

Diana felt her blood freeze. She raised her chin before turning to face Lady Woodham.

"I thought you were up to no good," said her ladyship, coming into the room.

"Are you sure that is what you thought?" replied Diana.

"I have no idea what you are talking about," snapped her ladyship.

"Perhaps you have good reason to fear me searching your room. Perhaps you have something to hide."

"What are you suggesting?"

"I am suggesting that, perhaps, your love for your blood son is so deep that you would do anything to make sure he inherits the title."

"What!"

"I am suggesting," continued Diana, "that you would like nothing better than to see my marriage to Julian ended before it has even begun, that you would dearly love to see him think his wife a murderess and seek an annulment before we can consummate this marriage and possibly produce a male heir."

"Young woman, you forget yourself."

"Do I? Pray tell, what is your beauty secret? How do you keep your skin so white?" Diana turned and picked among the bottles on the dressing table. "Arsenic?"

"You betray your breeding, or lack of it. I'll thank you to leave my room at once, and I shall try to forget we ever had this conversation."

Diana moved away from the dressing table. She stopped when she was shoulder to shoulder with her mother-in-law. "I shouldn't try to forget it if I were you. I should remember every word of it. And be very careful."

Lady Woodham's eyes opened so wide that they looked like huge marbles stuck into her face, and Diana was sure no one had ever talked to her in such a way her entire life. Diana smiled sweetly on her mother-in-law, feeling for the first time as though she, too, had grown in stature and power. "Goodnight. . . . *Mother.*"

Lady Woodham gave an outraged choke and Diana strolled off down the corridor, well pleased with her victory. It wasn't until she got to her room that she realized she could have made a tactical error. Had forcing Lady Woodham's hand been a wise thing to do? Perhaps she too would now find herself victim to the poisoner's hand. No. Lady Woodham was much too clever for that. She'd make sure her stepson was murdered and Diana was hanged for it.

Julian awoke feeling weak but well. There had been no poison in his milk. Perhaps he could trust Diana. He rang for his valet, who shaved and dressed him, then after fussing with his cravat, went to his study and sent for Diana's abigail.

She entered the study as if she were approaching the burning bush, curtseyed and whispered, "You wished to see me, your lordship?"

"I did," said Julian. "I wanted you to tell me about your old master, Mr. Hunt."

She looked confused. "What did you wish to know, my lord?"

"I wished to know about his health."

"He died quite suddenly," said Williams, and looked at the earl to see if that was what he wanted to know.

"Yes, I am aware of that. Did Mr. Hunt ever have stomach disorders?"

"Well," she said slowly, screwing up her round apple face, "he did have some stomach trouble. Off and on."

"Did he ever have stomach trouble when his sister came to visit?"

Williams took to chewing her lip.

Julian forced himself to appear patient, smiling encouragingly at her.

At last she said, "It seems, now that I recollect, that Mr. Hunt was often sick when his sister came to visit. But then, it seems he ate even more when she and Mr. Barnes was visiting. The doctor was always warning him he'd have gout if he wasn't careful, but he never listened."

Julian nodded. "Thank you, Williams. You may go."

"Yes, your lordship," she said, then dropped a curtsey and left.

Julian sat at his desk some time, thinking. What he needed was to talk to old Hunt's lawyer. He went in search of his wife.

He found her walking in the garden. At the sight of him, she smiled.

"Have you breakfasted?" he asked.

"I had some hot chocolate in my room," she replied. A look of apprehension fell over her face. "Have you eaten anything from the sideboard?"

He smiled. How good it felt to see concern for him on someone's face! He shook his head.

"Good," she said. "You mustn't. If you insist on not trusting me, then for your own safety, you must also trust no one else. Not until this person is caught."

"Diana," he took her hand. "I drank the milk you brought me."

She searched his face. "Then. . . . you believe me?"

"Almost."

She nodded. "It is a start."

"You must tell me the name of Hunt's lawyer. It is important I talk with him."

She sighed a little sigh. "I wish you could simply trust me."

"Remember, it is my life at stake. I have put my doubts in the coffin. If I talk to the lawyer it will be the final nail on the lid, then I can bury them for good. You mustn't begrudge me that final nail, Diana."

"His name is Hewitt."

"Good girl," said Julian and kissed her forehead. "Can you entertain yourself until dinner?"

"I'm sure I can think of something," she replied.

As Julian kissed her hand, Diana saw something of the old sparkle in his eyes. "Until tonight," he murmured.

"Until tonight," she repeated, hope and joy waltzing in her heart.

He left and she went to sit on the garden bench. The spring sunshine fell warmly on her shoulders and she let her shawl slip.

That afternoon Diana had a talk with the butler. "I want a fresh bottle of wine opened for dinner tonight. Please pour out the wine left in the decanter, and don't allow anyone to sample it."

"Perhaps your ladyship is not aware that there is half a decanter left?" replied Hansen.

"I want it poured out nonetheless," said Diana firmly. "Do I make myself clear?"

"Yes, your ladyship," said the butler.

"And Hansen."

"Your ladyship?"

"If you or any of the staff take so much as a swallow of that wine it will mean your position."

The butler licked his lips and nodded. "Yes, your ladyship."

The entire family came down to dinner that night. Lady Woodham was her usual frigid self. Diana, watching Stephen's normal mocking smile turn bitter in the face of Julian's ebullient mood, wondered how she could have ever thought him her friend.

Julian seemed not to notice it. He waxed expansive on any number of subjects, from the fine, warm weather to the spring planting to the excellent dinner. "Cook has outdone herself tonight," he proclaimed.

"It is good to see you feeling so well," said Lady Woodham.

"It is good to feel so well," replied Julian. "The way I feel tonight I could live forever. I'll have more wine, Hansen."

"You shouldn't overindulge after being so ill," warned her ladyship. "It might give you stomach trouble."

"I think it will be a long time before I experience stomach trouble again," said Julian and smiled at his wife.

Diana smiled back. This was the man she'd fallen in love with. Would he come to her tonight?

Her sense of anticipation grew as the evening wore on. Julian was extremely attentive to her, even going so far as to kiss her hand while they awaited Hansen's arrival with the supper cart.

Shortly after supper, she excused herself and went to get ready for bed. After Williams had unpinned her hair and helped her into her nightgown, she dabbed some perfume on her neck and shoulders, then climbed into bed to hope. Perhaps she was deluding herself. Perhaps he was only pretending interest in her to somehow force his enemy's hand. The thought was a blow to the heart and it snatched away her joy and made her want to cry. You have used your share of people, she told herself glumly. Now you see firsthand how it feels.

The door from Julian's room opened and she gave a start. He stood framed in the doorway, a moonlit god, clad only in breeches.

He'd come. Misery fled. Diana sat up and breathed his name.

She watched him come to her. He had both grace and strength in his walk. He was all hard lines and muscle and his torso fascinated her. It was like flesh over stone. Hard. She looked to his face. His eyes were hooded, suddenly a mystery. Her body shivered in anticipation.

He sat on the edge of the bed and regarded her. "Were you asleep?" he asked softly.

She found herself unable to speak so she shook her head.

He took a lock of her hair in his hands, and she watched, fascinated, as he kissed it. "You are," he said, "the most beautiful creature God ever created. You are more beautiful than Eve."

She smiled at this and tried to ignore her body's nervous tremors. "And how would you know that, my lord?"

"I just know," he said. "You will have to trust me." He moved closer. "You are," he whispered and touched his lips to her cheek, "Diana, the goddess." His mouth travelled down her neck, and his breath left a warm trail that seeped deep into her body, chasing away the shivers. His hands slipped her nightgown off her shoulders. "And with my body, I thee worship," he finished and bowed his head to kiss her breast.

She kissed the top of his head. "I love you, Julian," she whispered.

He made no reply to this, only slid her down on the bed beside him and kissed her.

It is enough, she told herself. *It is enough.*

The following morning she awoke to find him still with her, his arm draped possessively across her middle. She cuddled in against him and he muttered in his sleep and pulled her closer. The night had been a night of surprises, more full of mixed sensations than she could ever have imagined. But the most wonderful feeling of all had come when Julian had finally pulled her against him and murmured, "Sleep well, my goddess." And now, here she was, still in the shelter of his arms. She wished they could remain in this bed forever. It was safe here. Love lived here.

Julian stirred and moaned.

She looked over her shoulder at him and he opened his eyes and smiled.

"How are you feeling this morning?" he asked. "Are you very sore?"

She felt suddenly embarrassed and shook her head, hoping he would drop the subject.

He grinned at her. "It does get better, I promise."

"You'll hear no complaints from me, my lord," she said.

He kissed her ear and pulled her close against him. Bare skin on bare skin. And broad daylight! She felt her cheeks warming.

"Ah, the maidenly blush lives on," he observed. "Well, I suppose a woman does not make the transformation from virgin to wanton overnight. Although," he added, lowering his voice as if someone were eavesdropping on them, "you came very close last night."

Now her cheeks were on fire. "Julian!" she scolded and pulled away, wrapping the sheet around her.

"A fine time to worry about your modesty, madam, after I have already carefully inspected every inch of you," said Julian, and kissed her shoulder.

She said nothing but remained wrapped and he grinned and jumped out of bed.

She watched him, marvelling again at the firm line of sinew and muscle. It was so foreign, so completely masculine, and so very fascinating.

"Well, and what shall we do today?" he asked. "Do you fancy a drive?"

She hated to dampen his enthusiasm by bringing him back to painful reality, but this was as good a time as any. "No," she said. "I think I shall remain in bed today. I am not feeling well."

He looked at her in sudden concern. "What is it? Why didn't you say something earlier?"

She shook her head. "There is nothing wrong with me, really. I have a plan."

His face sobered. "Very well. Let me hear it."

* * *

Diana didn't appear at the nuncheon table.

"Where is your bride?" asked Stephen.

"She's not feeling well," said Julian. "I think, perhaps, what we need is to get away, take our honeymoon trip." He turned to his stepmother. "Now that you are so much better, there's really no need for us to stay. Jamison can look after estate matters for me for a month. And a change of scene and a warmer climate would do Diana good."

"Has she developed consumption overnight?" asked Stephen.

"Utter nonsense," said Lady Woodham. "The climate here is perfectly fine. We are having an unusually warm spring."

"We shall go anyway," said Julian, undaunted.

"Indulging that woman," muttered her ladyship. "Why, it's absolutely scandalous."

"You can hardly begrudge the lady her bride trip, Mother," said Julian.

"It is more than she deserves. She should be grateful simply to be Lady Woodham."

Julian shrugged.

"She is playing you for a fool," continued his stepmother.

"I rather enjoy playing the fool," he replied.

"Faugh," said her ladyship in disgust. "Let us talk of something else before my appetite leaves me completely."

"By all means," said Julian pleasantly. "Shall you feel up to attending church this Sunday?"

"No," snapped her ladyship.

Julian smiled. He knew exactly why his stepmama had no desire for spiritual food. It would mean being seen sitting in the same pew with her upstart daughter-in-law. "Well," he drawled, "if you will both excuse me, I have work to do."

He sauntered out of the dining room and off to his study, and lounged about there until he heard the sound of voices floating down the corridor. He waited a few minutes longer, then went back to the drawing room. He headed straight through this room and through the door into the dining room he'd just left. He took a post in the corner back of the door, where he would have a good view of the sideboard, and anyone wishing to tamper with the wine decanter in it, but wouldn't, himself, be immediately observed.

He'd waited little more than an hour when a stealthy figure glided into the room and over to the sideboard.

"Thirsty?" asked Julian, pushing away from the wall and strolling up to his stepbrother.

Stephen jumped. "Julian! You startled the wits out of me." Julian noticed his stepbrother's hand slip behind his back. "Actually, I was thirsty and came in for a bit more of that burgundy," said Stephen.

"So am I, now I think on it," said Julian, strolling over to the bow window and looking out. "Pour us both something."

"Very well," said Stephen.

"Rather a nice day," continued Julian. "Do you fancy a ride?"

"Why not?" replied Stephen, unstopping the cut crystal bottle.

Julian was next to him the minute he had it unstopped and grabbed his hand, shaking loose the vial from his hand. It fell to the floor between them, colorless liquid seeping from it. Julian stretched his lips in a mock smile. "I never thought you had the nerve for such a thing, Stephen. I thought to find my dear stepmama here. Did you poison her as well?"

"Go to hell," snapped Stephen and yanked his hand free.

"So, Mama in her extreme agitation merely overdosed herself and thus gave you inspiration. Is that it? Or maybe she thought to buy time by bringing on a near fatal sickness. Perhaps she thought to somehow accuse Diana of poisoning her. It was all very convenient, Diana being the last one who saw her before she took violently ill. Being the clever fellow you are, I suppose you figured to murder me and be rid of my wife all in one felled swoop. What a weak thing you are, Stephen. Poison is a woman's tool, you know."

Stephen merely shrugged.

"I suppose," continued Julian thoughtfully, "if poison had not worked you would have made sure I met with some sort of accident. And my poor bride?"

"She does have a habit of losing husbands, doesn't she?" said Stephen. "I'm sure she'd have found herself another before you were even cold in your grave." He turned back to the decanter. "I need a drink."

Before Julian could say or do anything, Stephen picked up the decanter and whirled around, wielding it like a club.

Julian put up his hand to ward off the blow, but too late. The last thing he saw before glittering darkness was his brother's face, full of hatred and determination.

Seventeen

Stephen stood for a moment over his fallen brother. Julian's head was drenched in wine, and it pooled out from his fallen body like blood. In spite of the very real blood oozing from the gash on the side of his head, Stephen knew he wasn't dead. The fool had put up his hand in time to lessen the impact of the decanter.

This wasn't how he'd planned things. What to do now? He stood for a moment, biting his lip, planning wildly. He could still make this work, but he'd have to act quickly, before Hansen came in and found the mess in the dining room.

He knelt beside Julian and hoisted him onto his shoulder. He staggered under the heavier man's weight, and by the time he got to a standing position he was panting. Hunched under his heavy burden, he went into the drawing room and deposited Julian on the sofa, then hurried back to the dining room to collect the valuable vial. As soon as he'd taken care of Julian, he'd find Hansen and accuse him of dipping into the wine and leaving the mess. Later, of course, everyone would assume that Julian, troubled once again by the pain of illness, dropped it. He hurried to the study, where he poured a fresh glass of wine from the decanter his brother kept there.

He smirked as he stole back to the drawing room. It was all so easily explained, really. Julian's cunning little black widow of a wife finally managed to give him a fatal dose of arsenic. Somewhere between the dining room and the drawing room, he'd fallen and hit his head. Poor Julian. Everyone had tried to warn him; his own family, even David Barnes. What an inspiration Barnes had been! Stephen still had his damning letter, fished from where Julian had thrown it and then forgotten it.

He went to the sofa where Julian lay sleeping like a baby and cradled him against his shoulder. "Drink this," he whispered. "I'll feel so much better."

"Put that glass down."

Stephen gave a start and wine sloshed over his stepbrother's cheek. He looked up to see Diana standing in the doorway. The sight of the pistol in her hand caused his eyes to widen. Nothing to do but brazen it out somehow. "What can be the meaning of this?" he demanded. "Julian has fainted, and I am trying to revive him." Her hand was shaking. She could never pull the trigger.

"Step away from him," she commanded.

Very well. He could take care of her and then return to his brother. He could still work this out. Tie her up? Knock her unconscious? A double suicide, perhaps? "Diana, put the pistol down. You have no idea what you are doing. I am sure you have no knowledge of firearms. You are liable to hurt someone."

"I fully intend to hurt you if you do not move away from my husband," she said. "And if I were you I would not be too sure that I know nothing of firearms. I know a great many things. I know about poison, and I know about greed."

He tried another tack. "There is enough for both of us."

"Move away from him, Stephen," she said, taking a step closer.

Slowly, Stephen laid his brother back against the sofa cushions. Julian moaned. Good God. Did he have a head of iron? He couldn't be coming to already! Still holding the goblet of wine, Stephen rose from the sofa and came toward Diana. "You don't want to shoot me, Diana," he crooned. "You cannot afford to look so guilty. What would my mother do if she came into this room and found me shot and my brother unconscious?

She would haul you off to the magistrate before you could even draw breath to protest your innocence. So, you see. We need each other."

"Leave this room," she commanded.

Stephen continued walking slowly toward his victim.

Diana watched him approach, willing her hand not to shake. She had never been so aware of the presence of her heart in her body or of her blood marching loudly about her head. When she'd faced the highwayman, it had been only her life she'd stood to lose. Now, not only her own life but Julian's depended on the shaking hands that held the pistol. Stephen was almost to the doorway now. All she had to do was get him out of the drawing room. Then she would go to Julian and stand guard over him until he awoke. Now he was even with her. One more minute. . . .

The sudden wash of wine in her face shocked her, and she blinked and spluttered. Stephen tore the pistol from her hand and she let out a screech. He clamped a hand over her mouth.

"Now look what you've done," he growled, and began dragging her across the room. "This is the end of you," he panted. "You will disappear. I'll bury you out there in the park. I'm sorry you won't rest in sanctified ground, but since you killed your first husband, you hardly deserve to rest there, any way."

Even now, when she had more pressing concerns, she wanted to scream, "I did not kill him!" But her mouth was covered.

"We caught the creature with the poison in her hand," Stephen continued. "Alas, it was too late to save my poor brother."

Julian would die. She would die. No, this wasn't right! They were meant to be together. She bit Stephen's hand, causing him to tear it away. Letting out another scream, she squirmed and kicked him.

He grabbed her in a viselike grip and hauled her the rest

of the way across the room to the French doors. He yanked the cord from the draperies and looped it around her neck.

Air! She couldn't breathe. She sank to her knees, hoping to escape, but he sank with her. Vaguely, she was aware of someone's voice. Julian?

The pressure on Diana's neck suddenly stopped and she tore away the cord and gasped for breath. Looking up, she saw Hansen with the pistol in his hand aiming it at Stephen. Tripping over her gown, she crawled away. She heard a moan coming from the sofa. Thank God. "Julian," she croaked, and half crawled, half ran to him.

A footman entered the room and Diana heard the crunch of carriage wheels on gravel.

"It would appear we have company," the footman said to Hansen. "What should we do?"

Keeping his eyes on Stephen, the butler handed his underling the pistol. "Keep this trained on him. I shall answer the door."

The butler left in stately majesty, shutting the drawing room door on the socially unacceptable scene. The footman swallowed, then said to Stephen, "I am afraid I shall have to request you not to move."

"Julian," said Diana, stroking her husband's forehead.

His eyes fluttered open and he gave her a weak smile. Then he closed them again and mumbled, "Shouldn't have thought myself invincible."

The sound of voices outside the door were insistent. A moment later, in stepped Lady Dalton, followed by her husband and a protesting Hansen. She raised a delicate eyebrow and said, "Do we intrude?"

Lady Woodham did not come down to dinner that night. She remained prostrate in her room, allowing only her abigail to minister to her.

Stephen was bound for Dover, where he would set sail for

a life of banishment on the continent. It had been supposed by the family gathered that his mother would join him there as soon as she was able.

"I must say, Julian, it was most rude of you to pack up and leave London without so much as a by your leave," observed his cousin. She shook her head at him. "Such a trick, making us chase you across England just to learn whether or not you were married."

Julian looked to Lord Dalton. "I am sure that information was of the utmost importance to Tony."

"Of course it was," Lady Dalton answered for her husband, and the two men exchanged smiles.

"I should say it was a good thing we did," observed Lord Dalton. He lifted his goblet, then hesitated. "I say, is this safe to drink?"

Julian laughed. "I had a fresh bottle brought up."

Lady Dalton shuddered. "I still can hardly credit it." She looked thoughtfully at her cousin. "Julian, when you were experiencing such ill health last year, do you think. . . . ?"

He shrugged. "I suppose we'll never know. But it wouldn't surprise me to learn my dear stepmama had been contributing to my poor health. Nor would I be amazed to learn she'd been responsible for my father's death. With me away, who would be around to ask any questions?"

"Terrible," said Lady Dalton. "Well, you are safe now, and so you may now devote yourselves to the task of living happily ever after," she finished beaming on Diana.

Diana was finding it difficult to stay awake. The strain of the day's events had left her feeling so limp, even the excitement of seeing her friend had long ago lost its power to buoy her up. She smiled weakly at Louisa.

Louisa looked at her and frowned. "I think, perhaps, an early evening would be in order. And you had best put some more cream on that neck," she added.

Julian smiled at Diana. It wasn't his usual mischievous smile. There was a tenderness in it she'd never seen before and she found herself suddenly longing for a chance to indulge a good cry.

"I think we shall both retire as soon as dinner is done," he said.

"I didn't mean you should leave us that early," complained Louisa. She sighed. "But I suppose Tony and I can amuse ourselves with a rubber of piquet."

"Your playing is atrocious," said her husband. "Perhaps, we, too, should retire early," he added, and waggled his eyebrows at her.

"Hansen," commanded Julian. "Bring on the dessert."

As the couples bid each other goodnight, Diana experienced the same nervous trembling she had the night before. It seemed to take Williams forever to help her out of her gown and unpin her hair. Then there were the ugly bruses on her skin to be attended to. Just remembering her violent struggle with Stephen made her feel slightly ill. *Never mind,* she told herself firmly. *You are safe now, and so is Julian.*

By the time her maid finished, nerves had given way to exhaustion and she fell into her bed and pulled the covers over her. She knew her husband would come to her, but as she waited, she found it hard to keep her eyes open. *I'll just rest them,* she told herself, letting her heavy lids pull a curtain of dark against the candlelight.

At some point, she was vaguely aware of the bed moving, of a strong body pulling her close and whispering, "I love you." She was dreaming, of course. Julian had never professed such a thing, not even last night in the heat of their lovemaking. Well, it was a wonderful dream. She sighed happily and sank deeper into slumber.

A gentle tickling on her cheek dragged her toward consciousness. She kept her eyes shut, determined to stay asleep, and brushed at it. The thing caressed her skin again and she opened her eyes to see her husband leaning over her, stroking her skin with a feather. It was morning, a new day. She smiled up at him and stretched.

He grinned. "I have been waiting this age for you to waken, sleepy head. A fine wife I have taken. You were sound asleep when I came to you last night." He pulled her into the circle of his arm and she snuggled in against him.

"I tried to stay awake," she said.

"My little heroine," he whispered into her hair. "It's no wonder you were exhausted. I'll never forgive myself for being so arrogant and stupid as to think I could handle Stephen alone."

"You are bigger than he," said Diana helpfully.

"When a man is fighting for his life, size is only half the battle. My stepbrother was a cunning and desperate man. I should have been prepared for trickery."

"I'm glad I didn't wait for you as you had instructed," said Diana. "And I am certainly glad I happened on that pistol in your room."

"There was no ball in it," he said. "Lucky for us all Stephen was unaware of that."

"Oh, Lord," she said weakly.

He hugged her and kissed her hair. "I will never be able to banish from my mind the horrifying sight of him with that cord around your neck. It is a terrible thing to struggle to consciousness only to see your wife being murdered before your very eyes."

"It is a terrible thing to be the wife being murdered," added Diana heartily.

"You risked your life for me."

She heard the awe in his voice and felt embarrassed. "As you did once for me," she reminded him.

"I don't know what I would have done if something had happened to you, Diana." Instead of saying anything more, he kissed her.

It is enough, she told herself, and wound her arms around his neck.

He moved his lips from hers and touched them to her cheek, then her neck. "I love you," he breathed.

This was no dream. She was wide awake. "Say it again," she begged.

He obliged.

It was a miracle. Tears of joy sprang to her eyes and she kissed his forehead and whispered, "With my body, I thee worship."

Epilogue

Huntsman Rest! Thy chase is done.

—Sir Walter Scott

Diana sat at her escritoire and looked out her sitting room window at the white dusting of snow on the ground. The skies were gray and heavy, and any moment she expected to see more flakes falling to make a lovely, thick Christmas blanket. Now that Mama and Mathilde had safely arrived, she didn't care what the weather did.

Contentment wrapped her so snugly these days she found it hard not to keep drifting into pleasant daydreams, and now her letter sat forgotten as she looked at the snow and wondered what her husband was up to. She had a strong suspicion she'd find Julian in the nursery, watching their son toddle about, even though he'd announced his intention earlier to spend the entire morning working in his study.

She could hardly blame her husband for not being able to stay away from that room of old toys and enchantment. Their son was beautiful, with his thick tousle of burnished gold curls and his dark blue eyes. And besides physical beauty, he possessed a sweet disposition and a ready baby laugh which made spending time with him more pleasure than duty.

The thought of duty brought her back from her daydreaming and turned her attention once more to the half-finished letter before her. She hastily scratched, "The only news with which I have not yet acquainted you, dear Louisa, is the unexpected death of Mary Barnes, which took place last week. Word has it she was eating biscuits in bed and somehow got a bit of one lodged in her throat and choked to death on it. I must confess that I am not sorry. I know Reverend Bellows would be shocked to hear me say such a thing (so of course I shan't within his hearing), but to you, dear friend, I can confide, especially since you are one of the few who know my whole history. It somehow seems appropriate that the wicked creature should meet such an end. I suppose if Reverend Bellows knew Mary Barnes's dark secret he would at least have to agree that she, indeed, reaped what she sowed. Now the only two who know the truth about her are her son and myself.

"I have a feeling David won't wish to remain in the neighborhood after this. Spinney Hall will hold too many dark memories even for him. Perhaps you should convince Tony to buy it for you for a birthday present. I know you already have Windymere House, but wouldn't it be fun to be neighbors?

"I apologize for the shortness of this letter, but that is all I can find of interest to tell you. And besides, I have just remembered something which demands my immediate attention. We hope to see you all at the Park soon."

Grinning, Diana signed the letter and readied it for the post, then hurried to the nursery to see her son and husband. It was going to be a lovely Christmas.

ABOUT ARSENIC

Once upon a time I read something about women ingesting arsenic to make their complexions more white. (Oh, what we'll do for the sake of beauty!) Of course, after having plunged neck deep into writing this book I went back to check my source and couldn't find it. In a panic, I called Melissa Lynn Jones, the queen of research, and I'm deeply indebted to her for finding me all kinds of interesting information on the subject of arsenic in beauty treatments.

Arsenic has been used by the vain for centuries. In seventeenth-century Italy, ladies could purchase a colourless preparation of liquid arsenic called Aqua Toffana (after Signora Toffana, who concocted it). This liquid didn't come with printed directions; private instructions were given to the lady at the time of purchase. It wasn't until after some six hundred husbands had died of arsenic poisoning that Signora Toffana was arrested and executed as the most prolific poisoner of the century. Arsenic has been introduced in medicine both internally and externally. As far as I can deduce, it was also used both ways cosmetically.

For my readers who are used to more humor in my books, I can only say that a girl has to be serious once in a while. I hope you enjoyed Diana's adventures. If you did, let me hear from you!

ZEBRA REGENCIES
ARE THE
TALK OF THE TON!

A REFORMED RAKE (4499, $3.99)

by Jeanne Savery

After governess Harriet Cole helped her young charge flee to France—and the designs of a despicable suitor, more trouble soon arrived in the person of a London rake. Sir Frederick Carrington insisted on providing safe escort back to England. Harriet deemed Carrington more dangerous than any band of brigands, but secretly relished matching wits with him. But after being taken in his arms for a tender kiss, she found herself wondering—*could* a lady find love with an irresistible rogue?

A SCANDALOUS PROPOSAL (4504, $4.99)

by Teresa DesJardien

After only two weeks into the London season, Lady Pamela Premington has already received her first offer of marriage. If only it hadn't come from the *ton's* most notorious rake, Lord Marchmont. Pamela had already set her sights on the distinguished Lieutenant Penford, who had the heroism and honor that made him the ideal match. Now she had to keep from falling under the spell of the seductive Lord so she could pursue the man more worthy of her love. Or was he?

A LADY'S CHAMPION (4535, $3.99)

by Janice Bennett

Miss Daphne, art mistress of the Selwood Academy for Young Ladies, greeted the notion of ghosts haunting the academy with skepticism. However, to avoid rumors frightening off students, she found herself turning to Mr. Adrian Carstairs, sent by her uncle to be her "protector" against the "ghosts." Although, Daphne would accept no interference in her life, she *would* accept aid in exposing any spectral spirits. What she never expected was for Adrian to expose the secret wishes of her hidden heart . . .

CHARITY'S GAMBIT (4537, $3.99)

by Marcy Stewart

Charity Abercrombie reluctantly embarks on a London season in hopes of making a suitable match. However she cannot forget the mysterious Dominic Castille—and the kiss they shared—when he fell from a tree as she strolled through the woods. Charity does not know that the dark and dashing captain harbors a dangerous secret that will ensnare them both in its web—leaving Charity to risk certain ruin and losing the man she so passionately loves . . .

Available wherever paperbacks are sold, or order direct from the Publisher. Send cover price plus 50¢ per copy for mailing and handling to Penguin USA, P.O. Box 999, c/o Dept. 17109, Bergenfield, NJ 07621. Residents of New York and Tennessee must include sales tax. DO NOT SEND CASH.

ELEGANT LOVE STILL FLOURISHES —
Wrap yourself in a Zebra Regency Romance.

A MATCHMAKER'S MATCH   (3783, $3.50/$4.50)
by Nina Porter

To save herself from a loveless marriage, Lady Psyche Veringham pretends to be a bluestocking. Resigned to spinsterhood at twenty-three, Psyche sets her keen mind to snaring a husband for her young charge, Amanda. She sets her cap for long-time bachelor, Justin St. James. This man of the world has had his fill of frothy-headed debutantes and turns the tables on Psyche. Can a bluestocking and a man about town find true love?

FIRES IN THE SNOW   (3809, $3.99/$4.99)
by Janis Laden

Because of an unhappy occurrence, Diana Ruskin knew that a secure marriage was not in her future. She was content to assist her physician father and follow in his footsteps . . . until now. After meeting Adam, Duke of Marchmaine, Diana's precise world is shattered. She would simply have to avoid the temptation of his gentle touch and stunning physique — and by doing so break her own heart!

FIRST SEASON   (3810, $3.50/$4.50)
by Anne Baldwin

When country heiress Laetitia Biddle arrives in London for the Season, she harbors dreams of triumph and applause. Instead, she becomes the laughingstock of drawing rooms and ballrooms, alike. This headstrong miss blames the rakish Lord Wakeford for her miserable debut, and she vows to rise above her many faux pas. Vowing to become an Original, Letty proves that she's more than a match for this eligible, seasoned Lord.

AN UNCOMMON INTRIGUE   (3701, $3.99/$4.99)
by Georgina Devon

Miss Mary Elizabeth Sinclair was rather startled when the British Home Office employed her as a spy. Posing as "Tasha," an exotic fortune-teller, she expected to encounter unforeseen dangers. However, nothing could have prepared her for Lord Eric Stewart, her dashing and infuriating partner. Giving her heart to this haughty rogue would be the most reckless hazard of all.

A MADDENING MINX   (3702, $3.50/$4.50)
by Mary Kingsley

After a curricle accident, Miss Sarah Chadwick is literally thrust into the arms of Philip Thornton. While other women shy away from Thornton's eyepatch and aloof exterior, Sarah finds herself drawn to discover why this man is physically and emotionally scarred.

Available wherever paperbacks are sold, or order direct from the Publisher. Send cover price plus 50¢ per copy for mailing and handling to Penguin USA, P.O. Box 999, c/o Dept. 17109, Bergenfield, NJ 07621. Residents of New York and Tennessee must include sales tax. DO NOT SEND CASH.

Taylor-made Romance from Zebra Books

WHISPERED KISSES   (0-8217-3830-5, $4.99/$5.99)
Beautiful Texas heiress Laura Leigh Webster never imagined that her biggest worry on her African safari would be the handsome Jace Elliot, her tour guide. Laura's guardian, Lord Chadwick Hamilton, warns her of Jace's dangerous past; she simply cannot resist the lure of his strong arms and the passion of his *Whispered Kisses*.

KISS OF THE NIGHT WIND   (0-8217-5279-0, $5.99/$6.99)
Carrie Sue Strover thought she was leaving trouble behind her when she deserted her brother's outlaw gang to live her life as schoolmarm Carolyn Starns. On her journey, her stagecoach was attacked and she was rescued by handsome T.J. Rogue. T.J. plots to have Carrie lead him to her brother's cohorts who murdered his family. T.J., however, soon succumbs to the beautiful runaway's charms and loving caresses.

FORTUNE'S FLAMES   (0-8217-3825-9, $4.99/$5.99)
Impatient to begin her journey back home to New Orleans, beautiful Maren James was furious when Captain Hawk delayed the voyage by searching for stowaways. Impatience gave way to uncontrollable desire once the handsome captain searched *her* cabin. He was looking for illegal passengers; what he found was wild passion with a woman he knew was unlike all those he had known before!

PASSIONS WILD AND FREE   (0-8217-5275-8, $5.99/$6.99)
After seeing her family and home destroyed by the cruel and hateful Epson gang, Randee Hollis swore revenge. She knew she found the perfect man to help her—gunslinger Marsh Logan. Not only strong and brave, Marsh had the ebony hair and light blue eyes to make Randee forget her hate and seek the love and passion that only he could give her.

Available wherever paperbacks are sold, or order direct from the Publisher. Send cover price plus 50¢ per copy for mailing and handling to Penguin USA, P.O. Box 999, c/o Dept. 17109, Bergenfield, NJ 07621. Residents of New York and Tennessee must include sales tax. DO NOT SEND CASH.